"Gracie?"

Gracie sighed. She loved to hear her name on his lips, and then she remembered herself and took a quick step back. There were tears in her eyes as she laid her hands on his shoulders.

"Father said you'd been shot." Her chin trembled and she bit her lip to keep from crying. "He said you didn't trust us anymore." Tears hovered on the edge of her lashes. "Does that mean you don't trust me, either?"

Jake stifled a groan. My God, how could he answer her? For all he knew, she could be the one who pulled the trigger. Just because she was beautiful as sin, and just because there were tears in her eyes, did not make her an innocent woman.

But he had to play the game. It was why he'd come.

SHARON SALA
writing as
DINAH McCALL

CHASE THE MOON

HarperTorch
An Imprint of HarperCollinsPublishers

This is a work of fiction. Names, characters, places, and incidents are products of the author's imagination or are used fictitiously and are not to be construed as real. Any resemblance to actual events, locales, organizations, or persons, living or dead, is entirely coincidental.

❦ HARPERTORCH
An Imprint of HarperCollins*Publishers*
10 East 53rd Street
New York, New York 10022-5299

First HarperTorch paperback printing: December 2003
First HarperCollins paperback printing: October 1997

HarperCollins ®, HarperTorch™, and ❦ ™ are trademarks of HarperCollins Publishers Inc.

Printed in the United States of America

Visit HarperTorch on the World Wide Web at www.harpercollins.com

10 9 8 7 6 5 4 3 2

Life is about taking risks.
This book is dedicated to the men
who aren't afraid to take them,
and to the women they love.

Jefferson Memorial Hospital
Cutter, Wyoming
1963

The baby's heartbeat fluttered erratically, like a butterfly caught in an oncoming storm. Tiny fingers curled and uncurled spasmodically as immature lungs, not yet ready for this world, struggled to breathe in and out. Three days into this life and already John Jacob Baretta was losing ground.

Joe Baretta stood beside the incubator, watching as the younger of his twin sons went about the business of dying. He reached out, yearning to hold the child he and Angie had made with their love, wanting to touch him while he still breathed. Instead, his fingers curled on top of the small plastic box in which his son was housed.

As Joe stared down at the baby, it was almost more than he could bear. A box. Johnny Baretta had gone from the warmth and security of his mother's belly to a goddamned plastic box. Pain filled him, threatening to send him to his knees, and just when he would have given in to it all, someone touched him on the arm. He took a shaky breath and looked up.

Mary Denton had been nursing for twenty-two years. She'd seen babies born and babies die, and it had yet to get easier when one was lost. She knew this man's history. She knew how long he and his wife had been trying to have children. Her heart ached for them. After all these years, to have been given two sons, only to have one snatched away just days after he'd been named was too cruel.

She needed to say something because Joe Baretta was coming undone. She pointed to the other incubator nearby.

"Did you see that they took the IV out of Jacob John's arm today?"

Joe blinked, trying to focus on the other incubator. That baby lay quietly, satisfied from a recent feeding. His tiny arms and legs were not pierced with needles and tubes, and his skin glowed a healthy pink. Except for his small size, he seemed to be thriving.

"He took a whole ounce and a half of formula, too. I fed him myself."

Joe nodded. He knew. He knew everything there was to know about his sons . . . everything except how to find the courage to give one of them back to God.

Suddenly an alarm sounded and a monitor gave a warning beep. Joe's heart jerked with fear as the nurse thrust her hands into the incubator. As she worked, he turned a frantic gaze to John Jacob's tiny chest. It wasn't moving.

"Oh God, no . . . please no," he whispered.

In that instant, the baby's little belly gave a spasmodic twitch, and they watched as John Jacob Baretta gave life another try. For now, Joe's prayer had been answered.

Mary Denton turned to check a monitor. *Please, little fellow, don't die on my shift. I don't think I can take this again.*

"It's okay," she told Joe. "He's still with us."

Joe gazed at her through tear-filled eyes. "But for how long?"

Then he shook his head and walked away. He was already a half hour late. Dropping his gown and mask into a basket by the door, he dragged himself down the long hall toward Angie's room. The closer he came, the more intense his sorrow. How could he celebrate the birth of one child while facing the death of another?

Inside the nursery, Mary Denton tried to concentrate on her duties and not the imminent threat of the baby's death, but it was almost impossible. Half an hour later, the nursery door opened again. Dr. Scott came in, already masked and gowned.

"Well now, let's see how they're doing," he said, picking up Jacob's chart.

Nurse Denton could see the doctor's eyes brightening as he scanned the notations. Quietly, she stood to one side, assisting as ordered, but all the while never more than an arm's length from the doctor's side as he examined Jacob John Baretta from stem to stem.

"You know, for a preemie, this little fellow is doing quite well," he said, and peeled off his rubber gloves, tossing them in the trash before donning a fresh pair in order to examine the other twin.

He turned to the other incubator in which John Jacob was lying. "Now then, little fellow, how about you?"

It didn't take long for his brows to knit across his forehead. When Mary Denton saw this, she knew what he was going to say before he said it. Even then, her stomach rolled, and she clenched her teeth when the words came out of his mouth.

"Is the father in the hospital?" he asked.

"He was. I believe he might still be with his wife."

He looked up. "Tell him not to leave. I don't think the baby will make it through the night."

She nodded, unable to speak.

Wayne Scott hated this part of his job. It always made him feel as if he'd failed, although he'd learned long ago to accept that there were aspects of life that no amount of doctoring skills could control.

"I'll be down in ER if you need me," he said softly, and gave the baby one last glance before leaving the nursery.

Again, all Mary Denton could do was nod. When the door shut behind the doctor, she looked back at the ailing baby, staring intently at his tiny

face. His color was so ashen, and he was so small—
so alone. Her focus moved from John to Jacob.
There was such a contrast between the two.

She told herself not to think about things she
couldn't change, but for once her heart wasn't listening to her head. She kept glancing from one
baby to the other. There was something about the
way they were lying that bothered her. Something
she couldn't quite put her finger on. She started to
turn away, when it finally occurred to her. Later,
she would call it a revelation, but for now all she
knew was that what she was about to do could cost
her a job.

Although the babies were in separate incubators
now, Mary knew that for the past eight months
they'd shared one of a different sort. Somehow, it
didn't seem right for baby John to be alone
when . . .

Without giving herself time to think, she pushed
Jacob's incubator up beside John's, then lifted both
lids. Careful not to disturb any of John's tubes and
needles, she moved Jacob into the incubator with
his ailing twin.

Her heart was racing as she finally stepped back.
Now the babies were lying face-to-face, almost
nose to nose, trading breaths and once again sharing the same space.

"God, please don't let me regret this," she whispered, and turned away to check the setting on one
of the monitors. A few moments later she looked
back, then gasped in disbelief.

Jacob—the larger, the stronger, the firstborn—

had thrown his arm across his little twin's shoulders. To the nurse, it looked as if Jacob was holding John in an embrace, but she knew that this must have been the way they'd shared the space in their mother's belly. More often than not, they must have been face-to-face, arm in arm, heart to heart.

She bit her lip, trying hard not to cry, but it did no good. The scene was too precious to ignore. She stood and watched, marveling at the two separate beings that had been created from a single spark of life.

And the long night passed.

The shift was changing, and already word was spreading through the hospital about what Mary Denton had done. Wayne Scott had heard the scuttlebutt on his way up from the cafeteria. He'd tossed his coffee cup in the trash and headed for the second floor of the hospital with his heart in his mouth. He liked and admired Mary Denton. Hell, if the truth be known, he'd even depended on her instinct to guide his decisions more than once, but this time he feared she'd gone too far.

When he exited the elevator, his heart dropped. Joe Baretta was standing outside the nursery with his arm around his wife, their gazes fixed upon the viewing window. His mind was reeling from the implications of a lawsuit the little hospital could hardly afford, when Joe saw him coming. The look on the young father's face stunned Wayne Scott into momentary silence. It was fortunate that he never got his apology out, because he would have had to take it all back.

"My God, Doctor Scott, what made you think to put the babies together like that?"

Before Wayne Scott could answer, Angle Baretta laid her hand upon his arm.

"Thank you, Dr. Scott. Thank you for giving Johnny a chance."

He knew there was a fixed smile upon his face because he could feel his cheeks beginning to tense, but for the life of him he didn't know how to answer. He turned toward the nursery, staring in mute confusion at the single incubator that had been pushed nearer the window. His gaze moved to the monitor and the rows of gauges to which the ailing twin was hooked, and his eyebrows arched in disbelief.

"Excuse me," he said quickly. "I'll talk to you just as soon as I finish my examination," and he bolted for the nursery door.

Mary Denton was making final notations on the babies' charts, while the morning shift nurse was swaddling a newborn that had arrived just before dawn. When Dr. Scott burst into the nursery, Mary looked up and then froze, awaiting certain wrath. Yet she knew if she had it to do all over again, she wouldn't have changed a thing.

Dr. Scott nodded as he began his examination. "Good morning, Denton."

She clutched at the pen in her hand for something to hold.

"Dr. Scott."

His exam was silent but thorough. Twice he took the charts from her hands and checked, then rechecked the findings with what he was witnessing now, almost unable to believe what he saw. Yet the facts—and the babies—were speaking for themselves.

Somehow, baby John was gaining ground. For the first time since he'd been born, his vitals were stabilizing. He'd quit fighting the tubes and needles, and now lay almost dormant beneath the sheltering arm of his brother, Jacob.

Wayne Scott had been practicing medicine for twenty-one years, and he still didn't believe what he was seeing. He shook his head and handed the charts back to Mary Denton. At the door, he paused to stare at the incubator again, then up at the nurse who'd risked her job for a small baby's life.

"Denton."

She tensed, but her chin was firm, her eyes level with his as she answered, "Yes, sir?"

"Well done."

Only after she heard the click of the door as he shut it behind him did she take a breath, and when she did, it felt like a sob.

The Baretta Ranch
Cutter, Wyoming
1968

The moon shone down on the bare backyard. The grass that Angie Baretta had worked so hard all summer to grow was brown now, dead from last week's frost. In less than a month, winter would be setting in. Between school and chores, Jake and Johnny Baretta's playtime was already limited. With the onset of winter, daylight would shorten drastically. And now, at a few minutes short of midnight, the five-year-olds were doing all they could to get the good out of light by which to play—even if it was only moonlight.

"Ooh, look at it now!" Johnny pointed as a straggly cloud briefly passed across the face of the moon. "It looks like the old man in the moon has a beard!"

Jake giggled, and then clasped a hand to his mouth and looked over his shoulder, almost certain that Daddy would suddenly come barreling through their bedroom door and send them back to bed.

"Jake, do you wanna go play?"

Jake hesitated. As the taller one by half an inch and the heavier by three quarters of a pound, he considered it his duty to temper what the family called Johnny's wild streak. He looked back at the door. It was still closed. He listened. The house was quiet.

He looked back up at the moon. It beckoned.

Impulsively, he took Johnny by the hand and, guided by the light of a full moon beaming through the windows, led him down the hall and through the kitchen.

Johnny was all but dancing with delight as they slipped out onto the porch. At once the night air of late fall seeped through their flannel pajamas, chilling their bare feet. But they didn't feel it. All they saw was the moonlight spreading upon the ground and the wide open spaces of a Wyoming night in which to play.

Forgetting that they were supposed to be quiet, they both burst into a shriek of delight and bounded off of the porch toward their swing set at the end of the yard.

Inside the house, Angie Baretta sat straight up in bed, unaware of what had awakened her, but with twins, her motherly instincts were always on over-time. She came out of bed in one leap.

Joe turned over, watching through sleepy eyes as Angie bolted down the hall toward the boys' room. Out of habit, he got up to follow. Angie's in-tuition was hardly ever wrong, and from the speed with which she'd left their bed, it looked as if something was definitely up.

As he reached the hallway, he heard Angie scream.

"Joe! Their beds are empty!"

Now a spurt of worry hit him, too. And even though he trusted her word, he had to see for him-self. Sure enough, the bunk beds were bare, the covers thrown back, the pillows kicked to the foot of the bed.

"Are you sure they're not hiding?" he asked.

Angie glared. "They're not here. I know."

But before he could think what to do, he heard a squeal, then an answering giggle, and shoved the curtains aside.

"The little devils," he muttered.

Angie ducked under his arm to look out the window and then groaned. "Oh my Lord! They're barefoot. They'll catch pneumonia!"

Joe laughed and gave Angie a friendly pat on the rump before kissing her cheek.

"There's a hell of a dew. Grab a couple of towels to dry their feet. I'll run the little beggars inside."

"Have mercy, Joe. How on earth am I going to get them raised?"

"With patience and a smile, honey." Then he added, "And maybe a little luck."

"That's easy for you to say," Angie said. "Now go get my boys."

"Yes, ma'am." He winked as he left.

Playing in the glow of moonlight was like nothing the boys had ever done. Even the simple act of swinging took on new joy. The rush of air against their faces seemed softer, the shadows beneath the leafless tree that much darker. Buildings looked less defined beyond the fenced-in yard where they were playing, although they knew where the barn and the shed and the smoke house were standing.

Their father's wrath had been forgotten in the forbidden pleasure, so when they heard his voice suddenly booming out across the backyard, they froze in sudden panic.

"Jake! Johnny! You two get in here right now," Joe Baretta shouted.

They bailed out of the swings in unison, their little bare feet hitting the cold ground in splats. As always, they looked to the other for assurance.

Whatever was coming, they could face it just fine as long as they had each other.

Joe shivered, then hid a smile as he watched the boys coming toward him hand in hand. The little idiots. It was cold as hell out here. When they reached the porch, their heads were hanging low. He grabbed them both, forcing them to look at him.

"What on earth were you boys trying to prove?" he asked angrily. "Tomorrow's a school day, and you should be in bed."

Two pairs of teary green eyes gazed up at him in mute defeat. He couldn't bear the expressions on their faces and scrubbed his knuckles playfully across the crown of each head as he shooed them inside.

"What were you guys doing out there?" he asked as he shut and locked the door.

They turned, a look of amazement on their faces, as if they couldn't believe he'd had to ask.

"We were chasing the moon," they said in unison.

He rolled his eyes and headed them down the hall. Already he could hear Angie running a tub of water and figured she planned to warm them up with a hot bath before putting them back to bed.

"Boys!"

They both paused and turned in unison. "Yes, Daddy?"

"I don't want you to pull this stunt again, do you hear me?"

"Yes, Daddy."

"Besides, you can't catch the moon, only shadows, and maybe pneumonia, if you don't get out of those damp clothes."

The twins looked at each other and exchanged secretive grins. They knew better. Not only had they chased the moon, but twice they'd almost caught it.

Chapter 1

New Zion, Kentucky
Present day

*G*racie Moon stood at the edge of the river, her fishing pole float bobbing in the water. Her blue jeans were old, her T-shirt soft and well-worn. Her hair was long and black, and this morning in honor of her fishing expedition, she wore it in a single braid down the middle of her back. She teetered back and forth on the tips of her toes, while her eldest brother, Brady, watched from the shore.

Suddenly the float went under, and she gave the pole a yank.

"I caught another one!" The fish came flying out of the water and up on the bank where it promptly unhooked itself and began to flop.

Brady laughed and ran to catch it before it got back in the water. Holding it firmly by the lip, he threaded the stringer through the fish's gill, adding it to the stringer of fish that she'd already caught. He held it up for inspection.

"Father is going to love breakfast this morning," he said. "Fresh panfried fish is his favorite."

"I know," Gracie said. "And fishing is my favorite thing. It works well together, don't you think?"

Droplets from the mist were clinging to Gracie's face and hair. Brady grinned down at her and tweaked her nose. Eleven years separated them in age, and he'd been her champion ever since she could remember.

"Remember the day you baited your first hook?" he asked.

Gracie laughed. "Yes, and you made sure I didn't forget it. Mother made spaghetti that night, and every time you took a bite, you held up the spaghetti noodles, dangling them like worms over your mouth before you slurped them down your throat."

"Didn't you know it's a brother's duty to aggravate younger siblings, especially sisters?" He hugged her, just because he could.

Gracie spun out of his arms and reached for her fish. "Come on," she said. "Father's probably wondering where I've gone."

Brady shook his head, "He won't worry. He knows I would never let anyone hurt you." A shadow darkened his eyes as he added, "Ever."

Gracie rolled her eyes. "Oh, Brady, you treat me as if I'm still a child."

She picked up her pole and the stringer of fish and started back up the mountain to the compound where her family dwelled.

Gracie's words were still echoing in Brady's head as he stared into the swiftly moving water. When he glanced up she was already out of sight. He sighed, picked up his rifle, and followed her up the path. She was right. Father would be waiting.

The sun was little more than a promise on the horizon when John Baretta stepped outside his small one-room cabin to greet the day. Due to an early-morning fog, visibility was almost nonexistent, and he knew by the time the sun came up and the moisture in the air began to rise, it would get worse before it got better.

Right now, he could almost appreciate the wisdom of an old man who'd uprooted his family and retreated to the uppermost regions of these Kentucky hills. Elijah Moon was a pacifist. A man who had created a community on these desolate mountains that he called New Zion. Fed up with the world, and saddened by the loss of his wife of forty-eight years, he'd rejected everything except God and family.

John closed his eyes, savoring the softness of the mist upon his face. Here in the early-morning quiet, it was almost as if the last one hundred years had never been. Far away from what Elijah called the rot of civilization, the peace on the mountains seemed close to holy.

But John Baretta knew that when the fog burned off, it would be impossible to hide the truth of what New Zion had become. In spite of the old man's dreams, his eldest son, Brady Moon, had turned New Zion into a hotbed of militia-minded people seeking revenge, and blaming everyone except themselves for their troubles.

Six weeks ago, John Baretta had arrived in Little Rome, Kentucky, posing as the last surviving relative of the recently deceased Lady Crockett. It wasn't the first time the Bureau of Alcohol, Tobacco, and Firearms had sent him undercover, but this time it was proving to be one of the most difficult cases. However, like his brother, Jake, who worked for another agency of the federal government, John Baretta was very good at what he did.

Coming into Little Rome as Jake Crockett was easier than he'd imagined. The late Lady Crockett did have a grandson named Jacob Crockett. But she hadn't seen him since he was a baby, and neither had anyone else in Little Rome. So while the real Jake Crockett was safely behind bars in a California maximum security prison, John Baretta was living a lie behind a criminal's name.

To John, the irony of it all had been the name he was given to use. It wouldn't be hard to answer to the name Jake. As children, he and his twin had often traded identities. They were so identical that once in a while even their parents had to look twice to see which twin was which.

John inhaled slowly, savoring the clean, fresh scent of the piney woods and listening to the moisture dripping from the leaves on nearby trees.

In the last few weeks, he'd become a part of the group, almost by name alone. Lady Crockett's husband, like so many in this part of the country, had long been a vocal supporter of the right to bear arms. And Jake Crockett made no bones about having served time in prison. His antigovernment rhetoric alone had made him a welcome member of New Zion.

But as welcomed as he'd been, in a few days he planned to leave. He had seen and heard all he needed to have warrants issued and everyone connected with New Zion convicted and imprisoned. And while he felt satisfaction for a job well done, he knew he was going to have one regret, and that was Elijah Moon's only daughter, Gracie. Because of where she lived, she was going to be brought down with the rest, and he would have bet his entire career that she was innocent of Brady Moon's intrigue.

Off to his left, a limb cracked. The sound echoed like a muffled gunshot and John jerked, then turned. When a woman emerged through the mist, he relaxed, smiling a slow, easy smile. Moisture had collected on her long, black braid, as well as on her shirt and jeans. If the sun had been out, John knew that she would have been sparkling. Yet, Gracie Moon didn't need the sunshine to sparkle. That came from within.

She kept coming toward him, and his gaze never wavered. When she was less than a yard away, he spoke, savoring the way her name felt on his tongue.

"Morning, Gracie."

Gracie Moon didn't pretend surprise. From the moment she started up from the river, she'd known exactly where she would be going. At his greeting, she paused.

"Good morning, Jake. You're up early."

His grin widened as he noted the stringer of fish she was carrying.

"Not as early as you, it seems. You've already caught breakfast, I see."

Gracie lifted the fish. "Would you like one? I'd be glad to share."

The idea of eating fresh panfried fish instead of another bowl of oatmeal in the great hall was appealing. He didn't need a second invitation.

"Don't mind if I do," he said softly, and took the stringer from her hands. "But I like to pay for my keep. How about if I clean these for you?"

She smiled and looked away. The single dimple in her right cheek popped in and out of place so quickly John almost didn't see it. When she looked back, her brown eyes were dancing.

"I like to fish, but I hate to clean them. I was hoping you'd offer."

He laughed, and it came back at him, bouncing against the trees and the fog in a muffled burst of sound.

"Come on," he said. "I'll walk you back to your cabin. You shouldn't be out on these mountains alone, anyway."

Sure of their destination, they soon disappeared into the mist, unaware that they had not been alone.

Brady Moon stepped out of the trees. He carried a rifle slung over his shoulder by a strap, and his

clothing was as dark as the expression on his face.
He didn't like Jake Crockett, and he liked even less
the royal treatment his father had given him.
Brady was a covetous son. He was the eldest of Elijah's eight children and felt it was his right to be
the favored one as well. While he pretended to
himself it was so, he knew that Elijah Moon shared
himself and his love equally with all of his children.

Then he heard the sound of Gracie's laughter as
she and Crockett walked still farther away. As he
stood there, a thoughtful expression crossed his
face.

"Come on, Crockett, ride down the mountain with
me," Brady pleaded, and the wide, engaging smile
upon his face became wider as he continued. "Besides, I could use a strong back to help me load the
supplies."

It was the last thing John wanted to do, but he'd
been put on the spot. Elijah was coming toward
them, his long, white beard shifting against his
body with every stride. Gracie walked beside him,
her hand beneath his elbow to steady the old
man's gait.

"I'd promised to help Gracie plant peas," he
said.

Gracie laughed, her dark eyes dancing beneath
the bright light of the sun. "Such dedication should
be rewarded. Please, go to town with Brady. Kay or
Annie will help."

John didn't have another excuse to offer, and

Gracie's claim that one of her sisters-in-law would help was true. The entire family lived in a communal atmosphere. What one had, they all had.

"Then I guess that settles it," he said to Brady. "Let me get my hat."

Moments later, he slid in beside Brady and leaned back in the seat.

"I'm your man," he said nonchalantly.

Brady grinned and fired up the truck.

The wind funneling through the open windows of the cab picked up speed as they started off the mountain toward Little Rome.

"Do you make this trip often?" John asked.

Suddenly, there was tension in Brady's voice. "What trip?"

"You know . . . off the mountain to get groceries."

The tension eased and he shrugged. "It depends. Usually every couple of months, I guess."

John nodded. Now what the hell do I talk about? That question set off bells I don't want ringing.

Suddenly a buck bounded in and out of the road ahead. It happened so quickly John could almost believe he'd imagined it. Almost, but not quite. The majesty of the animal was still there in his mind, even though it was already gone.

"Wow, did you see that?" John asked. "I'll bet he was at least a twelve-pointer. He better stick to the trees or he'll wind up on somebody's table."

Brady's eyes narrowed. "Yeah, and if those damned bleeding hearts in Washington had their way, we wouldn't have a gun to hunt with. There are people up here who would starve to death if someone took away their right to bear arms."

John nodded. He knew that the ban on assault weapons had absolutely no impact on someone who wanted to hunt for food. The ban had nothing to do with pump shotguns and deer rifles. And the push to make the "cop-killer" bullets illegal wouldn't have a thing to do with selling bird shot or ammunition for some young man's squirrel gun.

But tell that to fanatics who lived to "play war" and whose livelihood consisted of buying and selling illegal weapons and making plans to get even with a faceless government.

Just as they started around a bend in the road, the truck started to list. Moments later the familiar flap, flap, flap could be heard of a tire going flat.

"Damnation." Brady pulled over.

John got out on one side as Brady exited the other. The left front tire was sitting on the rim.

"Oh, well," Brady said. "It won't take long to fix."

He scooted beneath the bed of the pickup to undo the jack and the spare. Moments later another string of curses could be heard, and this time, they were more virulent.

"What's wrong?" John asked, as Brady came up from under the truck.

"No jack. Somebody took my jack." He kicked at the flat and turned in a circle, frustrated by the news. He looked at John, then down at his watch. "Well, there's no help for it but to go back to the compound and get one."

John started around the truck when Brady held up his hand.

"Why don't you wait here by the truck? There's no sense in both of us walking. We're not more than a couple of miles away, and if someone gives me a ride back it should only take a half hour or so."

"Sounds good to me," John said. He glanced into the thick growth of trees around him with interest. "Maybe that old buck will come back and we'll have ourselves a little chat."

Brady combed his hand through his thick red hair, and laughed, his teeth gleaming white in the bright light of day.

"You're a card, Crockett, and that's a fact," he said, waving as he started back up the mountain.

John grinned. It never hurt to stay on the good side of a man like Brady—just in case.

Minutes went by until a quarter of an hour had passed. John got bored sitting inside the truck and got out to stretch his legs, kicking at a rock in the road as he headed toward the ditch on the other side. He was almost there when the hair suddenly rose on the back of his neck. It was that instinct for survival that made him jerk, and because he did, the bullet that came down off the mountain hit him hard in the shoulder instead of square in the back as it had been meant.

He grunted from the impact as it slammed him facedown in the dirt, and for a moment he couldn't think—couldn't move. Then an instinct for survival pulled him to his knees, and he started crawling, falling more often than not as he made his way across the ditch and into the woods.

Once inside the cover of the trees, he pulled himself to his feet, clutching at the pain in his chest. The bullet had exited somewhere between his shoulder and his heart. Blood was pumping out in gushes, staining the blue denim of his shirt a dark, ugly black.

Jesus, help me.

It was his last coherent thought as he started to run.

Chapter 2

*T*he pain hit just as Jake Baretta was walking out of a cantina in Tijuana. Like a shaft of fire, it exploded in his shoulder, from the back to the front, and although he hadn't heard the gun, he knew that he'd been shot. Grabbing his chest, he staggered, then fell and rolled, and when he came upright, he had his gun in his hand. The woman beside him screamed and ran back inside, shouting something in Spanish he didn't have time to interpret. He was too busy trying to breathe.

Son of a bitch.

It took a few seconds for him to realize that not only was he not bleeding, but he was pretty sure he hadn't been shot. With a skill born of long years on the job, he carefully scanned the area and came to the conclusion that the only person in sight with a gun was him. The pain began to dissipate, and his skin turned clammy with fear. He didn't have to wonder what had just happened, he already knew. He wasn't the one who'd been shot—it was John.

His gut clenched. He holstered his gun and

started running for his car. The woman he'd been with came out of the cantina, screaming at the top of her lungs, but he didn't stop. He had to get to a phone. Somewhere, his brother was in trouble.

Ron Hudson, the deputy director of the Bureau of Alcohol, Tobacco, and Firearms, stood by as Joe and Angie Baretta leaned over their son's bed. His heart ached for them. John Baretta was dying, and there was no getting around the fact. Hudson had known and worked with John for almost nine years. Danger was always a factor in their job, but somehow, he'd believed John to be immune.

Behind him, the door to the room suddenly opened, and an agent sitting just inside stood, ready to block the way of intruders. Instead, it was John's doctor, making his rounds.

"Would you mind waiting outside for a few minutes?" He stepped aside, expecting everyone to leave the room.

At the stricken look on the Barettas' faces, Hudson decided to intervene. Considering John Baretta's condition, what could it hurt?

"Doc, if you don't mind, we'll stay. Okay?"

The doctor caught the inference all too well. The asking had only been a formality.

"As you wish," he said.

Joe Baretta took his wife and moved to Hudson's side as the doctor began his examination.

"Thank you, Mr. Hudson," Joe said.

"No problem." Hudson glanced toward the bed. "How's he doing?"

Joe couldn't answer. He feared the worst and didn't have it in him to say it aloud.

Hudson searched for a change of subject and remembered that John's brother was due anytime.

"So, I'm told your other son, Jake, is on his way."

Joe nodded.

Hudson rocked on the heels of his shoes and then stuffed his hands in his pockets. *Goddamn, but I hate this part of my job.* He glanced at the doctor, wincing when a strident beep sounded on one of the machines to which John was hooked. He took a deep breath and tried conversation again.

"You know, I still can't get over the fact that John's brother was already on the phone with Washington and wanting to know what had happened to John before we even knew he'd been hit."

At the mention of Jake's name, Angie Baretta took a deep breath and covered her face. Her husband touched her arm and then looked at his son's boss.

"They've always been that way," he said. "You know . . . if Jake broke his nose, John's bled, too. If John got the flu, Jake threw up as well, even though he wasn't sick. That kind of thing."

Ron Hudson shuddered. "That's almost impossible to believe."

Joe looked at his son, lying so still on the bed, and gently shook his head. "Not for people who've raised identical twins."

Ron nodded, although he didn't really buy the theory of psychic connections between identical siblings.

Across the room, the doctor made some notations on John's chart and then handed it to his
nurse before heading their way.

Angie Baretta took a hesitant step forward.

"Doctor?"

The longing in her voice was impossible to miss.

"I'm sorry, Mrs. Baretta, but there's nothing more
I can do. Your son lost too much blood before he
was found. His kidneys have already shut down.
I'm afraid it's only a matter of time before—"

Angie Baretta's cry of despair silenced the rest
of the doctor's explanation. There was nothing
else he could say, and moments later, he left the
room.

Hudson turned away, unable to watch the grief
spreading upon their faces. He felt sick inside—
sick of the violence in his job, sick of losing too
many good men, and sick as hell that it was going
to happen again.

His radio squawked, and a disembodied voice
gave a brief announcement.

"Chief. Helicopter arrival imminent. Less than
five minutes out."

Ron touched Joe's arm. "That should be the one
with your son. As soon as it lands, I'll bring him
in." He bolted for the door, glad to have something
to do besides watch a man die.

When he got to the hospital roof, he was surprised to see that it was almost dark, but the landing pad was well lit. He looked up, watching as the
incoming helicopter started its descent. The force
of the rotors sent wind slapping at the sides of the

building and all but knocked him off of his feet. He grabbed the edges of his jacket and squinted against the force.

Before the helicopter had time to settle, a door suddenly opened, and a tall, dark man emerged. Momentarily silhouetted against the backdrop of the city lights and the landing lights on the helipad, he looked like he'd come out of hell, and Hudson remembered that Jake Baretta worked for an agency of the government that few even knew existed. Dressed in black, from his boots to a jacket and turtleneck shirt, Jake Baretta started toward Ron Hudson in a lope, and Hudson was reminded of a big panther about to spring. He had an overwhelming urge to run before he was overtaken and eaten alive, and then reality surfaced as the man spoke.

"Are you Hudson?"

Behind them, the helicopter did a quick ascent, making an answer impossible to be heard. Ron nodded instead.

"Take me to my brother," Jake ordered.

Hudson turned and led the way.

Jake was scared. As scared as he'd ever been in his life. He could feel John's spirit slipping away. And when he walked in the room and saw his parents' faces, he knew his worst fears were about to come true.

"Mom. Dad."

They turned in unison, and then held out their arms. With a weeks' worth of black whiskers on his face and dressed all in black, Jake Baretta might have looked like the mercenary he'd been pretending to be, but inside he felt like a child—lost and alone, so very alone. Even after their arms encircled him and he clutched at them in desperation, the feeling didn't lessen. He wondered if when John died that he might die, too.

Angie Baretta was sobbing quietly against Jake's chest. The sound pierced his heart.

"Come on, Mom. He's tough as nails. I ought to know, right? Let's don't count him out yet."

Joe touched Jake's arm and then shook his head. "Not this time, son. I think we're all out of miracles."

Jake pushed away from them and moved to John's side. The bandage on John's shoulder was right where he'd expected it to be, and he touched his own arm in disbelief. Even after all these years, the magic between them was still there.

Black hair was matted to John's forehead, and Jake reached out and gently brushed it back. To everyone's surprise, John's eyes suddenly opened, and there was a sense of recognition on his face that none would have believed possible.

Jake stared, his gaze fixed into the wide, beseeching stare of his other half, and then he straightened and turned. His features were immobile, revealing nothing of what he was thinking. He turned and stared at the people gathered around John's bed.

"Get out."

Hudson jerked in reflex. The tone of Jake's voice was so sharp, the words almost hurt.

"Look, son, we can't just—"

"Get out. Now."

His parents were the first to respond. They'd seen far too many secret moments come and go between the boys not to know this was something Jake felt had to be done. They left without question.

Jake glanced at the guard by the door. "And take him with you."

For a reason Hudson couldn't fathom, he found himself obeying the odd request.

When they were finally alone, Jake turned to find John clutching his hand. He leaned down and laid his cheek against his brother's face, and even then, he felt the life and the warmth slipping away.

"John . . . Johnny . . . what did they do to you?"

John struggled for breath, fighting against the blackness that kept pulling him down. This was Jake—his brother—the other half of himself. He held on for dear life, using Jake's strength to get it all said.

Images came and went in his head so fast that it was like watching his life rewind. He licked his lips, blinking as he suddenly saw his mother's face, and then it was gone. When he opened his eyes, Jake was still there, waiting—just as John had known he would be. He took a deep breath, and a hollow feeling began to appear around his heart. Urgently, he gripped Jake's hand, and Jake leaned closer. If John could, he would have smiled. Jake always understood.

"Johnny, tell me. Who did this to you?" Jake asked.

John Baretta exhaled. It was little more than a soft, helpless sigh, but with it came the words he'd been trying to say.

"The moon . . . chase the moon."

And then he closed his eyes and let go.

Jake Baretta had heard it said that the quicker the spirit leaves the body, the faster that soul will reach heaven. At the moment John's eyes fell shut, Jake felt something move past him, like a breath of air. He knew before the monitor flat-lined that his brother was gone. Grief such as he'd never known swept through him, and he laid his arm across his brother's chest and hid his face on the pillow beside John's head.

"No," he whispered, and tried to pull John back from where he'd gone. "No," he said louder, begging God to give him back. "No!" he groaned, and started to rock John in his arms. "No!" he raged, but John was too far away to hear his brother's cry.

Out in the hall, Joe and Angie Baretta heard Jake's cry of disbelief and gave way to the grief they'd been holding back.

"Oh, Joe, how are we going to live without him?" she sobbed.

Joe held her close as his tears fell down upon her hair. "We'll find a way," he said softly, while his own heart broke. "Somehow, we'll find a way."

Ron Hudson kicked at a trash can out in the hall and headed for the men's room. It wasn't that he was ashamed to cry, it was just something he liked to do in private. A short while later, he came out, unprepared for the man who awaited him.

"We need to talk," Jake said.

Ron blinked in disbelief. Somehow, he'd been expecting Jake Baretta to be consoling his parents, not spoiling for a fight.

"I'm really sorry about John," Hudson said. "He was a damned good man."

Jake wanted to scream. He wanted to cry. He wanted to rage at the heavens for taking John from them. But Jake wouldn't have found solace in the letting of grief. For him, that would come after he watched the man who'd shot his brother in the back take his last breath.

"I know what John was," Jake said softly. "What I need to know is where was he when this happened."

"I'm sorry, but that's classified infor—"

Jake took Hudson by the arm. It was a firm, no-nonsense grip that shouldn't have been threatening, and yet somehow it was.

"Look, Hudson. I have a classified clearance that's probably higher than the president's. I know what John did for you. What I need to know is where I'll be going."

Hudson's mouth dropped. "What the hell are you saying?" he asked.

"I'm telling you that you're going to send me back to wherever John was as whoever he was pretending to be. And I'm not coming out until I bring the damn back shooter with me. Understood?"

Hudson shook his head. "No way, Baretta. Use your head. Not only is that impossible, but it would be suicide. You'd be made on the spot."

Jake wouldn't let go. "I'll be in your office to-morrow by nine A.M. You make sure my parents get home safely with John's body, but don't let anyone know that he's . . . that he's . . ."

Jake swallowed harshly. It was impossible to say the word.

Hudson thrust a hand through his hair. "I need my head examined for even considering this," he muttered.

"Just trust me," Jake said, and moments later he was gone.

It was 9:00 A.M. on the dot when Jake Baretta entered the outer office of Ronald P. Hudson, Deputy Director of the Bureau of Alcohol, Tobacco, and Firearms.

A pretty woman in a pale green suit looked up and smiled.

"John! It's been ages since we've seen you. Welcome back!"

Jake flinched but managed a smile and a nod. He didn't know who the hell she was, but it didn't really matter. What mattered was that he'd passed the first test, as he'd known he would.

"Love that jacket," she said, as she picked up the phone and buzzed the inner office. "Mr. Hudson, John Baretta to see you." A pause, then another smile as she glanced back at Jake. "You may go in."

"Thanks," Jake said gruffly, and hurried past.

He'd impersonated John a hundred times in their lives, and vice versa, but this was the first time it gave him the creeps. It almost seemed sacrilegious, but then he remembered his mission and pushed the thought aside. He kept telling himself— *Whatever it takes. Whatever it takes.*

Even though Ron Hudson was prepared for a similarity, he was completely unprepared for the exact same face. Last night it had been concealed beneath a week's worth of whiskers, and the mercenary-style clothing Jake had been wearing was so unlike John's style. But today, dressed in boots and jeans, a blue denim shirt, and a brown bomber jacket, Jake Baretta *was* John. They were one and the same.

"Well, hell," Ron said.

Jake's heart lurched again. Hudson was going to go for it. He could see it in his face.

"I want all the details, including where John was shot and who found him. I want to know everything he knew going in, and whatever he told you coming out."

Hudson suddenly frowned. "It'll never work," he said.

"Why not?"

"The scar. You would have to have a scar from the bullet wound."

Jake shucked his jacket and unbuttoned his shirt, peeling it back from his shoulders, then letting it fall to his waist as he held out his arms and turned around in place.

"Take your pick."

Hudson's breath caught, and for the first time since the issue had been raised, he began to consider it.

"What about your boss?" he asked.

Jake paused in the act of rebuttoning his shirt and looked up.

"Let's just say it's been taken care of."

Hudson knew that was all the explanation he was going to get. Impulsively, he got up from his desk and walked to a set of cabinets on the opposing wall. He opened a drawer and pulled out a file as thick as a man's fist.

"This is all John knew going in. We don't know what he learned while he was there. He wasn't conscious long enough when he came out to talk about it. A trucker found him sprawled at the edge of a highway outside of Little Rome, Kentucky. He was airlifted to Lexington. We were alerted later and had him transferred here to D.C. After that, you know the rest."

Jake's rage grew. Picturing his brother alone and dying on a highway gave him ideas that were better left unthought. He took the file and then flopped down in a nearby chair.

"What are you doing?" Hudson asked.

"Getting ready to meet the enemy."

Hudson sighed and picked up the phone. "You're a hard man, Jake Baretta. But where you're going, that just might be a plus."

Jake didn't bother to answer. He was deep in the file, too busy tracing his brother's last steps. A few moments later a name jumped out at him, and his heart skipped a beat. The family John had been sent to investigate was named Moon. A look of shock spread across his face as he remembered John's last words.

Chase the moon.

Tension drew a knot in Jake's stomach. John had been investigating some people named Moon. Damn! Jake wondered if John had been trying to name who'd shot him, or had his mind been wandering back to the happier days of their youth? Jake shuddered, then cast away the thought, focusing on nothing but the facts before him. If one of them did shoot John, did that mean his cover had been blown?

If so, then going back to Kentucky as Jake Crockett was like asking to be gut-shot, then waiting to die.

Gracie kicked at a pebble as she walked toward the cabin. Her arms were tired from hoeing weeds in the garden, and she was hot. As she passed by the empty cabin where Jake Crockett had been staying, her eyebrows knitted into a frown. It still didn't make sense. Although they'd done little more than talk, she thought he'd liked her. Her heart was heavy as she looked away. Obviously not, or he would have at least said good-bye.

She paused by the toolshed long enough to put up her hoe and was in the act of shutting the door when she heard footsteps behind her. She turned. It was Taggert Brown's wife, Moira. Gracie waved a hello, trying not to stare at the fresh bruise on Moira's cheek.

"Gracie, I'm glad I caught you," Moira said, and then glanced nervously over her shoulder.

Gracie frowned. She didn't have to ask to know why Moira was so nervous. Everyone in the compound knew that Taggert beat his wife, but no one seemed inclined to intervene. The terse remarks she'd made to Taggert on Moira's behalf had garnered a threat from Taggert and a scolding from her father. She'd had to settle for being Moira's leaning post instead.

Gracie brushed her finger lightly across the dark bruise. "Are you all right?" she asked softly.

Moira paled, then covered the bruise with her hand. "It's nothing," she said quickly. "Besides, I didn't come about me, it's my eldest. I know it's summer and school's out, but I wondered if there was something I could be doing to help him catch up. You know how behind he was in his math when school let out, I thought . . ."

Gracie smiled. "Do you want me to tutor him?" she asked.

Moira's voice rose an octave, giving way to the tension under which she constantly lived. "No! No! Taggert wouldn't hear of that," she cried, glancing over her shoulder again before continuing. "I thought maybe I could borrow one of your books, or some of those flash cards. I have a mind to help him some on my own."

Gracie nodded. "Of course, and it's a wonderful idea. All parents should take as much interest in their children's education as you do."

Moira Brown smiled, and in that moment Gracie saw the girl she must have been.

"I have a set of flash cards at the cabin. Come with me and I'll—"

"Oh, I can't just now," Moira said. "Taggert will be back any time now, and I'm not through with the wash. Maybe I could get them later, after supper?"

"That will be fine," Gracie said. "I'll be waiting."

Moira smiled her thanks and then turned, hastening away as quickly as she'd appeared.

Gracie tried not to be concerned. Moira Brown was a grown woman who was here by choice. She didn't have to stay with Taggert Brown if she didn't want to. No one was holding a gun to her head. And then she thought of the bruise on Moira's cheek and the countless other times she'd seen evidence of Taggert's abuse toward his wife, and wondered if she might be wrong. If Taggert was the kind of man to beat his wife, then he very well might be the kind to take a gun to her, as well.

Suddenly she shuddered. All thoughts of Jake Crockett's untimely exit from her life were forgotten as she headed toward her cabin.

The Greyhound bus was slowing down. Jake looked up from the newspaper he'd been reading, then tossed it in the empty seat beside him. It was July. Almost a month had come and gone since John's death. Enough time for a bullet wound to heal and a man to come back for revenge. It was going to be Jake's story, and it was a good one. Because of the trucker who'd found him and the ambulance call that had gone out, everyone in Little Rome had known about John's injury, but none knew anything past the fact that he'd been airlifted into Lexington. Hudson had assured him of that.

The bus pulled up to a café and parked. A few minutes later, Jake was standing in the street and watching the bus's taillights disappearing into the distance. A couple of people glanced at him, but it was nothing more than curiosity. He shouldered his duffel bag and started walking. Thanks to the map he'd seen of Little Rome, he knew where Lady Crockett's house was located. As Jake Crockett, all he had to do was go home. And if Little Rome was anything like small-town America, by nightfall, it would be all over town that Jake Crockett was back.

The milk in the refrigerator was sour. Jake poured it down the sink. He found a box of dry cereal in the cabinet, but when he poured some into a bowl, there were more weevils in it than raisins. At that point, he tossed it all into the trash and headed out the door to look for a grocery store.

Half an hour later he was pushing a cart up the bread aisle when he sensed someone staring at him. He looked up. There was a short, stocky man in bib overalls grinning at him from the end of the aisle. He tensed. *Damn. Someone I should know.*

The man approached and slapped Jake on the shoulder. "Crockett! When did you get back into town? When you left us in New Zion, we didn't think we'd be seeing you again."

Damn. One of the Zionists already. Remembering that he was supposed to be recovering from a wound to that shoulder, he winced from the impact of the man's hand and answered with a wary tone in his voice.

"Considering the condition in which I left here, that doesn't surprise me."

The man frowned. "What do you mean by that?" he asked, then added, "And what's wrong with your arm?"

Jake almost sneered. "As if the whole damn lot of you don't know."

The man bristled and then lowered his voice. "Just what do you mean by that? My father treated you like you were one of the family. Seems to me that you have a pretty poor way of showing your appreciation. Especially after the way you up and disappeared."

Jake was a pretty good judge of character, and this fellow seemed to be genuinely puzzled by his behavior.

"I didn't *up* and disappear," Jake drawled.

"The hell you didn't. I watched you and Brady leave. Thirty minutes later, Brady is walking back into New Zion to get a jack. I took him back to the truck myself and you were nowhere in sight. We were both pretty stunned. You were supposed to be keeping an eye on the truck and you were gone."

This was where it got tricky. Jake took a deep

breath. "I don't remember much of that day. The doctor said that was pretty common, considering the fact that I almost died."

The man's jaw dropped, and Jake would have sworn his surprise was sincere.

"Died? What? How?"

"Can't really say," Jake said. "All I know is I woke up in a hospital with a bullet wound in my back."

Horror spread on the man's face. "Shot? You were shot?" He touched Jake's shoulder again, only this time gently. "I'm sorry. I didn't know. I would never have thumped you so hard. Did I hurt you? Are you all right?"

Before Jake could answer, a sales clerk came around the end of the aisle.

"Oh, there you are, Aaron. I just wanted to tell you that we have your truck loaded and ready to go."

So this is Aaron Moon. It was good to have a face to put with a name. But if he remembered correctly, Elijah Moon had six other sons and a daughter. There would be other meetings that might not be as simple to get through as this one had been. He tossed a loaf of bread in his cart, reminding himself that he'd known it wouldn't be easy.

Aaron waved at the clerk. "Thanks, Eddie. I'll be right there," and then he turned back to Jake. "Come home with me. Father will be so glad to see you." He smiled to ease what he was about to say. "In fact, you were such a favorite of his that we were all a little bit jealous."

"Jealous enough for someone to want me dead?"

Aaron shook his head. "This isn't good. You shouldn't be thinking this way about us. Please, come back with me. Talk to Father. He always knows the right thing to do."

Jake's pulse leaped. So soon? He didn't know how to react. Instinct told him to play the invitation down. Instead of agreeing, he shook his head.

"I don't know how I feel about that anymore," Jake said.

Aaron frowned. "Okay. I won't force the issue. But don't think this is over. Father will not be happy to learn what has happened to you, and he will be especially upset that you could think one of us caused you harm."

When Aaron left, Jake breathed a quiet sigh of relief and pushed his cart toward the checkout stand. The first monumental meeting had come and gone, and the world had not come to an end. And then he amended himself. Not yet.

They came after dark. There was a knock on the door, and Jake's instinct was to turn out the lights and go for his gun. Instead, he laid aside the book he'd been reading and stood to receive his visitors.

Dressed all in black, from his coat to his pants to his shoes, with only a stark white shirt and a flowing white beard for contrast, the old man on the porch awaited an invitation to enter. Jake recognized Aaron Moon from earlier in the day, and while he didn't know the other young man beside him, he knew that the old man must be Elijah Moon. He took a chance.

"Elijah."

The old man stood without wavering, his pale blue eyes burning with an intensity that surprised Jake.

"Are you afraid to let me enter?" Elijah asked.

Jake was slightly taken aback by the old man's forthrightness. "No, sir. Just a little surprised is all." He stepped back and held the door. "Please come in." And when Aaron hesitated, Jake added, "All of you."

Aaron seemed relieved that he and his brother had been included in the invitation, and he started talking before they were all inside.

"I told Father and Burnett what had happened. They both wanted to come talk to you in person."

Jake nodded. "Have a seat," he said. "Sorry I don't have any refreshments to offer you, but I didn't buy anything but necessities. Anything more would have been more than I could carry home."

Elijah Moon touched Jake's arm, and Jake would have sworn he saw tears in the old man's eyes.

"We thought you just walked off the mountain after the tire went flat. My heart is heavy that you suffered alone when there were so many nearby who would have cared for you."

Suffered alone? Dear God, if it had not been for John's courage and strength, he would have died alone, too.

Jake refrained from showing emotion, but it was the most difficult thing he'd ever done in his life. He kept seeing John's face. Remembering John's eyes boring into his. Feeling the life slipping out of his brother's body. Hearing his mother's cries of anguish and his father's harsh sobs. Instead of answering Elijah, he turned away.

Burnett Moon stood abruptly. "Jake Crockett."

Jake turned.

"You look into my eyes and tell me that you think I could do such a cowardly thing as shoot you in the back, and I swear, as God is my witness, I will walk out of this house and never bother you again."

Jake stared. This man was younger than Aaron and slightly taller, but his clothing was similar, as was his manner. They seemed genuinely concerned that Jake not think badly of them, or their name. *Do it now*, Jake told himself. *Make your move now.*

He took a deep breath. *Forgive me, Johnny. If this is the bastard, he will pay.*

"No. I don't suppose I thought it was you." Jake looked at Aaron. "Or you." His gaze moved to the old man who stood tall, as if bracing himself for a blow by an unseen hand. "Or you, sir. I don't believe it was you." And when they would have interrupted, he continued, "But someone did, and your people were the last people I can remember being with."

Elijah Moon's gaze never wavered: "If you distrust us so, then why have you come back?"

Jake's gaze hardened. He was no longer pretending. "To find the back-shooting bastard and make him pay."

Elijah nodded. "That is fair. An eye for an eye. So it is written. So I believe." And then the old man stepped forward, placing his hands on Jake's shoulders and staring deep into Jake's eyes. "Come back to New Zion. We must prove to you that your enemy is not within our walls. If you feel the need, then I swear on God's holy name that I and my sons will personally protect you at all times until you can see for yourself that we are innocent of what you believe."

Jake relaxed his guard and nodded.

For the first time since he'd walked in the house, Elijah Moon smiled.

"Praise the Lord," he said softly. "Will you come now?"

Jake glanced around the house. "There are a couple of things I should do here first."

Elijah lifted his chin, and his beard shifted like a heavy fall of snow in a late-winter storm.

"So be it, then. I'll send someone for you tomorrow," he said.

Jake nodded. "I'll be ready."

Chapter 3

Jake counted fifteen small cabins, one long build-ing that looked like it could be a meeting hall, and at least a dozen small outbuildings of all sizes and shapes. In spite of the rustic appearance of the buildings, a couple of things surprised him. New Zion had electricity, and he suspected that there might be phones.

"Well, how does it feel to be back?" Aaron asked as he pulled up to a cabin and parked.

Jake glanced at the man behind the wheel, glad that for once he could answer truthfully.

"I'm a little nervous."

The smile on Aaron Moon's face drooped. "I'm so sorry you've suffered, but I'm even sorrier that it's caused you to distrust us."

Jake had no response to that. "What now?"

Aaron pointed to the cabin. "I thought you'd like to get settled. Father said you'd probably want to stay where you had before."

Jake gave the small cabin a closer look. *So, Johnny, this was yours, too?* As he got out, he felt comfort in knowing that he would be sleeping in the same bed in which his brother had slept.

Aaron grabbed Jake's bag. "Let me carry this for you. You'll probably need to be careful of your shoulder for a while."

Jake swiveled on the seat, meeting Aaron's gaze. "Yes, I'm still being careful."

There was no way Aaron could mistake the inference. Jake wasn't just being careful of his healing wound, he was going to be careful of everything surrounding him until he felt safe again.

"Fair enough," Aaron said, and preceded Jake to the cabin door, then opened it and stepped aside. "Welcome home, Jacob Crockett," he said quietly.

Jake couldn't help the surge of emotion that hit him when he walked inside the small two-room cabin. He could almost feel John's presence. He watched Aaron set his bag on the small dining table, and then let his gaze sweep the room in a silent inspection.

"Not much change here," Aaron said. "The pilot on this cook stove isn't too great, so I put a new box of matches on the counter." He laughed. "But you already knew that, didn't you? Remember how Gracie laughed when you said the stove needed a jump?"

Pain hit Jake deep. Being reminded of John's warped sense of humor was worse than he'd expected.

"I guess I'll let you get settled in," Aaron said, and started toward the door. He paused. "If you'd rather cook for yourself, just go to the hall and pick up whatever you need. You know how it goes. Up here, what's mine is yours, and vice versa. However, everyone is anxious to see you again, so if you feel up to it, come eat with us at noon. I'll save you a seat."

Jake decided he had to get over this feeling of lassitude and despair. Something like that could get him killed.

"I'll be there," he promised. "What time?"

Aaron gave Jake a quizzical look. "Same time as always. You know Father. He adheres to the old ways. Break fast at dawn. Dine at high noon. Sup at sundown when work is done."

Jake reached for his bag and started unpacking his things as Aaron shut the door quietly behind him, but as soon as he was gone, Jake dropped the shirt he was holding and sank down on a nearby chair, covering his face with his hands.

"God give me strength."

Less than an hour later, he was startled by a knock on the door, but even more so by the woman behind it.

All she said was, "Oh, Jake," and then walked into his arms.

He froze and tried not to panic. *Damn, Johnny, why didn't you warn me this would happen?*

Her arms were around his waist, her cheek against his chest, and he felt her shoulders trembling. Her long dark braid felt heavy against his hands as he tentatively returned her embrace. The thrust of her breasts, the feel of her slender body against his, were startling. He hadn't prepared himself for this, or for the supposition that John could have had a personal relationship with anyone here—no less with a woman as damned beautiful as this one. Worst of all, she thought he was John.

Gracie leaned against Jake's strength while still shaking from what she'd just learned. Last night her father did something he hadn't done in the two years she'd been there with him: He'd gone down the mountain. And she'd been even more stunned by the news he brought back.

Jake Crockett had come back to New Zion. But not for a visit. The way her father had told it, he'd come for revenge. When she learned why, it had nearly broken her heart. Jake had almost died and she hadn't known. The news had given an urgency to her need to see him again, and it had been all she could do to wait for his arrival back in their midst.

In the month he'd been gone, Gracie had been surprised by how much she missed him. When he left without warning, she'd told herself it was for the best. She had no business caring for a convicted felon, and especially a man who seemed to be as locked into New Zion as her father and his followers. But while she was standing within Jake's embrace, what she should do and what she wanted to do were two entirely different things.

In fact, she felt out of place in New Zion in a way none of the other women seemed to be. Most of them seemed to be as dissident as their husbands claimed to be, and the ones who weren't were under their husband's thumbs so tightly that what they thought didn't count. Gracie wasn't a hard-core feminist, but she was an independent woman, and until she moved up here to care for her father, she'd been of independent means.

She didn't adhere to the beliefs of the New Zionists, and most of all she hadn't planned on staying. But one month had led to another and another, and here she still was, alone among family, and lonely for friends.

It took a moment for Jake's shock to pass. He didn't know who she was, but he suspected that this was Elijah Moon's only daughter. From the files he'd read, Gracie Moon was the only unattached female in New Zion. He hoped to God this was Gracie, because if John had been seeing a married woman, then that would pretty much explain why he had been shot.

He said a prayer and took a chance.

"Gracie?"

Gracie sighed. She loved to hear her name on his lips, and then she remembered herself and took a quick step back. There were tears in her eyes as she laid her hands on his shoulders.

"Father said you'd been shot." Her chin trembled, and she bit her lip to keep from crying. "He said you didn't trust us anymore." Tears hovered on the edge of her lashes. "Does that mean you don't trust me, either?"

Jake stifled a groan. My God, how could he answer her? For all he knew, she could be the one who'd pulled the trigger. Just because she was beautiful as sin, and just because there were tears in her eyes, did not make her an innocent woman. But he had to play the game. It was why he'd come.

"I guess what it means is, getting shot in the back put me off balance. Trust isn't something that's happening yet. But I'm glad to see you, too. Does that count?"

Gracie ducked her head, fighting tears, and when she looked up, there was a sad smile on her face.

"Of course it counts," she said softly.

When her gaze raked the breadth of his shoulders, Jake knew she was thinking of his wound.

"I'm fine," he said quietly, and rolled his shoulder, as if giving the muscles some ease.

Gracie's gaze moved from his arms to his chest, then swept quickly down his body before she gave him a slightly startled glance, as if embarrassed that she'd been caught looking.

In that moment, Jake knew that whatever she and John had meant to each other, they had never been intimate.

"So, what's on the agenda for today?" Jake asked.

Okay, Gracie thought. *He needs to keep it ordinary and friendly. I can do that.* She pasted on a smile she didn't feel.

"The usual, I suppose. The women are putting up the garden vegetables for winter, and the men are doing whatever it is they do to get out of actual work."

Jake chuckled before he thought, and surprised a smile on Gracie's face.

"Well, at least one thing's still the same about you," Gracie said. "You laugh at my jokes."

Jake tensed. "Am I all that different?"

Gracie stepped back with her hands on her hips and gave him a long, serious look.

The motion pulled her T-shirt too tautly across her breasts for his comfort, and it gave him far too good a look at the lithe figure beneath her jeans. He made himself concentrate on her answer rather than what she looked like when she said it.

"You know, actually you are," she said.

He stiffened. The urge to bolt was strong, but he'd come for a reason, and a pretty woman's words weren't going to change his agenda.

"How so?"

She kept looking at him. At his eyes. At the shape of his mouth. At the cut of his chin. Finally, she shrugged.

"You look the same . . . but in a way you're very different. Harder, even colder." A gentle smile accompanied her apology. "But I suppose surviving being shot in the back would do that to anyone, right?"

"It made me hate," Jake answered.

Gracie touched his arm. "Just don't hate me."

Stunned once again by her quiet beauty and her seemingly innocent manner, he could do little but agree.

"I promise I'll try real hard," he said, and a slight grin tilted the corner of his mouth.

At the sight, Gracie laughed and touched the edge of his lip. "There you are, after all. All you needed was to come out from behind that frown."

The urge to touch her was overwhelming, and Jake wondered if the need came from him, or if it was that lingering part of Johnny that he would always carry. He stepped back, letting his smile widen even more.

"So, now that you're here, how about giving me the nickel tour? Has anyone new moved in or out? Is there anything going on that I should know about?"

Gracie grinned. "Is that all?"

"No, actually, if you're not doing anything special, Aaron said I could get some food from the hall and bring it here. Want to help me carry it?"

Gracie laughed. "If you promise to clean my next stringer of fish again, it's a deal."

She took him by the hand and out the door they went. Moments later, Jake found himself walking through the compound and listening carefully to everything she was saying, as well as what she was not. And while absorbing the sights, his mind kept going back to what she'd just said about fish.

John hated to clean fish. In fact, he would have done anything to get out of the job. That little bit of information told Jake more about how John must have felt about Gracie than anything else she could have said. For some reason, the knowledge that his brother might have liked her—even loved her—made him feel worse, not better.

Elijah Moon was sitting in a cane-back rocker on the front porch of a moderate-sized cabin and reading intently. As they passed, Gracie called out to him.

"Father, I'm going to show Jake where we built the new smoke house."

Elijah looked up. When he saw Jake, he put down his Bible and stood.

Gracie smiled at her father and murmured an aside to Jake. "He looks like Charlton Heston's version of Moses, doesn't he?"

Jake almost chuckled. It would be easy to let himself be beguiled by this woman and her family. Although he had yet to see any signs of a hard-core militia, there had been too much documentation in the ATF file to ignore.

Elijah's smile was as true as the one in his eyes. Jake found himself smiling back.

"Good morning, Jacob."

"Good morning, sir," Jake said.

Elijah shook his finger in Jake's face. "You know better than that. I still answer to the name I was given."

Again, Jake found himself being put on the spot of needing to know tiny little details that only John had known but had taken with him to the grave.

"Good morning, Elijah."

The smile on the old man's face widened. "Praise the Lord, but it is a good morning at that."

Gracie touched Jake's arm. "Give me a minute, okay?"

Jake waited, watching the tenderness with which she coaxed her father out of his coat and pulled his chair farther back into the shade. Then she disappeared into the house and returned moments later with a tall glass of lemonade and a plate of cookies.

Elijah pretended to fuss, but Jake could tell that he was more than willing to partake of the cold drink.

Gracie leaned down and kissed her father's cheek, then smoothed the hair upon his head, as if he were a child.

"You didn't eat enough breakfast. Eat some of my cookies or you'll hurt my feelings, okay?" She put a cookie in her father's hand, then laid his Bible back in his lap. "There. Now you don't have an excuse left in you not to do as I say."

Elijah's smile was gentle as he watched Gracie jump from the porch. "You get more like your mother every day."

"Why, thank you, Father. As I remember, she was the only one of us all with any sense. Maybe there's hope for me yet."

She gave Jake a quick glance and then resumed their walk, assuming he would follow, which he did.

As they passed each cabin, Gracie inadvertently gave away the much-needed identity of the inhabitants by calling hello or pausing to admire a quilt in progress or to pick up a toddler who'd taken a tumble in the dirt.

Jake absorbed it all, including the way the women behaved around Gracie. It didn't take him long to realize that, both by dress and behavior, she was somewhat of an outsider.

The women Jake saw were plainly dressed and unadorned in any way. Their faces were devoid of makeup, their hair straight and slicked back in tight, ungainly buns, or hanging loose and heavy in hippie fashion. Their clothing was looser and much less revealing than Gracie's. About half of them wore dresses that hung way past their knees, while others dressed in some pseudomilitary style: baggy camouflage pants and oversized olive drab shirts. Jake could only wonder what their men looked like.

Off to their right, a slender woman with long brown hair was hanging out clothes. Each time she stooped to pick up another garment, she seemed to pause before straightening. Jake frowned, thinking to himself she must be in pain. No sooner had he thought it when Gracie suddenly veered toward her. At the sound of their footsteps, the woman turned, and Jake found himself staring at the old bruises on her cheek and the lack of expression on her face.

"Here, Moira, let me help," Gracie said, and took the heavy wet clothes out of the woman's hands.

"No, no, there's no need."

The two women shared a long look that gave Jake food for thought. There was a bond between them that had nothing to do with kinship.

Gracie finally smiled, and Jake's breath caught at the beauty of her face.

"I didn't say you needed help, I want to help," Gracie said, and persisted in hanging the clothes.

A flicker of worry came and went on Moira's face as she reluctantly accepted Gracie's help. She kept giving Jake nervous glances between handing Gracie the clothespins.

Gracie paused and glanced at Jake, then winked before turning back to Moira.

"He won't say anything," she promised.

Jake was stunned. What the hell would there be to say? And better yet, who to?

When they were finished, Gracie hugged the woman and then turned to Jake.

"Okay, now, where were we?"

"On our way to the supermarket?" he quipped.

Gracie laughed and Moira turned away, trying to hide her smile. Jake pretended he didn't notice, but he couldn't help wondering what on earth had frightened that woman enough to make her afraid to show a simple smile.

As they walked on, it occurred to him that, except for Elijah, he had yet to see a man. He glanced down at Gracie. She looked calm, almost serene, and he decided to test his luck again.

"You were right about the men," he said. "Looks like they all shucked out of here."

The smile moved past Gracie's mouth, leaving a frown on her forehead.

"Oh, you know where they are," she said, and paused to stare up at the mountaintop looming above them. "You used to be up there with them." The tone of her voice changed, and Jake felt her disapproval as she muttered beneath her breath, "Grown men playing at war."

Jake decided to test her reaction. "Playing? Is that all you think they do?"

She stumbled, and Jake caught her by the arm before she could fall.

"Darn tree root," she said quickly, and looked away.

He didn't press the issue, but could tell that he'd hit a nerve.

It wasn't until the noon meal was about to be served that the men began straggling back, and when they did, Jake got his first good look at the people with whom John had been living.

They came in the eating hall by twos and threes, sweaty and smiling, tossing jokes back and forth among themselves as they walked toward a bathroom in the back to wash up. At least a dozen men filed through, with Aaron and Burnett among them. Their wives were in the kitchen, stirring great pots of vegetables and taking large pans of meat from the ovens. Children of all ages played inside and outside of the building. And, in spite of their mothers' constant calls to come inside, seemed unwilling to stop long enough to sit down and eat.

Jake had chosen a seat in a corner of the room. The fact that it was near an open window was not an accident. He still wasn't convinced that they hadn't somehow discovered John's true identity and were just waiting for their strength in numbers to finish the job they'd first botched.

Burnett was the first to see him. He smiled and waved as he walked past. Aaron looked up, nodded solemnly, and hung his hat on a hook as he, too, moved toward the washroom in back. One after the other, the men looked at Jake; some little more than a quick, nervous glance, others staring openly. Some of them smiled; others frowned and looked away, as if embarrassed to be caught staring. Only one man met his gaze straight on, and when he did, the flesh crawled on the back of Jake's neck.

The man was huge. His overalls were faded and the side buttons undone, obviously to give him more room to breathe. His boots were black and dusty and of combat style, while his shirt was missing both sleeves. Jake suspected that was because of the size of his arms, rather than for comfort and coolness. The skin on his face was as slick and tight as a baby's bottom, while his eyes were all but lost in the folds of fat pushing up on his cheeks.

The grin he gave Jake was more like a sneer. Jake returned the look and was thankful when he was out of view.

Damn. What the hell was that all about?

It was obvious to Jake that they'd all been informed of what had happened to him, as well as why he'd come back, but he couldn't decide if their nervousness hinged on guilt or a wariness, since he was back in their midst and bent on revenge.

Finally, the food was on the table and everyone had taken a seat, including Jake. At Elijah's insis-

tence, he was sitting at his right hand, while Gracie
was on Elijah's left. From the way everyone was
staring, the placement of Jake's seating was obviously significant, but he didn't know why. He
caught more than one set of raised eyebrows and
heard the low murmurs of disapproval. But he
didn't give a damn whether they liked where he
was sitting or not. In fact, he welcomed their dis-
sent. At least he might learn something if one of
them had the temerity to speak out.

Elijah stood, and the silence that spread through
the room was impressive. Jake caught himself holding his breath. When the old man began to pray, the
words echoed in the long hall, rumbling like far-off
thunder, then building to a great crescendo.

"Father, we are gathered here today in your
presence, about to eat from the bounty of that
which you have given us. Make us worthy in your
sight. Keep us always in your heart, just as you are
always in our prayers."

Feet shifted on the floor, and someone dropped
a fork as one of the men lifted a platter. And then
Elijah startled them all by adding what was obviously an unusual addendum to his prayer.

"And Lord, if there are any among us who have
sinned against you, or our fellowman, cast him
from us and do with him what you will."

Elijah returned to his seat as if nothing untoward
had happened, but this time the silence in the room
came from shock, not reverence, and to a person,
every adult, including Gracie, looked at Jake.

Jake ignored the innuendo and picked up a bowl

of new red potatoes, taking some on his plate before passing them to his left.

"Elijah, how about some spuds?"

The old man tucked his beard between the table and his chest and reached for the bowl.

"Don't mind if I do," he said.

And the moment passed.

After the meal, the children were excused and the women cleaned up while the men gradually left the room. A few headed to their respective homes, claiming chores that needed to be done, while more than one took up residence on old army cots beneath the large, shady trees and started to snore.

Jake walked out of the building beside Elijah and Burnett. The trio parted as Burnett took his father's arm and started toward Elijah's cabin. Jake paused in the shade of the porch, surveying the small community of New Zion and thinking to himself that, except for the electric line that had been strung through the trees and up the mountain, this place looked like something out of the 1700s. Land had been cleared and cabins built from the trees they'd cut down. The few head of livestock they had were corralled close to the houses, while chickens roamed free, pecking everywhere they went.

"Damn, Crockett, since Elijah's firstborn isn't here to defend his rights, you're sure struttin' your stuff."

Jake pivoted, searching the group of men at the edge of the building for the owner of that accusation. The big, overall-clad man stepped out of the crowd, daring him to argue.

"What do you mean by that?" Jake asked.

"I mean, you settin' in Brady's seat and all as if it was yours for the takin'."

Ah. I should have known the biggest man also had the biggest mouth.

Jake kept staring at the man, absorbing his words as the threats they really were.

Jake stepped toward him with an attitude they couldn't miss. "I didn't sit anywhere I wasn't invited to sit."

The giant smiled, and his eyes seemed to disappear in the flesh, although Jake sensed he could see everything all too well.

"Well now, I suppose you could look at it that way," the man said.

"Come on, Taggert, let it rest," someone said.

"Yeah, Brown, don't start something you can't finish."

So this was Taggert Brown. The knowledge hit Jake harder than he would like to admit. Taggert Brown had a file of his own within the file on New Zion. He'd been arrested and jailed more times in his life than Jake had seen fit to count, and each offense had to do with guns. From assault with a deadly weapon to brandishing firearms in public places. The man was a walking testament to the mess the justice system was in. If life had been fair, Taggert Brown would have been languishing behind bars for the rest of his life. But here he was,

challenging Jake because he knew that there was
no one around to make him pay.

*Was it you, Taggert Brown? Were you the cowardly
bastard who shot Johnny in the back?*

Even as Jake asked the question in his mind, his
rage grew, and it made him take chances he might
not have otherwise taken. He took another step
forward, putting himself well within striking distance of Taggert's ham-sized fist.

"If you've got something else to say, then say
it," Jake said. "Otherwise, I suggest you shut up.
And before you start reminding me of manners I
might be missing, I'll remind you that my manners—and my back—have been shot all to hell.
I'm past caring what you or anyone else thinks. I
came up here for a reason, and I'm not leaving
until it's done."

Shocked by the viciousness of Crockett's unexpected attack, the men moved together like a
swarm of flies, taking comfort in their numbers.
Even Taggert was speechless. But it didn't last
long.

"So, are you sayin' you ain't goin' to work out
with us no more?" Taggert asked.

Jake's eyes glittered a clear, cold green. "If you
mean by working out, am I going to go play war in
the woods with you boys again, then hell no."

Although several of the men had decided to
move away, Taggert didn't know when to let matters drop.

"I'd like to know how come," he said loudly.

"Ever'one up here has a duty. Ever'one has a part to play."

Jake tapped a finger in the middle of Taggert Brown's tight, fat belly. "That's just it, Taggert, my friend, someone up here doesn't play fair."

Taggert frowned, at a momentary loss for words, and then his gaze moved from Jake to the women who were exiting the building, and Jake watched as the man's anger refocused on a new target. Jake turned and then his stomach knotted. *Oh, hell.* It was the woman from the clothesline.

"Moira, go get me some rags. I've a mind to clean my gun."

The woman broke free from the others and started running down the road toward the cabins.

Jake suddenly understood her behavior, and it made him sick. He glanced back at Taggert Brown and then down at his hands. Short, thick fingers. Ham-fisted hands. Hands capable of brutality. He swallowed his ire and tried not to think of that woman having to bend to Taggert Brown's will.

And then suddenly it was all too much, and Jake walked away. All the way across the compound, he could almost believe there was a gun aimed straight at his back—knew exactly how it would feel when the bullet hit him—and wondered if he would have the strength to make a run for it as John had, or if he would drop on the spot.

But the shot never came, and he made it to his cabin without further incident. After closing the door behind him, he shoved a chair beneath the knob and then leaned against the door until his legs stopped shaking and his heartbeat returned to a regular rhythm. He made himself forget the woman called Moira. She wasn't why he'd come. And for that matter, Gracie Moon couldn't matter, either. He'd come to find John's murderer, and nothing else could matter.

He sighed wearily as he looked around. The sparse furnishings of the cabin reminded him of how transient his time there really was, and he crawled onto the bunk that was his bed and laid down on his back, staring up at a knot on a rafter above his head. He stared until his eyelids grew heavy. And just before he fell asleep, he thought he heard Johnny calling out his name.

"I won't tell if you don't tell."

Jake eyed the pie cooling on the table and then glanced nervously over his shoulder. Finally, he shook his head.

"And I won't tell if you don't tell."

Johnny grabbed two forks from the kitchen drawer.

"I've got the forks. You get the pie," he whispered, and headed for the back door, holding it open as Jake came toward him, holding the warm apple pie in front of him like a coveted work of art.

Easing the back door shut, they headed across the yard to their hideout behind the chicken house, positive that their theft had gone unnoticed. But no sooner had they turned the corner and sat down to eat than Angie Baretta came flying around the chicken house with a switch in her hand.

Both boys looked up, and then at each other, in panic.

The pie was between them, the forks were in their hands. They'd been made.

"We weren't—"

"Just hush!" Angie said, brandishing the switch she was carrying. "It's bad enough you stole the pie. The least you could do is have the grace not to lie when you're caught."

Both boys ducked their heads in shame. John started to sniffle, but Jake's guilt swelled within his heart, and he refused to cry. Instead, he bit his lip and waited for the switch to fall.

Angie had other plans for her two eight-year-old thieves. "Well," she said. "What are you waiting for?"

Startled, they looked up.

They echoed in unison, "Mama, what do you mean?"

"You wanted it," she said, pointing at the pie with her switch. "Then you better get started."

John looked at Jake. Jake looked at John. John started to cry.

At this point, Angie almost relented. Tears in those big green eyes always did her in. But this time, she knew they needed to be taught a lesson.

"Eat!" she ordered.

And they did. Sniffling and sobbing through the entire apple pie, and to the boys, it tasted more like sawdust with every bite. When there was nothing left in the plate but crumbs, she took the plate and both forks and left both boys with guilty consciences and a bellyache it would take days to get over.

Jake's stomach hurt, and he knew if he never tasted another apple pie in his life it wouldn't be too soon.

"Johnny."

"What?" Johnny groaned, rolling over on his side and wishing he could puke.

"Are you sorry?"

Johnny gagged. "Oh, Jake. I don't ever want to eat pie again."

Chapter 4

*T*hree days had come and gone since Jake had taken up residence in New Zion, and it felt like three weeks, instead. Everywhere he went, he knew he was walking where John had walked, seeing what John had seen, breathing the same damned air.

But not even John's spirit could make him feel as if he was still in control. Every day he fell like he was living on a precipice, and that the moment he fell asleep, he would roll off and plummet to his death. Except for Elijah, Gracie, Aaron, and Burnett, he was a virtual outcast. Even Elijah's other sons gave him a wide berth. And the men who were in Taggert Brown's inner circle didn't dare give him the time of day for fear of repercussions from Taggert.

Jake could not have cared less whether he won a prize for congeniality, but he cared a whole lot that he wasn't able to take part in their practice skirmishes. How, he wondered, was he going to find a way to investigate what was going on up the mountain, when his every move was being watched? Every day that he spent down here in the compound was a day further away from discovering the truth about John's death. He wondered if he'd been fooling himself.

And then the mood within the camp began to change. It didn't take Jake long to figure out why. Brady Moon, Elijah's oldest son, was due back at the end of the week. Even the children playing outside their houses began shouting his name as they played, and then squealing in pretend terror when another would give chase.

He watched their games, saw the sticks they used for guns, and the way they often rolled and played dead. Although he and Johnny had played much in the same manner when they were children, somehow these children's games had taken on a mock vendetta of a more personal nature. When he and Johnny had played, there were good guys and bad guys. But these children weren't just playing cops and robbers. He heard their shouts. He heard their squeals, and when he saw how they played, he knew exactly where their confusion had come from.

A little redheaded boy who wasn't even school age darted out in front of Jake, screaming at a child who was running behind him.

"Take that, you governant pig!" He tossed a rock in the air, and when it fell in front of the other child, he stopped and pointed. "That was a hand 'nade. You're 'apposed to get bowed up now."

The other child compliantly dropped to the

ground and started rolling and moaning in pretend horror.

Shocked by what he was seeing, Jake turned away, almost stepping on Gracie, who was emerging from between two cabins with a basket of green beans on her hip.

"Talk about timing," she said, and handed him the basket before going back for the other one at the end of the garden row.

Jake stood with the basket, watching the way she walked, then looking absently at the rich bounty growing in the garden behind her, feeling the freshening breeze as thunderheads gathered in the sky above. A fly buzzed past his ear. A bead of sweat rolled out of his hair and down the back of his neck. He felt suspended in time. The beauty of the mountain was here for anyone to see, but because of the actions of the people living in the midst of the majesty, it somehow seemed tarnished.

Gracie lifted the second basket, bracing it against her hip as she hurried to catch up with Jake, and then she realized he hadn't moved. In fact, there was a look in his eyes that almost frightened her.

"Jake?"

He blinked, then let his gaze fall to her face. She, like this place, was almost too beautiful to be real. That heart-shaped face. Those dark-brown eyes. The sensual cut to her lips and that black rope of hair. He wondered what she would look like with it loose.

"Jake! What's wrong?"

His stare was unwavering, and then in the middle of the silence in which they stood, a child's strident cry could be heard.

"Kill him, Junior. Kill Uncle Sam."

Jake took a slow, deep breath, and in that moment Gracie's gaze locked with his and their shared dismay was impossible to ignore. As the children barreled past them on the run, Gracie came to herself in time to shout.

"Billy! Michael Joe! You, too, Junior. You stop that this instant, do you hear me. That's no way to play."

They froze, stunned by the admonition of the woman who was family to one and teacher to the others.

"But Aunt Gracie, Daddy says it."

And then they bolted, shocked by their own temerity, and leaving Gracie pale-faced and shaking.

"Dear God," she said softly, and set down her basket before she dropped it.

Jake didn't know what to make of her behavior. Why should she be so surprised? Was this for his benefit, or was she really that naive?

"That was my nephew," Gracie said.

"Which one?" Jake asked, watching their hasty retreat.

She shook her head and pressed a finger against her lips, unable to voice her fear. Never had she felt so out of place.

"Which one, Gracie?"

Startled by his insistent tone, she pointed. "The

little redhead. He belongs to my brother Mark." She took a deep breath. "Sometimes I feel like I'm wasting my time up here."

Picking up her basket, she started toward her cabin. He followed her, still carrying the basket of beans.

"Then why do you stay?"

She paused. "Because of Father. I promised Mother I would look after him." A sweet sadness seemed to come over her. "A promise is a promise, you know."

After the promise he'd made to himself about John, there wasn't anything Jake could say to refute her statement.

"You haven't always lived like this, have you?"

She smiled, and her eyes took on a faraway look.

"Goodness no. I was living in Atlanta and teaching school . . . until Mother died."

"I'm sorry," Jake said. "If you told me before, I guess I'd forgotten."

She shook her head. "No, it's all right, and I don't think we ever talked about me . . . at least, not the me I was before I came here."

"Did we talk about me?" he asked.

There was an odd expression on her face as she set her basket down on the porch. Then she took the one he'd been carrying and set it in the shade as well.

"Tell me, Jake, have you forgotten so easily? You were only gone a month."

"Doctor calls it short-term memory loss and blames it on the fact I nearly died. Sometimes I think I'm getting better, and then something like this comes up and it makes me feel like a fool."

Gracie flushed. "I'm sorry. I didn't know."

"Don't let it bother you. I'm not exactly advertising the fact," he said.

Gracie folded her hands in front of her, studying the way the early-morning sunshine made shadows on his face. It was such a fine face. Such a strong face. Somehow, she always had trouble picturing it behind bars.

"No," she finally said. "We didn't talk about you, either, although I know where you've been."

This time it was Jake who looked away. It took him a moment to regain his thoughts.

"So, you were a teacher."

Her mood lightened. "Still am, only up here, I'm not getting paid."

"Where do you hold school?" he asked.

She pointed toward the hall where they ate. "In there, only it's summer, remember? We're sort of on vacation."

Just then Elijah came out of the cabin, and the moment between them was broken.

"Well, well," he said, looking at the brimming baskets of beans. "What a fine bounty. God is good."

Gracie grinned. "Yes, he is, Father. And we could have used His help picking the darned things."

Elijah waggled his finger in his daughter's face, although his devotion to Gracie was obvious.

"Daughter, do not jest with the Lord. He gave you a strong back for such purposes."

Gently she pushed her father into his rocker and shoved the basket of beans at his feet.

"And he gave me this wonderful father, who I'm sure is going to help me—"

Elijah smoothed his beard and pretended to scowl. "Hush your fussing and just bring me a bowl. I'll snap beans until I fall asleep. After that, you're on your own."

Gracie gave Jake a quick glance. "What would happen if I brought two bowls instead of one?"

Jake looked down at the baskets and knew that Elijah wouldn't last long enough to be of much help. There was such an expectant look on her face that he couldn't say no.

"Then I suppose that I'll snap beans until I fall asleep, too. After that you're—"

Gracie grinned and bolted into the house before either one of them could change their mind.

It took a bit to get settled into the routine, but Jake found an odd solace in the mindless task. Long after Elijah's hands had gone limp and Gracie had taken the bowl from his lap, leaving him to sleep, Jake sat on the steps in the shade of an old man's world and wondered where it had all gone wrong.

Some time later, a sudden round of gunfire shattered the peacefulness of the day, and Jake stood abruptly. Gracie came out of the cabin, drying her hands on a towel.

"They've come too close to the cabins," she said, frowning as she looked up the mountain. "They don't usually come this close." She glanced down at her father, who seemed to still be dozing.

Jake remained silent, watching. Gracie thought he looked poised to run and misinterpreted what she saw.

"Do you miss it? Being with the men, I mean?"

Another round of gunfire shattered the silence, and Jake watched mothers coming out of the cabins to check on the whereabouts of their children.

Jake shifted his stance, then relaxed as the sound began moving back up the mountain, out of hearing distance.

"Is it because you're still distrusting?" Gracie asked.

"What do you think?" he said harshly. "I've been in a lot of bad places, and I've been hurt plenty of times before, but I've at least had the pleasure of seeing my enemy's face."

Gracie bit her lip and looked away. She hated this thing that was between them. This guilt. This shame. It hadn't been there before. She longed for the happier times, when Jake would look at her and laugh and not judge what she'd just said or done.

"Brady will be back in a couple of days. Maybe he can help you find sense in it all."

John's face popped into his mind, and Jake felt an overwhelming urge to cry.

"There *is* no sense to be made of this," he said, and walked away, leaving her with a basket of beans ready to be canned.

It started to rain around midnight—a hard, pounding rain that ran from the roof and onto the ground in strong, steady streams. Jake rolled out of bed and dashed to the window, slamming it shut just as a gust of wind splattered raindrops against the panes. Moments later, a loud clap of thunder rocked the chair near his bed, and then lightning followed. The crack was shattering, and it sounded as if the mountain itself were coming apart.

"Damn." He went in search of something to dry up the puddle on the floor.

Once that was done, he thought about going back to bed but knew sleep would be impossible, at least until the storm had passed. He tossed the wet towel in the sink and reached for his jeans, which he slipped on in the dark. Fearful of scorpions underfoot, he reached for his boots and was in the act of pulling the last one on when a sound came to him over the storm.

Puzzled, he went to the door, then listened again. When it came once more, he stepped out on the porch. Someone was persistently ringing the school bell that hung from a scaffolding near the great hall.

Only slightly sheltered from the blowing rain, he stood near the edge of the house, watching as light after light appeared in the houses and people began running toward the sound. Instinct told him that something was wrong, very wrong. Following the crowd, he bolted off the porch and into the rain. He was almost at the great hall when he heard the woman screaming.

Gracie was near tears and shivering from wet and cold as she tried unsuccessfully to calm her sister-in-law's fears. Her brother Matthew seemed stunned as he clutched their baby to his chest, while the two young boys standing in the midst of the gathering people had become the unwanted center of attention. While their presence in this crowd was out of the ordinary, it was the one who was missing who had caused all the fuss. Gracie's heart ached for Matthew's wife, and it was all they could do to keep her from running out into the storm.

"Kay, please, sweetheart," Gracie crooned. "Calm down. There are plenty of us here. We'll find Timothy."

"Then why are we standing here?" she screamed, looking to her husband, Matthew, for support. "Why aren't you doing something? For God's sake, please! We've got to find him."

Jake came in the doorway just in time to hear Kay Moon's plea. He grabbed Burnett's arm.

"What happened?"

Burnett was near tears. "Matthew and Kay's oldest boy, Timothy, slipped out of the house after dark and went to the river with some other boys to noodle for fish."

Jake groaned as he looked out into the storm. "Oh man, and they don't know where he is?"

Burnett pointed to the two small boys who sat huddled together on a nearby bench.

"They were the last ones to see him. They said when it started to storm, they all headed for home. They thought he was right behind them."

"When did they see him last?" Jake asked.

"I don't know."

"But, I do, Daddy."

Both men turned at the sound of the small child's voice, then Burnett knelt and grasped his son by the arms.

"Michael Joe? Were you with them?"

Jake touched Burnett, trying to ease the shock and anger he saw on the man's face.

"Is he yours?" Jake asked.

Burnett was stunned, thinking about his baby out in the dark with those boys.

"Yes," he said. "And he's only six."

Jake thought back to a night when he and John had slipped out of the house to play in the moonlight. But they'd been in the wide-open spaces of Wyoming, not the thick woods of a Kentucky mountain, and certainly not wading in a river and trying to catch fish with their hands. He knelt in front of the little boy.

"Michael Joe? Is that your name?" he asked.

The child nodded.

"Can you tell me where you saw Timothy last?"

The little boy looked out the doorway into the storm and winced when another bolt of lightning flashed, momentarily lighting up the sky.

Burnett put his hand on the child's head, "Mikey, don't be afraid," he said softly. "You're not going to get in trouble. We just want to find Timmy, okay? Now, answer Jake. Where did you see Timmy last?"

"Down by the old beaver lodge. He fell in the river down by the lodge."

"Jesus, have mercy," Burnett whispered, and lifted the boy into his arms just as Gracie walked up.

The storm wasn't letting up, and Jake knew that time was of the essence.

"Burnett, can you show me exactly where?" Jake asked.

Burnett nodded, then thrust his son into Gracie's arms. "Gracie, take Michael Joe to Annie. And tell her not to let him out of her sight. He was out with the boys."

Gracie gasped, and then hugged the little boy in disbelief.

"Where are you going?" she yelled as they started out the door.

Burnett shouted over his shoulder, "To the beaver lodge. Michael Joe said he last saw Timothy near the beaver lodge."

And then he and Jake bolted out the door.

Rain hammered their faces, making it difficult to see. As they passed Jake's cabin, he grabbed Burnett by the arm and yelled, "Wait! I'm going to get a flashlight."

Burnett nodded, and moments later, Jake came out on the run and handed it over. "You know these woods better than I do. You lead. I'll be right behind you all the way."

The emergency lantern had a narrow beam, but it was bright and strong, and it cut a welcome swath through the stormy night.

Limbs slapped the men in the face as they ran

down the side of the mountain toward the river below. Once Jake thought he could hear some of the men behind him, and then he became so focused on getting through the trees without being beheaded by a low-hanging limb that he forgot to listen.

He heard the river before he saw it. It was no longer the slow meandering flow of muddy water. Runoff from the storm had turned it into a frothy torrent of uncontrollable power.

Lightning flashed just as they reached the edge of the riverbank, and Jake's heart dropped. In that brief period of illumination, he'd seen enough to know that if a child had fallen into that hell, he probably wouldn't come out alive.

Burnett stood beside Jake, anxiously sweeping the flashlight back and forth across the raging torrent.

"God help us all," he said.

Thunder rumbled, and Jake's bare back was stinging from the blast of wind-blown rain. "Where's that damned beaver lodge?" Jake shouted.

"Somewhere over to the right," Burnett yelled back, and swung the lantern in that direction, slicing through the darkness with the path of light.

Jake began to run along the edge of the river without taking his eyes from its glow. Once he stumbled over tree roots, and twice he staggered, catching himself only moments before falling flat on his face. The last time he fell, he came up on all fours, his gaze still fixed on that slim beam of light. But before he pulled himself upright, something caught his attention, and he started to yell.

"Burnett! Move it back to the left! A little more! A little—"

They both saw the boy at once, clinging to what was left of a decomposing beaver's lodge in the middle of the river. Even in that weak glow, they could tell the child's strength was almost gone. His arms were locked around a dead tree that was protruding out of the water. His shirt was missing, and his eyes were closed. Jake's heart dropped. Each time the river surged against the child, it looked as if he would follow the flow, and then something within him seemed to rally and he continued to cling.

Jake started running back the way he'd come, passing Burnett as he ran.

"Don't move and don't take the light off him," he shouted. "I'm going in after him, and I need to start upstream."

Burnett didn't argue, and he couldn't have moved if he tried. He was frozen to the spot by the horror, fearing he was about to witness the drowning of them both.

Seconds later, he heard a loud splash and resisted the urge to look. Instead, he started shouting at his nephew, praying he would be heard over the sound of the river.

"Timothy, hold on! We're coming for you, boy!"

The moment Jake surfaced, he knew he was in trouble. He'd been in deep shit more than once in his life, but never had he been less in control. The power of the flood lifted him up and then slammed him down as a floating tree slid past. It was only by the grace of God that the tree missed him and that he stayed afloat. Even as the water was carrying him downriver, he kept trying to swim to the opposite shore, hoping that the trajectory would sweep him by the lodge.

It was all but hopeless. Water swept up his nostrils and down his throat, choking and rendering him momentarily helpless as he struggled for breath. And then he thought of the child who'd had enough will to hang on when a lesser man might have given up the fight, and he plowed through the water even harder, kicking with all the strength in his long, powerful legs.

On the opposite shore, Burnett Moon stood helplessly, holding a light for a drowning man. And then suddenly men burst out of the tree line behind him and came running toward him, adding their lights to his single beam, until there was a small but steady spotlight centered on the drama being enacted before them.

Out of the dark, an old man's powerful voice was suddenly heard, and the demand that he made on them all was too powerful to ignore.

Elijah Moon stood at the river's edge with his gaze aimed at heaven. And as the rain continued to fall on them all, he lifted his arms and shouted, "Pray! Pray to a merciful God that they will be delivered."

Unaware that more men had arrived, Jake continued to flail through the muddy rush, and over the boil of the water he heard voices. Help had arrived, but from where he was they were of little use. Fearing that he would lose sight of the boy's location, he kept his focus on the light, and as an unusually large surge of water lifted him up, he could see that the boy was about to let go.

With a helpless roar of rage, he quit fighting the flood and as he came even with the lodge held out his arms. The child slipped off of the limb and into the water, sinking almost instantly. From the river's edge, a great sound of despair rose up through the storm, and to a man, they each believed the two were gone.

But Elijah Moon had spent all of his life believing in the power of prayer, and when he shouted for the men to turn their lights downriver, they did so without question. In that moment, one of them spied a dark head bobbing with the flow, and a great shout went up.

"There they go!"

They started running along the riverbank, waving their flashlights and dragging their ropes.

Fortunately, when the men left the great hall, they'd formed two groups. Both had gone down the mountain, but while some of them had made for the beaver lodge, the others had gone farther downriver to start their search, and walked upstream, thereby covering more ground in a shorter time.

It was ironic that Taggert Brown was staring into the river when lightning lit up the sky. And when he saw the pair of heads bobbing in the thick of the water's flow and recognized Jake Crockett, he couldn't believe his eyes.

His hesitation was brief. While he would have willingly let Jake Crockett drown, there was enough decency left in him not to sacrifice the child for his own purposes.

"There!" he shouted, aiming his flashlight into the river. "There's someone in the river! Throw out a rope."

Timothy Moon was eight years old, and Jake knew unless a miracle happened, he would never see nine. He'd caught the boy within seconds of passing the lodge, but he'd known the moment he pulled him out of the water and close to his chest that it might already be too late. He'd never touched skin as cold as this boy's and feared he might already be dead. It was all he could do to keep their heads above water, yet somehow he did.

The rain had lessened, but the thunder and lightning still ripped through the night. It was during another quick flash that Jake saw the three men on the shore ahead. In that moment, before the sky went dark, he saw their mouths open and shouting something he couldn't hear. But he didn't need to hear them to know what was being said, because he could see the ropes they were throwing into the river—right in his path.

He was swept past the first one, almost before he knew it, and when it slipped through his hand, his heart dropped. A second or so later, another one caught him around the throat, almost choking him senseless before it slipped off.

"No, damn you, no!" he roared, and held out his free arm, letting it trail through the water like a sweep.

Just when he thought he'd missed the chance, rough, scratchy hemp slapped the middle of his palm, and Jake grabbed on for dear life, quickly wrapping it around his wrist and welcoming the pain as his body was abruptly jerked against the current.

Taggert Brown felt the tug on his rope and shouted aloud, "He's got it! By God, he's got it! Help me!" With a mighty grunt, he began pulling the rope, aware that at any moment, Crockett could lose his grip and he and the boy would be swept to their deaths.

Hand over hand, they pulled, and the three men became four—and the four, six—and the six, eight—until with their combined strength they hauled Jake Crockett and Timothy Moon from the midnight flood.

One second Jake was in water, and then the next thing he knew he was being dragged out and up the rocky edge of the riverbank with the boy still clutched against his chest. Choking and coughing and spitting up water, the sensation of being stationary was startling, but not as much as when he looked up and saw that he was surrounded by a ring of lights. For a moment, he wondered if he had died and gone to heaven. Then he heard Elijah Moon's voice and relaxed. Unless God and Elijah were on more than speaking terms, he was still on earth.

A light lowered, and he felt a touch on his forehead, then on his chest. Someone was kneeling beside him. As he struggled for breath, a man's hand moved through the glow to sweep across Timothy's back. Jake's teeth were chattering as he held the child close.

"I don't think he's breathing," Jake said.

"Help them," Elijah said.

Hands came out of the darkness, gently prying the child from Jake's arms, and when he was gone, Jake felt a moment of loss before his training surfaced. "He's going to need CPR. Does anyone know CPR?"

A murmur went through the crowd, and with it, Jake's hopes plummeted. He was almost too weak to breathe for himself, let alone a small child, but they'd come this far. He'd have to give it a try.

"Put him down," he ordered, and someone threw a coat on the ground then laid the boy upon it as Jake crawled to his knees to begin resuscitation.

Before he could begin, he heard a cry, and the circle of light parted. It was Gracie, and from the looks of her, she'd run all the way. She was soaked clear through. Her clothes were plastered to her body, and her hair was heavy and dripping as she leaned over the child on the ground. But there was a lilt in her voice that was impossible to mistake.

"I can help," she said, as she dropped to her knees.

To Jake, she was an angel from heaven. "Give her room," he ordered, and the circle of light widened as she bent down, sharing her breath with her brother's child.

Chapter 5

Someone threw a coat over Jake's shoulders, and followed it with a pat of appreciation. All around him he could hear the murmurs of disbelief regarding the near-miraculous feat he'd accomplished. But he knew differently. He wasn't a hero. He'd seen a child in trouble and simply reacted, using his government training. Jake found it more than ironic that the organization these people so despised was responsible for him being able to pull Timothy from the flood. But he cast all that aside as he bent to Gracie's aid.

"Let me help," he said.

She rocked back on her heels, and only then was he aware she was crying.

As Jake examined the child, Gracie peeled off her raincoat and stood above them, using it as a shield to protect them as best she could.

"Father, we need an ambulance," Gracie said.

Elijah didn't respond, but continued to pray in a loud and fervent voice.

The strongest of the winds had passed, but the

rain still continued to fall. It was a cold, miserable drizzle that seeped into your bones. Gracie shivered, unable to believe that her father would not answer her plea. She repeated herself in a louder voice.

"Father! We need an ambulance!"

His focus wavered, and he came out his vigil of prayer to stare down at the scene before him.

"Whatever happens is God's will."

Gracie glared. It wasn't the first time she and her father had disagreed on such things, but it was the first time she'd had the impetus to challenge him. She'd be damned before she'd let her own flesh and blood be the scapegoat for Elijah Moon's beliefs. She shoved her raincoat into Burnett's hands.

"Here! Hold this."

"Where are you going, Gracie?" he asked.

"I'm going to call for an ambulance, and if the storm has knocked out the phone in the hall, I'll be back with a truck. Either way, that boy is going to the hospital."

Elijah pointed at her. "No, daughter! Up here, we take care of our own."

She spun, and there was such anger in her voice that it startled everyone, including Elijah. "Well, someone didn't do such a good job tonight." Then she pointed at Jake, who was still performing CPR. "He risked his life to save your grandson, and he's still trying. How dare you minimize what he did by leaving the rest of the rescue up to God. Don't you think God had a little bit to do with what has already happened?"

Unwilling to wait for an answer, she started up the mountain when a shout stopped her in her tracks.

"He's coming around!"

Gracie heard Timothy begin to cough up the water he had swallowed.

As the child moaned, his father, Matthew, lifted him from the ground and cradled him against his chest. Jake took a deep breath and was struggling to get up when someone slipped an arm beneath his shoulders.

"Thanks." He glanced sideways to see who had come to his aid.

It was Gracie Moon who'd offered herself as a crutch. And in that moment, the look he and Gracie shared was enough to rock his world.

Stunned by the unexpected bond that sprang between them, Gracie found herself speechless. It wasn't until Jake spoke that she thought to blink, and it was what he said, rather than the way he said it, that made her react.

"Run, Gracie. You bring back that truck. Because if you don't, that boy will die."

She didn't question him. All she knew was that she was thankful someone had the good sense to act. With full intent of doing as he'd said, she turned to go when Aaron stepped out of the shadows and into her path.

"No, sister. I'll go. You've already done your share."

Stunned by what he viewed as betrayal by his own family, Elijah's voice began to shake.

"No, Aaron, not you, too?"

Aaron threw up his hands. "For God's sake, Father. Look at Timothy! He's your grandson and he's only eight years old. He deserves a chance at life."

Without waiting for an answer, Aaron quickly disappeared into the night.

Having witnessed the battle of wills between their founder and two of his own, the men seemed anchorless, as if there was no one left to make a decision. As weak and weary as he was, Jake knew it was going to be left up to him.

"I'm totally disoriented as to where we are, but I think it would be wise if you started moving the boy up the mountain to meet the truck as it comes down." When no one spoke, he added, "It would save a lot of time—and maybe his life."

Instantly, a party was formed, with Taggert Brown leading the way. Since Aaron was already gone, Burnett stayed behind, aware that Elijah would need assistance getting back to New Zion.

Burnett gave Jake a long, considering look, and then shook his head. "Here," he said. "I brought your boots. Thought you might be needing them."

An understanding passed between the two men. By the very act of picking up the shoes Jake had kicked off when he went in the water, Burnett had shown faith that Jake would need them again.

Jake took the boots, and as the old man and his son left, he turned away and walked to the river's edge, then sat down to put them on. He looked up at the sky. The storm was passing. He looked down into the river, then combed his fingers through his hair and closed his eyes.

His voice was just above a whisper as he realized how close they'd both come to dying. "My God, my God."

Someone touched his back, and he turned. It was Gracie. When he stood, she stepped beneath his arm, then put hers around his waist.

"Lean on me," she said.

In that moment, hidden by the shadows of the night, Jake Baretta felt tears come to his eyes. *Lean on you? Oh God, Gracie Moon. If only I could.*

"I'm all right," he said quickly, and would have pulled away, but she quietly refused to let go.

"I know you are," she said softly. "But I'm not. I need to touch you to know that you're still alive and kicking." She took a deep breath, and then shuddered. "I came out of the woods just as you were swept by the beaver lodge. When I saw both you and Timothy go under, I thought you were dead."

He couldn't clearly see her face, but he heard all too well the emotion in her voice. Because he was aware of the dangers of becoming involved with this woman, he tried to make light of what she had said.

"You know what they say, 'Only the good die young.' "

He felt her grip tighten as she turned him toward the path that ran along the river's edge. When she spoke, she sounded almost angry.

"Shut up. Just shut up, Jake Crockett. No matter

what you or anyone else thinks, I know you are a good man."

It was so much more than he'd expected to hear that he did as she said. Silently, they made their way up the mountain, and when they came out of the tree line and into the clearing of New Zion, Jake felt as if he'd come home. And then he remembered why he'd come and what these people had done to John, and quickly set that feeling aside.

As they entered the compound, Gracie glanced ahead to her father and Burnett. Her father's steps were dragging, and she knew why. She'd defied him in front of his sons and in front of the other men. She knew she would hear about it later, but right now, she had other things on her mind.

"Burnett, see that Father gets some hot tea before going to bed. He's bound to be chilled to the bone."

Elijah turned, speaking to Gracie for the first time since their argument below.

"I'm not a child. I know how to take care of myself," he said.

"Sometimes I wonder," she said.

When Jake started toward his own cabin, Gracie caught him by the elbow. "Oh, no you don't, mister. You're coming with me to the hall. Father isn't the only one who needs to be doctored."

"But—"

"May as well go along with what she says," Elijah said. "Gracie's just like her mother, God rest her soul. When she sets her mind to something, nothing will sway her."

Jake sighed. He wanted nothing more than to take a hot bath, get into dry clothes, and sleep for a week. Yes, his back was stinging, in some places actually hurting, but he'd had worse and survived it alone. It was disconcerting to have someone actually care.

He glanced down at Gracie. She was standing in the yellow glow of a security light with her hands on her hips and her wet clothes clinging stubbornly to her body, as if they dared not droop unless she gave them permission. He decided that was probably her "teacher look" and almost smiled.

She met his gaze and shivered, trying to assure herself it was because she was wet, and not because of what she was feeling.

"Well, are you coming?"

He muttered something beneath his breath.

"If you're trying to intimidate me with curse words, you're going to have to do better than that. Living among seven brothers, I've pretty much heard it all."

Jake grinned. Damn, but this woman was something, and that was a fact.

"Well, hell, don't mind if I do," he drawled, and offered his arm, as if they were going for an afternoon stroll.

His capitulation surprised Gracie.

"You have the makings of a complete jerk," she said shortly, and started toward the hall without seeing if he would follow.

Jake's grin disappeared as he fell into step be-

hind her. There wasn't a damn thing funny about
the sway of her hips or the way that long, black
braid bounced against her back. When they finally
reached the shelter of the hall, he wasn't smiling at
all. In fact, it was all he could do to focus on the
roomful of waiting women and children instead of
Gracie Moon's backside.

Bare-chested, with his blue jeans wet and hanging low on his hips and his boots squishing with
each step that he took, he felt pretty intimidated by
the assortment of female eyes gazing upon his person. He started to go back.

"Look, Gracie, why don't I—"

She turned and glared.

He sat down.

"Moira, will you please bring the first-aid kit?"
Gracie asked.

She hastened to do Gracie's bidding, while the
others gathered around. Jake heard Gracie's gasp
and knew that they'd seen his scars. Actually, it
wasn't so bad, considering where he'd been and
what he'd done to get them. But he supposed to
these women, a couple of bullet holes and a few
knife scars was an appalling sight.

When Gracie saw his back, she took a slow, deep
breath and sat down. Besides the fresh bruises and
scratches, he had two deep cuts and more old scars
than a man had a right to bear. Her touch was gentle as she traced the ridges of scar tissue, but her
voice was trembling.

"Oh, Jake. Did you get these in prison?"

He looked over his shoulder, only then aware

that he was all but surrounded by the females of New Zion.

"All but this one," he said shortly, pointing to his shoulder. "That one came with your compliments."

The women gasped and stepped back. Gracie paled, but stayed where she was.

"Not mine, it didn't," she said shortly. "Now turn around and sit still."

Taggert's wife, Moira, glanced nervously at the half-naked man in their midst, then handed the first-aid kit to Gracie.

"If you run out of disinfectant, I have some in my cabin," she said. And then fearing she would be judged by her peers, she glanced at Jake again and added, "After what Aaron said you did for Kay's boy, I say we owe you."

Jake started to smile, and then winced as Gracie began wiping his cuts. He gritted his teeth.

"Have mercy, woman, what are you doing back there, digging for gold?"

A titter of laughter shifted through the room. And then a child cried, and another yelled as he fell off of a bench. Gracie looked up from her task long enough to speak.

"The men will be back soon, and the children need to be in bed." The alcohol-laden cotton swab dripped from her fingers as she glanced back at Jake. "Besides, you're all in my light, and since Mr. Crockett is not in any condition to compromise my morals, I suggest you go home."

Without needing further pushing, the women

gathered up their children and hurried out the door, leaving Gracie alone with Jake. For several minutes, she worked in silence, and then he began to hear more than the soft whisper of her breath.

He turned, unprepared for the tears running down her cheeks.

When their gazes met, she hiccuped on a sob and dropped the cotton and buried her face in her hands.

Jake was stunned. "Gracie?"

She didn't answer but continued to sob, her shoulders trembling with every breath. The urge to hold her was strong, and he attributed the feeling to nothing more than the heat of the moment.

"Gracie, what's wrong?"

She shook her head and turned away, and Jake found himself staring at the back of her neck. At the graceful way in which she sat. At the gentle tremble of her shoulders, and as he stared, everything around him became magnified a thousand times.

The sound of water dripping from the roof and onto the ground. The scent of wet clothes and warm bodies and the strong smell of disinfectant. Of the bloodstained cotton at her feet. He took a deep breath and felt his lungs expanding. Felt his blood surging through his body and knew that tonight he'd tempted fate and won. He found himself needing more than the verification that his heart still beat. He wanted to feel more than alive. He wanted—

His thoughts froze, and in that moment, he knew what he wanted. He wanted Gracie Moon.

"Come here," he said softly, tugging at her shoulders until she was forced to face him. "Why are you crying?"

"Because I thought you were dead. Because I didn't think I would ever hear your voice or see your smile again. I thought I lost that once and I don't want that to happen again."

Jake groaned and took her in his arms. "If we've made love before and I've forgotten it, then just shoot me now and make sure you finish the job. I'd hate to think I'd lost something that special."

Gracie buried her face against his bare chest and then laughed through her tears. "You are impossible."

Jake stroked her head, then her back, touching her over and over as one would a child, soothing her sobs until there was nothing left but an occasional shudder.

"We haven't done this before, have we, Gracie?"

She stilled but didn't look up.

"In fact, I'd lay odds that we've never even kissed."

He felt her tensing beneath his touch. "Have we, Gracie?"

He dropped his arms, then tilted her chin, forcing her to meet his gaze. "Don't you think it's about time?"

"Oh, God," Gracie whispered.

Jake's eyes glittered dangerously. "Don't disturb His rest, because He can't help you now."

He lowered his head, capturing the shock and surprise on her half-parted lips and slipping inside her mouth before she could stop his intrusion. Like the spy that he was, he sought out her secrets. The way she moaned when he bit the lower edge of her lip. The way her pupils dilated as he lifted her from the bench and pulled her across his lap. The way her nostrils flared as he traced the shape of her shoulders with his hands, and the gasp that she made as his thumbs drifted too close to the sides of her breasts.

"I want to make love to you, Gracie Moon."

She met his gaze head-on. "I know," she said quietly. "I can feel."

His chin tilted, as he braced himself. "But you're not going to let me, are you?"

She bit her lip and new tears filled her eyes. "No."

Even though he'd known what she would say, it was still a disappointment. "Are you going to tell me why?"

"Because I'm only going to make love to the man I marry, and I don't think you're the staying kind."

He froze. "Are you telling me you've never—"

"Pretty much."

Surprised by the unexpected tenderness he felt for her, he couldn't do anything but hug her. Thoughts swirled around his head that had no business being there. Traitorous thoughts. He'd been willing to sleep with the enemy, but he hadn't expected to feel compassion. And then he took a deep breath, admitting for the first time that compassion wasn't all he felt.

He hugged her once more, then scooted her off his lap and stood.

"Thanks for the first aid," he said gently, and satisfied himself with cupping her cheek. "You know what? I'm not the only one who's soaking wet. Don't you think you should get into something dry and get back to bed?" He looked up at the clock on the wall. "It's almost morning."

Gracie bent down and picked up the bloody cotton. When she stood and then walked away without looking back, Jake thought he'd never seen a more regal person in his entire life.

You don't belong here, Gracie Moon. And he knew in that moment that he didn't want her to be here when the place went under.

When Jake woke up, it was almost nine o'clock in the morning. He groaned, then stretched, realizing that there wasn't a place on his body that didn't ache. His stomach growled and he glanced at the clock, then groaned again. It was too late. He'd missed breakfast. That meant he would have to fend for himself, and at the best of times, he was a piss-poor cook.

Minutes later, he came out of the bathroom, drying his face and thinking of making some coffee when a knock sounded at the door. He reached for his jeans and then realized they were lying in a soppy puddle near the door.

"Just a minute," he shouted, and raced for the closet to get a clean pair.

"It's only me. Aaron."

Jake relaxed. "Then come in."

Aaron Moon entered bearing gifts, and when

Jake got a whiff of the fresh, hot bread and saw the jar of honey to go with it, he grinned.

"Why, Aaron, don't tell me you cooked?"

"Not unless it's over a campfire in the middle of the woods." He grinned as he set down the food. "SueEllen made an extra loaf this morning. And when you didn't show up at breakfast and considering the night you had, we all figured you'd be sleeping in. Everyone is grateful for what you did. Matthew came back this morning with the news. Timothy is going to be okay. Kay stayed with him at the hospital, but that was only for safekeeping. They'll be bringing him home tomorrow."

"That's great news," Jake said, fastening his jeans as he headed for the cabinet to get a knife.

"And it's all thanks to you," Aaron said.

"I would never have been able to get out of the water without the ropes. Everyone helped."

Aaron smiled. "At any rate, we're very appreciative. Enjoy!"

"Looks good," he said, cutting himself a generous slice.

Aaron frowned when he saw Jake's back. "It's a shame I can't say the same thing about your back."

Dismissing the remark, Jake got out a plate and poured honey on the warm heel of bread. "They'll heal."

"From what I can see, I suppose you should know that better than most."

Jake paused in the act of taking a bite, then set the food down, untasted. "If you have something to say, then you better get it said."

"It's impossible for me to believe that anyone here would do you bodily harm. It had to be a stray bullet from some hunter's gun."

Jake smiled a slow, deadly smile. "Now, how many hunters have you seen meandering into New Zion's territory? The way they talk down in Little Rome, this place is more than off-limits to outsiders."

"We took you in, didn't we?"

Jake looked down at the bread and honey, then up at Aaron. "Yes, I suppose that you did. But tell me something, Aaron. When the invitation first came, was it because I was Lady Crockett's grandson, or because I'd done time and might be of use in another capacity?"

Aaron paled. "Do you know what you're insinuating?"

Jake continued to push. "That's not an insinuation, it's an honest question, so are you going to give me an honest answer? Or are we going to hide behind this pacifist theory that no one but your father believes in?"

Aaron looked away.

"Who was the first one of you to suggest bringing me in? Who needed dirty work done and didn't want to do it himself?"

Aaron looked up, and Jake could see shock spreading over his face.

"Who was it, Aaron? Who would possibly want a convicted felon in your midst? And what would he want of me, unless it was to aid and abet in—"

Aaron shook his head. "It's not what you think. Brady was only being—"

"Ah, yes. When, by the way, is Brady expected to return?"

"Some time tomorrow." And then he waved nervously toward the food, anxious to change the subject. "Enjoy. You deserve it and more."

"Thanks," Jake said. "And you be sure and tell SueEllen thank you, too."

Jake picked up his plate and walked to the window, taking a bite of the bread as he watched Aaron Moon scurrying across the compound. He could see Aaron wasn't going home. He was heading toward a group of men who were standing beneath the big spruce outside the hall.

"Yeah, spread the news, brother Aaron. Be sure and tell everyone there that Jake Crockett is getting antsy."

Then he took another large bite of the bread, grunting with satisfaction as he paused to lick the honey from his fingers. When he had finished, he went back to cut another slice and missed seeing Gracie heading his way. And even if he'd been forewarned she was coming, there was nothing he could have done to stop her.

Gracie had wrestled with the devil all night, and he'd worn Jake Crockett's face. There was love in her heart for this man, as well as a touch of lust. What confused her was his on-again, off-again manner toward her and her family. She'd caught him staring at her more than once, and in those times, there'd been an expression on his face she'd never seen before. She knew he was still distrustful, and after she saw his back she understood why. But for the life of her, she couldn't understand why he should be judging her as well.

Morning hadn't brought her any satisfactory answers. Her father was still sulking about her defiance, and her heart hurt, thinking of what she'd refused Jake last night.

Even though she knew it was foolish, she wanted an excuse to touch him again. And she had the very best reason for doing so. Someone had to doctor his back. As the only single female in New Zion, she knew she would be pushing at dangerous boundaries by going to his cabin alone, but at this point, she didn't give a good damn. Some of these people in New Zion were her friends. Most of the others were her family. But they didn't hold two consecutive beliefs that she shared.

She thought of the job she'd walked away from in Atlanta, of the freedom she'd given up without a backward glance. Then she gave herself a mental kick in the pants and picked up the basket containing the first aid.

"Father, I'm taking some medicine to Jake. I need to tend to his back again. I'll see you later."

Elijah's mouth dropped as he looked up from his Bible, and his complexion turned an angry red.

"Do what you will," he said harshly. "By your actions last night, you've already proven to be a disobedient daughter. Why should you care if you heap shame upon my head, as well?"

Gracie paused in the doorway. "Yes, Father, I'm a real mess, aren't I? I quit a job that I'd trained long and hard for. I came to this . . . this . . . hide-out with you because I love you, and because Mother asked me to take care of you. But I did not bargain on being thrown back to the Middle Ages. I am not disobedient. That is a word used for children, and I am a woman grown."

She paused, and before she could go on she heard the faint but unmistakable sound of an explosion up the mountain. When he looked away and frowned, she knew that he'd heard it, too.

"What I'm wondering is, if you were so set on getting away from the bad things of this earth, then why does every man among us carry a weapon?" She took a breath. "And don't tell me it's to hunt for food, because the ammunition they are using would blow more of the deer away than there would be left to eat. Besides, there are enough canned goods in the storehouse to last us through Christmas, and that's nearly six months away."

She hadn't expected him to answer, so when he remained mute, she left, slamming the door on her way out.

By the time she got to Jake's cabin, there was blood in her eye. If he so much as crossed her, then God help the man, because she wouldn't. She paused on the threshold and knocked, and when he called out, "Who's there?" she lost her cool.

"If you'd open the door, you'd find out."

When the door swung open, he had a shirt in his

hands and a startled look on his face. But it was the drawl in his voice that made her laugh.

"Whatever it was, I didn't do it," he said.

She dumped her basket on a table, shut the door, and took the shirt from his hands.

"Turn around and sit down somewhere, and yes, you did."

Jake did as he was told, and then wondered why she was the only one who didn't seem the least bit fazed by his presence.

"What did I do?" He hissed as she swiped at one of the deeper cuts with a thick, disinfectant-soaked swab.

"You know what you did," she said angrily, and tossed aside the swab, only to reach for another.

Jake turned and grabbed her hand before she could arm herself further.

"Gracie, honey, do me a favor. Either doctor me, or give me what for, but for God's sake, don't do both at the same time. I don't think I can take it."

The anger slid out of her in a rush, leaving her weak beneath his gaze and sorry she'd let him bear the brunt of something he hadn't caused.

"Oh, dear." She dropped down on the side of his unmade bed without thinking. "I'm sorry. Father and I had an argument, and I was taking it out on you."

Jake's eyes narrowed thoughtfully as he kicked back in the chair. "What's all the fuss?"

Gracie looked up and got caught in the animal magnetism of a full-grown male.

"Don't you ever wear a shirt?" She flushed when he grinned.

To his credit, he did slip one on, but when he turned, it was still unbuttoned, and as he sat back down, it hung open just enough to tease her.

"Okay, I'm dressed."

She eyed him, then sighed. Naked, or wearing a full suit of armor, she supposed Jake Crockett would still be an intimidating man.

"Thank you."

He grinned and then stretched his legs out before him, crossing them at the ankles and leaning back on his elbows.

As he did, that damned shirt slid fully open, and Gracie glared. He was doing it on purpose. She tried to remind herself why she'd come but couldn't.

When her chin began to tremble, Jake relented. He stood abruptly and went to her side, sliding onto the bed beside her.

"I'm sorry. What's wrong?"

Gracie suddenly realized where she was sitting. Startled, she glanced up and got lost in the fire in his eyes.

"I was, uh . . . Father said I . . . that I never—"

Jake leaned closer but made no move to touch her, and all the while wondered who was being teased the most, him or her?

"You never what, Gracie Moon?"

She bolted off the bed like a startled deer, then pivoted, pointing an accusing finger in his face.

"Don't do that!"

He grabbed her finger and pulled her forward. "Do what?" He tugged a little harder. "You mean this?" He pulled until she stumbled forward.

Together they fell, he on his back, she on his belly. And for a moment, before reason surfaced, each of them considered the wisdom of moving past this position to the next.

"Why, Miss Gracie, I do declare," he drawled.

Sputtering beneath her breath and with her face as red as mountain berries, she socked him on the shoulder with her doubled-up fist.

"I suppose you think that was funny," she muttered.

Surprised by what he was feeling, Jake sat up. "Do you see me laughing?"

Unsure of what to say or do next, Gracie settled herself by gathering up the medicinal supplies she'd scattered on the table.

"Thank you for coming to take care of me."

Her fingers started to shake. "If you really meant that, I'd say you're welcome. As it is, I don't know how to take you, Jake Crockett."

Jake shoved himself up from the bed and had her in his arms before she knew he was coming.

"That's just the problem, Gracie Moon. I don't know how to take you, either."

Chapter 6

"Are you going to kiss me again?"

Her breathless question teased at his heart.

"Do you want me to?"

Her hesitation was brief. "Yes."

"Even though I'm not the staying kind of man you're looking for?"

She touched the side of his face, fixing her gaze on the intensity of his cool, green eyes, and ignored her conscience.

"Even though."

Jake had started out teasing, but he was sinking fast. She was so beautiful and too damned trusting. *Hell, brother John, why did you start something I'm not going to be able to finish?*

When he saw her reaching toward his bare chest, he grabbed her hands, pinning them behind her back and then pinning her between himself and the table.

"Are you sure?"

She slipped free of his grasp. "You ask too many questions."

And suddenly Jake was no longer in charge.

When Gracie's hands slid around the back of his neck and she leaned against him, all he could see was her mouth, slightly parted and waiting for him to come in.

With a groan, he let himself fall into her trap, knowing full well it might be impossible to get himself out. There was one thing about Gracie Moon that he hadn't expected. She was a passionate little virgin; a deadly combination for a man in dire need of a feminine fix.

"Ah, Gracie," he whispered, and then centered his mouth upon her lips.

When she gave back his kiss and whimpered for more, Jake felt himself losing ground. This wasn't supposed to be happening. But the longer he held her, the farther reality slipped away. He found himself turning with her in his arms. Knew he was walking her toward the bed. Felt it give beneath their weight as he rolled her beneath him. Wanted her stripped bare and begging.

That was when he realized it would never be enough.

He thrust a knee between her legs and moved into place, dissatisfied with the barrier of their clothing but unable to focus long enough to do anything about it. Her hands were locked around his neck, her scent was in his nostrils, and her hair was coming undone beneath his fingers.

Oh hell, oh Johnny, why her?

And then in the midst of their passion, a sound intruded. Gracie came out of a daze and blinked up at him in confusion.

"My sweet Lord," she whispered, unable to believe that she'd lost control of her every inhibition with just one kiss.

Jake ached as he raised himself up on his elbows and stared down at her. Outside, the noise was getting louder.

"From the sounds of things outside, either we're about to experience the Second Coming, or it's a lynch party headed my way."

Gracie gasped. "Oh no! Oh shoot! Get off of me quick!"

Jake groaned and rolled. "I'll move, but don't ask for speed. I'm not in any shape to run races right now, which doesn't bode well for my neck."

"Oh, do shut up." She raced to the window, carefully peering out between the curtains. "My father may seem strange, but he doesn't hang people."

"No, he only has them shot," Jake mumbled, and started buttoning his shirt.

Gracie fixed him with an angry glare. "I heard that. Besides, you've got to get over that stupid notion. Why on earth would anyone want to hurt you?"

Ignoring her question, Jake tucked his shirttail into the waistband of his jeans. "So, what's the big to-do?"

She looked out the window. "I can't see for sure. Someone just pulled in with an eighteen-wheeler." She leaned forward. "Good grief, it's Brady! What on earth do you suppose he's doing with that truck?"

Jake was at her side within seconds, searching the grounds for the sight of an unfamiliar face. But at this distance, and in the midst of such a celebration, it was difficult to sort one out from the other.

"There's only one way to find out, right?" Then Jake startled himself and Gracie by slipping an arm around her and yanking her to him. Before she could object, he stole a last, lingering kiss.

"You know what, sweet Gracie?"

Somewhere between infinity and heaven, Gracie found the good sense to answer him.

"What?"

"You might want to fix your hair before you go outside. You look awful pretty to me, but I'd be guessing that the well-loved look isn't going to go over real big with your brothers."

"Oh, no!" Gracie grabbed her hair.

"Feel free to use my hairbrush," Jake said, pointing toward the bathroom.

"I can't," she moaned. "It takes forever to brush it and put it up."

Jake grinned and winked. "You should have thought of that before you let me take it down."

"Then wait on me, damn it." Gracie began separating the long length into three thick strands.

Oddly enough, Jake did. And all the while he was standing and watching her twisting that hair into a braid, her words kept echoing in his head. *Wait on me. Wait on me.* What surprised him the most about himself was that he had.

She started pacing the floor around the bed. "Shoot, I can't find the rubberband."

Jake glanced down. "It probably got lost in the covers."

Holding the ends of her hair with her fingers, she tried not to glare. "Would you please look?"

He gave the bed a cursory glance. "Don't see it anywhere," he said, and then walked to the cabinet.

She stared in disbelief as he took the wire twist from a loaf of bread, then wadded the end of the wrapper beneath the loaf and stuffed it back in the cabinet.

"Here, you go. Improvise," and handed her a small green paper-wrapped wire.

"But that's a—"

Jake rolled his eyes. "Gracie, you'd wear out a saint's patience. I know what it is. The question remains, are you going to use it, or are you going to walk out of my cabin holding on to your braid with one hand and your unbuttoned shirt with the other?"

She gasped and looked down. Sure enough, there was just enough bare belly showing between the buttons that had come undone to suggest something scandalous had been going on.

Panicked, she looked to him for help. "Jake . . ."

He grinned and obliged by taking his time about fastening the buttons, while she frantically worked on her braid.

"Ready or not, here I come," Jake said, and walked out the door.

Gracie was right behind him, the basket of medicine and gauze hanging casually over her arm. Together, they sauntered toward the crowd gathered around the big rig as though it was an everyday occurrence. In fact, they were in the thick of it all before Aaron noticed them.

"Hey, Gracie, look who's back."

At the sound of his sister's name, Brady Moon looked up from inside the truck. He couldn't wait to see the look on her face when she saw the gift that he'd brought. He'd heard her talking to their father about a children's Bible. She was going to be so excited when—

And then his gaze moved to the man standing beside her, and he jerked as if someone had punched him in the belly. His vision blurred, and his head began to pound.

Stunned by the shock of seeing Jake Crockett standing upright and back in their midst, the bag of flour he was holding hit the floor with a splat, splitting the seams and showering everyone close by with a dense white cloud. Women screamed in dismay as the children began to squeal in delight.

No one except Jake and Gracie saw the look of horror on Brady's face. Gracie didn't understand why, but Jake did. Brady Moon looked like a man who'd just seen a ghost.

Chase the moon. Chase the moon.

Remembering John's last words, Jake went still. The urge to kill overwhelmed him as his fingers curled into fists, and his eyes narrowed in a cold, warning stare.

It was you, wasnt it? You cowardly, back-shooting son of a bitch, it was you.

He started walking toward the truck. Gracie ran to catch him.

"Jake, what's wrong?"

When he didn't answer, she reached for his arm. He shrugged her off and kept on walking.

Aaron was laughing and dusting at the flour on his brother's shirt when he caught a glimpse of Jake from the corner of his eye. He froze, then elbowed Burnett and nodded at Matthew. Brother after brother, man after woman, the silence spread until the only sound to be heard was the near-imperceptible whoosh of escaping air as the flour sack finally went flat. But Jake kept coming, and the crowd parted silently to let him through.

From his porch, Elijah Moon suddenly stood. Although age and stubbornness had blinded him to many things, he still recognized the growing danger of the situation.

Brady Moon had started to sweat. Every eye in the enclave was now pinned on the drama between him and Jake, and he knew it. With mere seconds between himself and ruin, he reacted in the only way he knew how. With a forced laugh of disbelief, Brady jumped down from the truck and headed toward Jake with open arms.

"Crockett, you worthless piece of shit. So you finally decided to come home."

But the look on Jake's face was enough to stop Brady several feet short of reaching his goal.

Brady looked around in confusion, playing his part to the hilt. "Hey, guys, what's wrong with this picture?"

Aaron stepped between the men, giving Jake his back as he faced his brother down. "Jake didn't walk off the mountain that day, Brady. He was back-shot. He crawled off and saved himself."

Brady didn't have to pretend. Just hearing how Crockett had saved himself was almost more than he could bear.

"I don't believe it!" He pushed Aaron aside and walked toward Jake with his hand outstretched. "Jake! Tell me this isn't so."

But Jake's answer wasn't soon in coming. He was too busy looking into the eyes of his brother's killer, and he didn't like what he saw. He'd been in the business too long not to know a pissant liar when he saw one, and Brady Moon was one of the best. If Jake hadn't seen his first reaction, he might have believed him, too. But he had, and it was too late now for Brady to hide the truth.

Finally Jake spoke, and the slow, sarcastic drawl was not lost on a single person there.

"I shouldn't have to tell you a goddamned thing, Brady Moon. You were there, remember?"

Gracie covered her mouth with her hands, stifling a moan of disbelief. And as hard as she tried to tell herself differently, she'd seen the look on Brady's face. It hadn't been one of surprise. It had been one of horror.

The crowd around them began to move back, and Brady felt himself losing ground. There was one trick he'd learned young that never failed to work, and if he ever needed a miracle, it was now. He took a step toward Jake with his hand outstretched, and as he moved, tears welled in his eyes and spilled down his cheeks.

"You can't believe that," he said softly, and the persuasion in his voice was directed at the onlookers, as well as at Jake. "You were my friend. I looked upon you as a brother." Now tears were streaming from his eyes, and he could hear the sympathetic murmurs of the women. He paused and beat a fist upon his chest as he raised his voice an octave. "Surely you don't believe this! I am not Cain! I did not set out to kill my brother!"

No, you killed mine. But Jake didn't say his thought aloud. All he did was turn and walk away, leaving the crowd in no doubt as to what Jake Crockett believed.

Sundown had come and gone, bringing an unnatural quiet over the compound. Inside the cabins, people spoke in hushed voices, talking over the events of the day. Brother spoke to brother in disbelief, each needing the other's reassurance that one of their own could not be capable of such a cowardly deed. And while the answers were positive, not a one of them could forget the look on Jake Crockett's face. Even if Brady hadn't been the one to shoot him, Jake's beliefs were to the contrary.

It set an uneasy mood within the New Zionists that they had never encountered. They'd come up there in a public show of rejection to what they considered government intrusion into their lives. They hadn't planned on the possibility of rejecting one of their own.

In Elijah's cabin, Brady sat at his father's side,

playing the part of the dutiful son, while in another room, Gracie's fear for her family grew. Elijah was a strong man, but she wondered how he could be so susceptible to Brady's lies.

"That was a very large load of supplies," Elijah said.

Brady smiled. He had this part down by heart. "Yes, Father, my business in Lexington is paying profits quite well." And when Elijah would have argued, Brady held up his hand with a smile. "Please, don't argue with me on this point. I had the business before New Zion was founded, and you know it. It's only right that we all share from the fruits of my labors."

Elijah heard, and while good sense warned him there was more going on, he was too willing to let Brady do as he chose, rather than buck him on certain points. Besides, in a sense, Brady was right. If there were profits to be made, sharing them was the godly way.

Instead of questioning Brady further, Elijah leaned back in his chair and closed his eyes, searching through his memory for a Bible verse that would apply. Nothing specific came to mind and he realized he was very tired.

"New Zion can be the land of milk and honey someday," he said.

Brady reached out and clasped his father's arm, his heart swelling with pride. "No, Father, with you at the helm, it already is."

Elijah took his son's words as his due. In his mind, New Zion was what he'd always dreamed

of creating. Another Garden of Eden in the decay
of today's society. And then he remembered Jake
Crockett's accusations and frowned. There was a
snake in Elijah's garden, and he wanted it stamped
out.

"You must find a way to make your peace with
Jake Crockett," Elijah said. "He is a good man. He
has need of us. It is our duty to show him the way,
to redeem him from the evils that befell him while
living in the cities." And then he added, "We must
discover the truth behind his story. If there is a man
among us who would commit murder most foul,
then he must be dealt with in a firm and just way.
That is God's law. That is God's will."

Brady smiled while his belly turned. Retribution
in any form other than that which he dealt out was
not something he wished to consider. He nodded
and listened as Elijah continued to talk, and all the
while he made plans of his own.

In the next room, Gracie lay wide-eyed and
sleepless, listening to their conversation. Yes, the
foodstuffs Brady had brought for their storehouse
were wonderful. If they had to withstand a long
siege, it would not cause them undue hardship.
But Gracie kept asking herself, if the life of New
Zion was supposed to symbolize peace and har-
mony, as the doctrine went, then what possible
siege could there be to withstand? And there was
something even more puzzling to her. Where had
Brady gotten the money to fund such a buy? There
was no way a body shop in Lexington could bring

in the kind of money needed for what Brady was buying.

Gracie wasn't the only one who was restless that night. Jake decided to take advantage of the change in their routine at New Zion to do some long-needed investigating. He had to find out for himself what John must have already known.

When the midnight hour was upon them, Jake shoved a chair beneath his doorknob and then slipped out a back window. Within seconds he was in the trees, and within a quarter of an hour, far up the mountainside and following a well-beaten path.

He walked into a booby trap thirty minutes into his search, and it was only by the grace of God and a rabbit that darted across his path that he was saved. The rabbit died. Jake could hardly mourn its passing for staring at the wooden stake with which it had been pierced. At that point, he stepped off the path and took to the trees, constantly on the lookout for more of the same.

It was with great relief that he finally walked into a clearing. And while he was pretty certain everyone in New Zion was home in their beds, he had no desire to walk into any more surprises. Circling the encampment, what he saw made his concern grow.

Bunkers dotted the landscape. Small sheds painted in camouflage colors nestled beneath large, overhanging limbs. To his right he saw wooden cutouts of life-sized people, and when he drew closer he realized they were riddled with holes. Bullet holes.

Off to the left, a long roll of razor-sharp concertina wire marked a far boundary. His nerves were on edge as he moved toward the sheds. If they contained what he suspected, then there was every possibility that they, too, would be rigged in some way to discourage intruders.

But to his surprise, the doors were only padlocked. It took but a few seconds to open them, and when he stepped inside and showed his flashlight around, his expression darkened.

Illegal assault weapons. Ammunition. Explosives. All the makings for everything from pipe bombs to holocausts. He backed out as quietly as he'd gone in, leaving everything, including the locks, in place. It was just as John's boss, Ron Hudson, had suspected. They weren't preaching the word of God in New Zion. They were planning to start a war.

As he started back down the mountain, his dilemma was growing. He'd come to avenge his brother's death, but there was more going on here than the murder of one man. What Jake had just seen could cause the deaths of many more innocents. Should he get this information to Hudson and let him bring them down now, or could he risk waiting, hoping to find proof that Brady had really been the one who killed John? Gut instinct told him that Brady was guilty, but that wasn't enough to take to the bank. Jake needed some kind of proof, and then God help Brady Moon, because he would show him no mercy.

By the time he reached his cabin, it was less than an hour to dawn. He stood in the tree line for several long minutes, making sure that he would not be observed. Finally, satisfied that nothing moved except the wind, he crossed the distance to his cabin, lifted the window, and went in the same way he'd gone out.

As badly as he wanted to sleep, he couldn't risk the luxury. He needed to be in the hall for breakfast. He wanted to look into Brady Moon's face. Then he would know what choice to make.

Jake met Elijah halfway between his cabin and the hall. The old man seemed burdened, and Jake wondered how much he really knew of what was going on.

"Good morning, sir," Jake said.

Elijah stopped, staring intently before nodding.

"I'm sorry about yesterday," Jake said. "I hope you know I will never be the instigator of trouble here. However, I will not run from it."

Elijah considered Jake's words, then nodded. "Fair enough," he said. "Come, walk with me to the hall."

Jake fell in beside him, shortening his steps to match the old man's slower stride. When they reached the hall, their arrival together did not go unnoticed.

Gracie came out of the kitchen carrying a tray of hot biscuits, saw her father with Jake, then watched as Elijah beckoned for Jake to sit at his side. Instantly, she searched the hall for Brady, knowing full well how he was going to react. When she saw his face, her belly clenched with fear. In that moment, she knew that Jake's suspicions were true. She'd never seen so much hate, and it was all directed at Jake.

Brady had convinced himself he had matters well in hand until Elijah walked in the door with Jake Crockett. After the confrontation they'd had yesterday, his father's public show of approval for Jake made it seem as if Brady was the one in the wrong. Clenching his fists, he muttered something to Aaron about going to check on the guns, and stalked out the door.

Gracie breathed a quick sigh of relief as she saw Brady leave. Whatever that meant, at least it had been postponed. She set the tray of biscuits in front of her father and gave him a good-morning kiss.

"I see you finally woke up," she teased, stroking the snow white hair on his head.

"It was a long night," he said.

Her smile became strained. "I know, Father. I heard you and Brady talking until all hours. You should have sent him home."

Elijah glanced at Jake, then back at Gracie. "There were things we had to discuss."

Refusing to sit silently while he was the subject of the conversation, Jake interrupted. "And did you get everything worked out to your satisfaction?"

Elijah began buttering a biscuit. "That remains to be seen."

And that was all the answer Jake was going to get. He reached for a biscuit and the jar of jam. It was strawberry, John's favorite. He looked down at the thick, ruby preserves and knew his decision was made. Because of Brady Moon, John Baretta would never taste strawberries again. Hudson would just have to wait to make his raid. Jake had a score to settle.

It was after dark when Brady walked up the steps of his father's house. The episode at breakfast had been eating at him all day. He needed to know what it meant. But before he could knock, Gracie met him at the door. She stepped outside, closing it quietly behind her.

Brady frowned. "I came to talk to Father."

Gracie put her hand on her brother's arm in a plea for understanding. "Not tonight, Brady. He's already asleep."

Her refusal surprised him. Heaped with the sidelong, questioning glances from men who were supposed to respect him, his beloved Gracie's rejection was one too many.

He shoved her aside. "You have no say in the matter," he said. "Get out of my way."

Gracie staggered, catching herself before she actually fell. Shock, coupled with an unexpected anger, filled her, and she grabbed his hand before he could turn the knob.

"I said, not tonight. He needs his rest, not a repeat of last night."

Brady reacted before he thought. He lashed out,

catching her cheek with the back of his hand. He felt no guilt for doing this. She was his sister. Sometimes a woman needed discipline from a person who cared.

"I'm sorry, Gracie, but you shouldn't have made me do that," Brady said.

Gracie's cry was as much from shock as from pain, but it was loud enough for one man to hear.

Jake had been sitting on his porch in the dark. He'd seen Brady crossing the yard to Elijah's cabin. When the door opened, he'd seen Gracie momentarily silhouetted against the light within, and then he had watched with growing suspicion as she slipped outside to meet her brother.

His belly knotted. Their behavior hovered on the edge of clandestine, and he stood, then moved back into the shadows, reminding himself that while the old man might not be aware of what was really going on in his New Zion, there was every possibility that his only daughter did. There was every possibility that she was up to her neck in the mess.

But his opinion quickly changed when he saw Brady shove her aside. Jake cursed beneath his breath, watching as Gracie regained her balance and began an entreaty again. His instincts were to go to her aid, but he reminded himself that he was the outsider here, not her. He stayed his ground until he heard the slap of hand against cheek. When she cried aloud and fell backward, he bolted.

Shaking with every breath, Gracie clasped a

hand to her cheek and felt blood. She would never have believed it possible, but she was suddenly afraid of her eldest brother.

"You did it, didn't you, Brady?"

He froze. Shocked by her accusation, he began to shout. "Shut up! You don't know anything about what's going on. All you know is to sniff at Jake Crockett's crotch like some bitch in heat."

Gracie gritted her teeth and crawled to her feet, standing toe to toe with him in spite of her fear.

"I know Father doesn't know about your little games up on the mountain. I know that the last thing pacifists should be buying are guns. I know—"

Brady drew back again, but his blow never fell. Instead, he found himself flat on his back and staring up at the man who stood astraddle his legs.

"You ever touch her like that again, and I'll make you sorry."

"Stay out of this, Crockett," Brady said.

Jake leaned down, grabbed Brady by the front of his shirt, and hauled him to his feet. His voice was soft, making what he said that much more deadly.

"Like hell."

"This is family business," Brady said.

"Then maybe we should go get your father. Since he's the head of the family, don't you think he would want to know what you just did to his only daughter?"

Brady paled. Everything was going wrong, and the last thing he wanted was for his father to get in the middle of this.

"This has nothing to do with him. It's between my sister and me."

Jake's voice became quieter still. "Elijah doesn't have much to do with anything going on up here, does he?"

Brady's face darkened, and he glanced at Gracie. Unblinking, she gave him back stare for stare.

Jake tightened his grip on Brady's shirt. "Don't look at her. Look at me!"

Anger surged as Brady pushed away from Jake's hands. "No, Crockett, you look at me. I'm tired of being accused of something I didn't do. I don't like you messing into things that are none of your business, but I have no intention of hurting you."

"Sorry I can't say the same. Now I'm guessing this little disagreement was because your sister didn't want your father's rest disturbed, so why don't you take yourself home before you do something else you might regret."

Brady spun and stalked off into the shadows, and when he did, Gracie went limp. If Jake hadn't grabbed her, she would have fallen at his feet.

"Look at me," Jake ordered, then tilted her chin when she was too slow in responding.

When he saw the flow of blood on her cheek, he started to curse, then held her instead.

Her voice shook. "You made an enemy tonight."

"Then he can just get in line with the others. He's damn sure not the first. Come with me," he said softly. "We need to get some ice on that and fast, or you're going to have one hell of a shiner by morning."

She followed without argument, and when he led her into his cabin and seated her in a chair, she covered her face with her hands and started to cry.

Jake set the ice on the cabinet and took her in his arms. "I'm sorry. If I'd reacted sooner, this might not have happened."

More than a little shocked, she struggled to gain her composure. "You were watching?"

He touched the side of her face and was surprised by the tenderness he felt for her as she leaned against the palm of his hand.

"I was sitting on my porch, enjoying the night. It was impossible to miss."

She pulled out of his embrace. "I don't belong here," she said quietly. "Brady is crazy, and he's ruining my family."

"They're all adults," Jake said. "They should know their own minds."

She shook her head. "No. You don't understand how we were raised. Father drilled complete obedience into us from the day we were born. We followed his will because we were taught to obey our elders. But while Father expects obedience, Brady craves adulation. He always did. I've never been afraid of him—until tonight."

"You left, why didn't they?"

She turned and then smiled, wincing when the act caused her pain. Jake reached for the ice as she answered.

"Mother was a feminist ahead of her time. I'm the only member of my family with a college education. I left home when I was eighteen and except for the occasional visit, didn't come back until Mother died."

"Then why do you stay now?" Jake asked, and then laid the ice pack gently against her cheek.

Gracie stared off into space, her eyes losing focus as her mind wandered back over the last two years. "I never meant to. It sort of just happened."

A sense of urgency hit Jake as he realized what he was starting to believe. Not only was Gracie innocent of subversive activity, but there was a distinct possibility that she could be in danger. Again, he considered contacting Hudson right away. Of telling him to send in the guns and clean out this nest of vipers before any more damage was done. But he knew if he did, a lost schoolteacher would be caught up in the sweep. Somehow, he couldn't bring himself to pull the plug. At least, not quite yet.

"You should leave."

The certainty in his voice startled her. "Why? What do you know that I don't?"

Hiding his feelings, Jake turned away to add fresh ice to the pack. Never had he been so aware of living a lie. Reapplying the ice with one hand, he cupped her cheek with the other.

"I know that your brother hit you once. Every statistic out there says he'll do it again."

"And would you care?"

Jake froze. The underlying meaning of that question scared him, because he already knew the answer. She rose and walked several feet away.

"Yes, Gracie, I would care, more than you know."

Turning, she stared at him thoughtfully for a long, long time, and then finally shook her head.

"You know, Jake, you're a real good man. I'd like to know what was missing in your life that set you on a wrong path."

Jake didn't move, although he felt a strong urge to take her in his arms.

"I suppose you might say, the love of a good woman."

"And if you had that now, what might you do?" This time Jake's answer came swiftly, surprising him as much as her.

"I'd be tempted to take her and run, and never look back."

Chapter 7

When Jake walked into the hall for breakfast and saw Brady sitting with Elijah, he was startled. But when he realized Gracie was absent, he got furious. Without thinking of the consequences, he went to Elijah. He could barely control his anger as he stared the old man straight in the face.

"Where's Gracie?"

Brady looked up, then away as Elijah took a drink of his coffee. "Said she wasn't feeling well."

Jake leaned closer. "Goddamn the both of you. Don't hide your shame at her expense. Either you go get her or I'll do it myself."

From Elijah's expression, Jake could see he didn't like being challenged, but right now Jake didn't give a damn. When neither man made a move to get up, he cursed beneath his breath and stalked out.

Moments later, he was at her door. He knocked and, without giving her time to answer, shouted, "Gracie, come to breakfast."

"I'm not hungry."

"You open this damned door or I'm coming in after you."

His hand was on the doorknob when the door swung open. Even though he'd been expecting it, the shock of seeing that dark, purple bruise staining the curve of her cheek made him sick.

She stepped aside, allowing him entrance, and as he came inside, his hand instinctively went to her face. She trembled at his touch and then closed her eyes, savoring the feel of Jake's hand against her skin.

He felt the ground shift beneath his feet and knew it wasn't a natural occurrence. The only thing rocking his world was Gracie Moon.

"Dear sweet Lord, you take my—"

He choked on the rest of what he was about to say and took her in his arms. She smelled sweet and felt soft and he'd never been so confused in his life.

"You aren't really sick, are you?"

She stiffened and looked up at him. "Is that what Father told you?"

He nodded, then leaned down and brushed his lips against the bruise, wishing he could absorb her pain. Gracie swayed against him. When her arms slid around his waist, his heart swelled inside his chest.

"Gracie, has your father seen your face?"

"Yes."

"What did he say?"

Gracie slipped out of his arms and turned abruptly, flaring the long skirt of her loose summer dress. When she began picking up the books on the pretense of cleaning up the room, Jake wasn't fooled. He'd seen the tears in her eyes.

"Gracie?"

She paused, glancing around at the confusion of clutter in the small two-bedroom home. It shamed her to tell him the truth.

"He didn't say a thing. He just picked up his Bible and started to read."

The old bastard. Hiding his head in Christian teachings while hiding from the truth.

The thought made Jake mad. He took Gracie's hand. "I came to take you to breakfast."

It would mean going against Elijah Moon's wishes again. But at the thought, a fire lit in her eyes. She smoothed down the front of her dress, then lifted her chin. It was way past time that someone did just that.

"Good," she said. "Because I'm suddenly very hungry."

He held out his hand and she took it.

Their arm-in-arm arrival raised eyebrows, but it was nothing compared to the hisses and gasps that spread across the hall when they saw Gracie's face. Annie handed their youngest to her husband, Aaron, and dashed toward Gracie.

"Gracie, darling, what on earth happened to your face?"

She glanced at Brady, refusing to be swayed by his hard, angry look. "Brady and I had a difference of opinion."

Annie gasped, her eyes narrowing angrily as she

gave her brother-in-law a glance before looking back at Gracie.

"When you've had breakfast, come to my cabin. I have something to put on that bruise that might help."

"Thank you," Gracie said. "I will."

"Where do you want to sit?" Jake asked.

"I'll just go in the kitchen and—"

"Gracie Moon, I asked you a question."

She sighed. When he wanted to, Jake could be a real hardheaded man. "How about over there," she said, pointing to a vacant spot near the doors.

"Looks good to me," he said. "Have a seat. I'll go get our food."

Gracie tried not to stare as Jake walked away, but he was too compelling a man to ignore.

Across the room, Elijah saw the longing on his daughter's face and frowned. He didn't consider the fact that at twenty-seven, Gracie was a woman grown and could make up her own mind about men. In Elijah's world, there were rules, and if he found out one had been broken, he would make certain that somebody paid.

The day passed with Brady Moon getting deeper and deeper into hot water with the citizens of New Zion. He had to do something to restore their faith in him, or his credibility would go all to hell. That evening he sought out Taggert Brown.

Taggert was sitting on his front steps, planing the bow of a rocker he was making and watching chickens scratching in the yard.

Brady pulled out his knife and started whittling on a scrap of wood. "Don't you think it's about time to put up those hens? You let 'em roost in the trees and something will get them."

Taggert didn't bother to look up. "I know how to take care of chickens," he said shortly.

Nervous tension settled between Brady's shoulders. He couldn't remember Taggert ever being this abrupt with him. Maybe a change of subject would soothe the way.

"So, how do you feel about Crockett's return? He isn't exactly trying to fit in, is he?"

Taggert looked up, and there was a cold, angry glare on his face. "You know, Brady, I don't like Crockett. And even though he saved your brother Matthew's boy, I don't give a shit what happens to him."

Brady started to smile. This was more like it.

"However," Taggert continued. "I got me a real big problem fighting alongside a back-shooter. And if I find out you was the one who shot Crockett in the back, then I might have to break your damned neck on the off chance it could happen to me, too."

Brady paled. Of all the men he was training, Taggert was the most deadly. A Vietnam veteran who suffered periodic bouts of flashbacks, Taggert was as likely to pull a gun on a man as to laugh in his face. The last thing Brady wanted was to get on the wrong side of him.

"Damn it, Taggert, not you, too? Surely you don't believe me capable of such a horrible deed?"

Taggert continued planing the wood without looking up at Brady. "I ain't sayin' I do, and I ain't sayin' I don't. All I am sayin' is, it would piss me off greatly if it happened to be so."

"Well, you're about to piss me off greatly, too. I expect to see you at maneuvers at sunup. I picked up some new firepower. We need a training session in breakdown and reassembly."

"I'll be there."

"See that you are."

When Brady got to Jake's cabin he had to make himself keep moving, because the urge to purge was upon him. Jake Crockett was a blight on New Zion, and Brady wanted him gone. But how to do it without completely alienating his father was a problem. Elijah Moon preached the word of God with fire in his eye and power in his breath. He might be aging, but his spirit was not.

Unaware that he'd been the topic of another conversation, Jake slept. And as he slept, a faint bit of moonlight from a new quarter moon came in through his window and showed down on his bed, casting long purple shadows on the floor.

Jake lay sprawled on the bed, his muscles twitching as his mind carried him through the dream.

Johnny Baretta stood poised at the bedroom window, ready to make his break. All he needed was Jake's promise that he would cover for him if need be.

"Well, are you going to do it or not?" Johnny asked.

Jake frowned. "You know if you get caught at that

dive, Dad will whip both our butts. You for going, and me for letting it happen."

Johnny grinned. *"They can't make you responsible for me, you're only seventeen. Besides that, you're my brother, not my father."*

"Sometimes I can't tell the difference," Jake muttered.

Johnny laughed. *"Better come with me. I hear the pussy is real good."*

A wry grin tilted the corner of Jake's mouth. *"Your brains are in your pants."*

"Yeah, well you're too damned noble for your own good."

They stared, one at the other, looking into mirror images of the other one's face. And yet as alike as they looked, they couldn't have been more different inside. The constancy in their lives was the unwavering faith they had in each other's trust.

Johnny ticked off the things Jake had to remember to do.

"When you brush your teeth, remember to put on my red gym shorts. Then when you get a snack later, wear your cutoffs. That way Mom will think she's seen the both of us. If she asks where I am, tell her—"

"Hell, I know what to say," Jake muttered. *"I've said it enough times before."*

Johnny laughed. *"Tell her I said good night, and that I've gone to sleep."*

Jake woke up with a jerk, and sat straight up in bed. The blue-white slivers of moonlight slicing the length of his legs made him shudder. It looked the way he felt—that he'd been cut in two. He rolled out of bed and went to the window, shoving the curtain completely aside as he stared up at the bit of new moon.

An ache bloomed in his chest that moved to his throat. He continued to stare until the sky began to shimmer, and he realized he was crying. Johnny was dead. He'd laughed his last laugh and breathed his last sigh. There was a hole in Jake's chest where his heart used to be, and the longer time passed, the wider it grew. Sometimes he feared it would open up too far and he would fall in upon himself and never come out.

He put the flat of his hand on the windowpane and closed his eyes. In his mind he saw Johnny's face once more, with devils dancing in his eyes and laughter in his voice. Someone up here had taken that away. And that someone was going to pay.

It didn't take long for Gracie's injury to become old news. In a place where women were subservient on a daily basis, a bruise on the cheek might be frowned upon, but it was not a thing upon which to dwell. However, the act had done something to Gracie besides bruise her face. It had become the first crack in the guilt that bound her to New Zion. She found herself thinking of her old life—of the education she'd worked hard to achieve, of the career she'd given up to come care for her aging father. And while she still loved him, it was becoming increasingly difficult to honor him.

The man who filled the thoughts of her days and

nights was not of her blood, but her heart. As much as she feared what Jake Crockett had been, it was the man she saw now whom she loved.

When it came time for school to resume, she refocused the days of her life to the children and the job that she loved and left her thoughts of Jake for the nighttime, when she could dream of him on her own.

"Aunt Gracie, do I have to call you teacher?"

Gracie smiled. Timothy was a character. He'd been asking her that since her first day after she'd come up the mountain.

"No, Timothy, you don't." And when she saw him giggle and elbow one of Taggert Brown's children, she saw fit to add, "However, you do have to mind me, remember?"

The giggle went out of Timothy as he adopted a more serious attitude. Gracie smiled. She knew the moment her back was turned that everything but school would be on their minds.

"Now get out your spelling books and turn to page four. Do the exercise at the end of the chapter."

The children sighed but did as they were told. Gracie turned to the portable blackboard and began writing down words for them to copy later.

A cool breeze was coming through the open window to her left, lifting the wisps of hair that had escaped her braid and feathering them against her face. Outside in a nearby tree, a squirrel suddenly scolded, while hens clucked to their chicks as they pecked at the ground. It was a day like many others had been, but for some reason Gracie felt more than alive.

Her skin was sensitive to her clothing, and she was aware of her body in a way that she'd never been before. As she wrote the words, she felt the weight of her breasts against the inside of her arms. When she moved from side to side along the blackboard, the muscles in her legs tensed in response to the rhythm of her walk. It was almost as if she could see farther, hear clearer, and breathe deeper than she'd ever done before.

The children's hushed voices faded into the background, and she paused at the end of a word and closed her eyes, stunned by the sensations coursing through her veins. Remembering what she'd been doing, she looked up, absently glancing out the window before resuming her task. As she did, her breath caught at the back of her throat.

Jake was standing beneath a tree and watching her every move. The look on his face was somewhere between lust and longing, and she wondered how long he'd been standing there, watching her. She turned away, trying to forget he was there. It was impossible. It was like trying to ignore being stalked by a wild animal.

Jenny Brown raised her hand. "Miss Gracie, may I be excused?"

Gracie nodded, and the child raced toward the bathroom at the back of the room as Gracie took note of the others at work.

"Don't forget the questions at the end of the chapter, too," she added. A collective groan swept the room, and she turned away to hide a grin, and in doing so, glanced out the window again. He was gone.

She sighed, and a few moments later realized that the awareness of herself she'd been experiencing was gone. Startled, she glanced back out the window.

Surely just being under that man's gaze hadn't caused all of that?

She let the notion slip, and not until the next morning when she walked into the room and found a single red apple waiting for her on her desk did she think of it again. It could have come from any of the children. But when she picked it up and lifted it to her nose, inhaling the sweet familiarity of the apple's fragrance, she knew it had come from him.

Instinctively she turned toward the window. Just as she'd guessed, he was watching her. And as he stood without moving, staring intently at her face, at her body, and at the apple she was holding, her pulse began to race.

He tilted his chin in a dare-me-to-leave attitude, and Gracie dared him right back. In a move that would have shocked her entire family, she licked the apple with the tip of her tongue and then took a bite, catching the juice at the edge of her mouth with the tip of her finger.

When she bit that apple, Jake shuddered. He stood beneath her scrutiny only a few moments more and then walked away before his body betrayed him. He kept thinking of that apple, and the way she'd lifted it to her lips before taking a bite, and groaned. As he went about his work, he kept thinking that if Eve had looked anything like Gracie Moon, it was no damned wonder old Adam had succumbed to temptation in the Garden of Eden.

Elijah was down at the hall passing the lazy Sunday afternoon by regaling the children with some of his favorite Bible stories. It was one of the few times that Gracie ever had the cabin all to herself, and she knew just what she was going to do. Tomorrow was another school day, and she wanted her hair to be fresh and clean to start off the week. She'd meant to wash it yesterday, but she'd been so busy that by the time she thought of it again, it had been too late.

But today was another story. The afternoon was still young, and if she washed it now, it would have the hours it needed to dry before going to bed. In a pinch, she could have used an electric hair dryer, but she preferred to let her hair dry naturally.

Anticipating a lazy afternoon outside in the sunshine while it dried, she headed for the bathroom to get her shampoo. She wasn't going to waste time by stripping down to wash it in the shower. Not today. The kitchen sink would have to do.

The water ran warm beneath her fingers as she ducked her head beneath the faucet. Soon, she had worked up a lather and was scrubbing her scalp with her fingertips and remembering her favorite salon in Atlanta with regret. One of these days she was going to get back to the real world, and when she did, the first thing she was going to do was have someone else shampoo her hair.

In the middle of rinsing out the soap, she heard the front door open and groaned beneath her breath. Her peace and quiet was over, but in a way she hadn't expected.

Brady stood in the doorway, staring at Gracie's backside and wondering how he was going to make things right between them. After striking her, he'd been saddened by the fact that it even happened. Gracie was his. She should know he would do anything for her. Of all his siblings, he loved her the most.

He frowned, thinking of Jake Crockett and blaming him for all the turmoil in New Zion.

In the midst of his thoughts, Gracie reached for a towel, wrapping it around her hair to catch the drips, and then straightened and turned. The shock on her face hurt his heart, and he spoke first, before she could order him out.

"I came to say I'm sorry."

Gracie frowned. For some reason, she felt as if she'd just been stripped beneath her brother's strange stare.

"Sorry for what?" she asked. "For hitting me, or for shooting Jake?"

Brady's face flushed a dark, angry red. "Gracie, do you hear yourself? Look at me!" He pounded his chest in frustration and took a couple of steps inside, closing the door behind him. "It's me, Brady! Your brother, remember? How can you believe that I would knowingly . . . on purpose . . . and with malice . . . shoot someone, and in the back?"

Said aloud, the idea did seem preposterous, but Gracie had been a witness more than once to her brother's persuasive style of behavior. She knew that he lied. She'd grown up seeing him do one thing and admit to another. Once, when she was five, she'd seen him kill one of her mother's chickens in a burst of anger and then heard him blaming the incident on Burnett without batting an eye.

Water dripped from beneath the towel and down her back, but she didn't flinch as she answered his demand.

"It doesn't matter what I think, does it, Brady? It's Jake you have to convince."

Brady paled. "I don't have to convince that son of a bitch of anything," he said softly. "I don't care what he thinks of me. You're the one I care about. Your opinion of me is what matters."

The pain on Brady's face was too much for her to bear. She looked away.

Brady took the opportunity to shorten the distance between them. He reached out, pulling Gracie into his arms and then rubbing the middle of her back between her shoulder blades as his soft whispers broke the silence between them.

"I'm so sorry I hit you. I don't know what made me do it. One minute I was in control and the next thing I remember was—"

Gracie stepped out of his arms, and when their gazes met, Brady paused in midsentence. He was the first to look away.

She turned to pick up a nearby hairbrush and comb, then walked out the back door and sat down on the steps. There was a knot in her stomach and a lump in her throat as she started combing the tangles out of her long, dark hair. For Gracie, his guilt had been confirmed when he was unable to look her in the eye.

Brady followed her outside, then stood and watched as she worked the tangles out of her hair.

"Need some help?"

"No," she said shortly, and continued to work.

A bitter smile twisted his lips. "There was a time when you used to beg me to comb out your hair."

Gracie closed her eyes, refusing to let herself remember the old days. She took a deep breath, stood up, and turned. "That was a long time ago, Brady. I'm not a little girl anymore."

An unnatural flush stained his cheeks as his gaze swept her shapely figure. "Damn you, Gracie," he muttered, and then turned and walked away.

Gracie didn't relax until she heard the front door slam. "Oh Lord," she whispered. When she lifted the comb to her hair, she realized that her hands were shaking.

The days moved into a week and then another and another. The harvest of the summer garden was coming to a close. The days were still warm, often hot, but the nights were starting to cool. Fall crops were beginning to mature, and the pumpkins in the fence row were turning orange. There was an expectant feel to the air. It was the time of waiting.

"Hey, Jake!"

Jake paused, hammer in hand, to see Matthew Moon approaching. He cocked his head in a quick hello, then hammered the last nail into place on the corral he'd been building.

Matthew leaned over the rail fence, his long brown hair sliding forward across his shoulders as he ran his hand along the wood.

"You've done a good job," Matthew said, eyeing the straight line of the fence posts, as well as the flat, hand-hewn planks that had been used as rails.

Jake wiped sweat from his forehead with the back of his shirtsleeve, accepting the praise for whatever it was worth. Ever since Timothy's rescue from the flood, Matthew had been going out of his way to make conversation.

"Thanks," Jake said.

Matthew propped his foot on the lower rail, then removed his wide-brimmed brown hat and scratched his head.

"Say, I came to tell you there is a man in Little Rome who's looking for you."

Jake froze. *Shit. Looking for me or for the real Jake Crockett?* "Oh? Did he give his name?"

"Yes, but I have to say I forgot it. I'm not good with names. However, I remember he was a real

estate broker. Said you'd called him some time
back about—"

Relief surged as Jake interrupted. "About selling
my grandmother's house! That's right, I did, but
that was ages ago, right after I'd come back to
town." Then he grinned. "Took his own sweet time
about getting here, didn't he?"

Matthew nodded. "Said to tell you he'd stay
over one day and then he'd be gone tomorrow.
Said if you're still interested in selling the place to
let him know. He eats his meals in the diner."

Jake glanced at his watch, then tossed the hammer into the bucket of nails and took off his gloves.

"Guess I'd better get a move on."

Matthew nodded. "You'll have to ask Father for
the keys to one of the trucks. I'd take you myself,
but I'm already late for drill. Brady is probably
having himself a fit as we speak."

Jake laughed. "I don't need a chauffeur."

Matthew's eyes were dark and solemn. "Well,
actually, you do. It's Father's rule, you know. The
vehicles are Moon property. No one drives them
but—"

A wry grin split Jake's face. "Hell, like I haven't
heard this before. No one does anything up here
unless Elijah or Brady gives the blessing."

Matthew looked away.

Jake laughed again. "Don't let it worry you. I
know how to beg with the best of them. And if he
won't let me drive one, I'll walk down. I've done it
before."

Matthew flushed. "You will never know how

grateful Kay and I are. We wouldn't have our son if it wasn't for you." He took a deep breath. "Sometimes I think about what would have happened to Timothy that night if you hadn't come back to New Zion. I'm not a strong swimmer. I don't know—"

Jake put a hand on Matthew's shoulder. "It's over. He's safe. Don't give it another thought. Thanks for letting me know about the agent. I'll go talk to Elijah now."

Jake rushed to his cabin to change his shirt, then headed to Elijah's cabin. He knew who was waiting for him down below in Little Rome. It was Ron Hudson. The real estate agent was the agreed-upon cover if Hudson ever needed to get in contact with him. Jake didn't know what had happened, but he was anxious to find out.

He knocked on Elijah's door and, when he got no answer, walked around to the back porch where the old man was fond of sitting. Sure enough, he found him there reading his Bible while Gracie sat nearby, peeling her way through a bushel of red apples.

At the sound of footsteps Gracie looked up, and her heart skipped a beat as she saw Jake. She dumped the apple she was peeling into the pan and stood.

"Hi there. It's good to see you," she said quickly. "Can I get you something cool to drink?"

He took a moment to absorb the beauty of her face, as well as the gentle manner in which she spoke. Today, her hair was down and tied back from her face with a piece of ribbon. The jeans she was wearing were a well-washed blue, and her brown plaid, long-sleeved shirt was rolled up to the elbows, revealing strong, tanned arms. Then he remembered why he'd come.

"No, but thanks," he said. "Actually, I came to ask Elijah a favor."

The old man looked up.

"Matthew just came from Little Rome. There's a man asking to see me." Jake could see a frown of rejection beginning on Elijah's face, but he continued as if not noticing. "I called him weeks ago about selling my grandmother's house. I have no need for it, and if it sits empty too long, it will lose value."

Elijah nodded. That much made sense.

"So, I was wondering if I might borrow one of the pickup trucks to drive into Little Rome. It shouldn't take all that long, and I'd be glad to pick up anything you might be needing up here in the meantime."

Even though Elijah saw the wisdom of the notion, the idea of someone outside the family using family property didn't sit well with him. Refusal was on the tip of his tongue when Gracie suddenly spoke.

"I'd be glad to drive you," she said quickly. "There are some personal items I've been needing at the drug store."

Elijah looked away. Well aware of womanly functions, he could not deny Gracie's right to feminine hygiene, but he didn't want to think about it. In spite of the fact that Gracie was taken with Jake

Crockett, Elijah still believed her submissive enough to his rules not to blatantly disobey.

"Daughter, I will ask you to drive safely, and be back before the evening meal."

Gracie kissed Elijah on the forehead and within minutes found herself behind the wheel of Elijah's black half-ton pickup.

With the windows down and the weight of New Zion left behind her, Gracie felt as light as the air tunneling through the cab. She laughed for the joy of just being alive.

Jake had hoped to go down alone, but if he'd had to have anyone accompany him, he couldn't have chosen a better companion. Gracie Moon already had a firm place in his heart, but he didn't want Hudson knowing that. Then she laughed, and he knew he didn't give a good damn what Hudson might think. Whatever happened, Jake would give his life to make sure that Gracie was not pulled under with the rest of the lot. He turned sideways in the seat, allowing himself to look but not touch.

"Care to let me in on the joke?"

Her dark eyes were dancing as she gave him a quick glance before focusing back on the narrow, winding road.

"No joke, just joy," she said, and tapped the brake gently as they started into a turn.

Jake knew what she meant. "Gracie?"

"Hmm?"

"As a kid, did you ever think about running away?"

Her smile slipped, but only a little. "Oh, sure. Hasn't every child?"

"Did you ever act upon it?" he asked.

She shook her head.

"Why?"

This time her smile slipped a little bit more. "Because I was Mother's good girl, that's why. Because I could never have brought myself to disappoint her, and because if I'd gone, then she would have been lonely."

Jake wasn't following her. "She wouldn't have been alone. Wouldn't your father and brothers have still been there?"

Gracie shook her head. "You can be lonely in a room full of people, Jake. But if you know who you are and are at peace with the world, it isn't hard to be alone." She sighed. "I'm afraid Mother didn't have much peace."

Her remark was so poignant, he couldn't help but touch her in some way. He reached out and tugged playfully at a long strand of her blowing hair.

"Are you lonely, Gracie Moon?"

The road straightened, and just for a moment, Gracie took her eyes from the road and gave Jake a long, intent stare. Finally, she shook her head.

"Not anymore."

Don't let her go.

Jake jerked. The thought came out of nowhere so fast he was taken unawares. He caught himself looking into the side-view mirror and over his shoulder.

Is that you, John? Do you know something I don't?

But there was no answer, so they finished the rest of the way to Little Rome in silence. It wasn't until Gracie passed the city limits sign that she spoke.

"Where do you want to go?"

"Matthew said the real estate agent would be at the diner. Do you know where it is?"

She nodded.

Jake glanced at his watch. "It's almost noon. If he's there, you can eat with us before you run your errands."

Her eyes lit, changing her expression to one of pure joy. She laughed again.

"Okay, this time you have to confess. What's so funny?"

When she pulled up to the diner and parked, the grin was still on her face.

"This is the closest thing to a date I've had in more than two years."

Something pulled at Jake, warning him, reminding him. But he couldn't get past the glow on her face. He leaned over, whispering close to her ear.

"Then you're in for a real treat, sweetheart. I'm hell on hamburgers and when it comes to apple pie à la mode, I'm impossible to resist."

Gracie turned and their lips met. The kiss they shared was soft and sweet. When she pulled back, there was a look on her face he'd never seen before.

"You eat your way to heaven, Jake Crockett. I'm betting on something else to get me there."

She got out of the truck, leaving him behind

with an ache below his belt and a fire building in
his blood.

"God help me," he muttered, and crawled out of
the truck.

Ron Hudson was relieved to see the tall dark-
haired man emerging from that black pickup
truck. After weeks and weeks with no news from
Baretta, he'd begun to get jumpy. It had caused
him to reconsider the wisdom of their earlier plan.
There were things that Jake needed to know, and
he hoped Jake had some things to tell him.

But when he saw Jake come into the diner with
a woman, he got a bit nervous. Playing it cool, he
looked up from his plate, pretending no more interest than he would any other person, and then
forked himself a big bite of fries.

Jake knew the rules.

He leaned over the counter, catching the waitress's eye.

"Excuse me, miss. But I'm supposed to meet a
real estate agent in here. I don't know what he
looks like, but his name is Joe Pete. Can you help
me?"

She glanced around the half-empty café, then
pointed. "There's only one stranger in here, so I'd
be guessing that's him."

He nodded. "Thanks, I'll give him a try." With
all the casualness he could muster, Jake headed
toward the booth where Hudson was sitting. "Excuse me, sir, but you wouldn't by any chance be
Joe Pete?"

Hudson laid down his fork and stood up. "At your service," he said with a smile. "And if you're Jake Crockett, I hope you are a forgiving man. Only recently I learned about your call to my business, and I can only blame the lateness of my response to the fact that my secretary was in the midst of an affair with the UPS man. Not only did my deliveries get screwed, but so did she." Then he glanced at Gracie and blushed. "Excuse me, miss. I shouldn't have said that."

Gracie grinned. In a way, it felt good to be treated as one of the guys instead of placed on some pedestal. "Think nothing of it," she said. "I have heard worse. I have seven brothers."

Hudson smiled and nodded, although his thoughts were in a whirl. Seven brothers? She has to be Gracie Moon!

Jake could see the shock on Hudson's face and his determination to protect Gracie as best he could hardened.

"I will talk business," Jake said. "But after we eat."

Hudson waved his arm magnanimously toward the empty seat opposite him.

"Please, won't you join me?"

Gracie slid in without a second invitation. Her mouth was already watering for something she didn't have to cook. Jake slid in beside her, and when the waitress started to hand them menus, Gracie refused hers.

"I don't need one," she said. "I already know what I'm having." The waitress pulled out her pad.

Gracie closed her eyes, picturing her favorite treat. "I want a cheeseburger and fries and a chocolate ice cream sundae, and I want the sundae first."

Jake grinned. "Dare I ask why you're going to eat your dessert first?"

She gave Jake a long, cool look. He had a sudden notion that she wasn't talking about food at all.

"I'm not a patient woman," she said. "If I can't have it all, then at least I will have had the best first."

Jake took a deep breath and Ron Hudson choked on a bite. The glance they shared was telling. They both looked away while Gracie sat among them, oblivious to the secrecy that bound them all.

Chapter 8

Still playing the part of a real estate agent, Ron Hudson got out of his car and stood in the street taking pictures of Lady Crockett's house while Jake and Gracie went inside.

"Look, Jake," Gracie said. "I think it would be better if I left you two alone to talk business. Why don't I come back in about an hour, and if there's anything else you need to do then, we can."

Jake nodded, and when she would have walked away, he caught her arm and pulled her to him. She wasn't prepared for the sweep of his mouth against her lips or the longing for something more than a kiss. When he turned her loose, her legs were shaking and her stomach was in a hard knot.

"What was that for?"

Jake's eyes narrowed thoughtfully as he rubbed his thumb across the lower edge of her lip. "Just something to remember me by."

Gracie turned away. As if she could ever forget him. "I'll be back in an hour."

She met Hudson coming in the door, and when

he'd gone inside, she shut it after him. For some reason, she had an urge to turn around and grab Jake and run. Instead, she got behind the wheel and drove away, leaving the men behind.

It didn't take Hudson long to ask, "Why haven't you contacted me, and what have you learned?"

Jake began to pace. "The place is a storehouse of explosives and firepower. They have enough illegal weapons up on the mountain above New Zion to start a small war, and about a dozen well-trained men ready to use them. They practice daily on what they call skirmishes or maneuvers."

"Have you been a part of that?"

Jake shook his head. "Hell no. Do I look like I just fell off the turnip truck? Someone shot John when he wasn't looking. I don't intend to make it easy for them to shoot another Baretta again."

"Then why did they accept you back in the fold?"

Jake shrugged. "I think it's as much a matter of honor as anything. I accused them of harboring a back-shooter. It appalled the old man so much that he insisted on offering me a place to stay to prove me wrong. I've been accepted up to a point, but it's touch and go on a daily basis."

"So, you don't have any idea who shot—"

Jake's expression went flat. "Oh, I know which son of a bitch shot Johnny. I just can't prove it. In fact, that's most of the reason why I didn't contact you."

"Who did it?"

"The eldest son, Brady Moon. For some reason, he hates my guts, and the feeling is mutual."

But Hudson wasn't satisfied. "And what's the

rest of the reason? By any chance, would it be that pretty woman who drove you into town?"

Jake turned, and there was an anger to his stance that almost frightened Hudson.

"Leave her out of it."

Hudson stared, unable to believe what he was hearing. "What the hell did you just say?"

"You heard me," Jake warned. "She's not a part of what's going on up there. She only stayed to take care of her father. She doesn't approve of what they're doing, and in fact, she and her older brother, Brady, have come to blows over it. Less than a month ago, the son of a bitch knocked her flat for arguing with him."

"That doesn't mean she's not involved."

Jake put a hand on Hudson's shoulder. It wasn't intentional, but Hudson perceived the threat just the same.

"Look, when you bring them down, I'll take great satisfaction in knowing I helped, but not at the cost of ruining an innocent woman's life."

Hudson knocked Jake's hand aside, standing toe to toe as he argued. "I'll grant you she's a beautiful woman, and she's probably great in bed, but that doesn't give you any reason to—"

"I haven't slept with her," Jake said, and then turned away to stare out a window. "In fact, I'd lay odds there hasn't been a man on this earth who's gotten past a couple of kisses." *Except me.*

Hudson sank into a chair, shaking his head in disbelief. "Well, shit. A virgin. No wonder you've lost your focus."

Jake spun, his voice shaking with anger. "To hell with you, Hudson. I haven't lost a damned thing except my brother."

Hudson's shoulders slumped. He was tired and worried, and Jake still didn't know the half of it. "Just so you know, Brady Moon is involved in at least a half-dozen illegal activities in New Orleans and suspected of others in Dallas. He's running drugs and guns and prostitution on the side."

Jake's anger cooled as reality set in. "That explains where he's getting the money to fund New Zion."

Hudson raked his fingers through his hair and arched his back. "New Zion isn't long for this world," he said.

Urgency deepened the tone of Jake's voice. "I've got to find a way to break Brady Moon. Somewhere inside of that bastard is the reason why John is dead."

"You've got yourself less than a week. On the basis of what you've told me, I'm going to be filing arrest and search warrants as soon as I return."

"How will I know when it's going down?"

"Someone will come to buy the house. When you come down to sign the bill of sale, we're going to go up."

Jake began to pace. "But what if I—"

"No buts, Jake. You've finished what John was sent to do. Time is running out for all of us."

Jake dropped into a chair as Hudson stood.

"For what it's worth, you've done a hell of a

job," Hudson said. "I would never have believed you could pull this off."

Jake looked up. "It isn't over yet."

Hudson drove away with the warning ringing in his ears.

Gracie pulled up to the Crockett house just as the real estate agent was driving away. She went inside, expecting Jake to be elated about the possibility of a sale. She wasn't prepared for the dark, brooding man sitting in the shadows.

"Jake?"

He looked up, but didn't move. "Back already?"

She nodded and took a step closer. "Are you all right?"

He didn't answer, and she would have sworn she saw tears in his eyes. Yet when she looked again they were gone, and she decided it had just been a trick of the light.

She slid onto the arm of his chair and put her hand on the back of his neck. His pulse throbbed against her fingertips and she began rubbing the muscles in his shoulders. They were all in knots.

"Are you sad about having to sell your grandmother's house?"

He pulled her across his lap and wrapped her in his arms. "Gracie, I never knew a man could be this sad and not be able to cry."

Her lips trembled. There was so much pain in his expression and voice that it made her physically ache. "Would it help if I cried for you?"

He closed his eyes and pulled her close until

their foreheads were touching. "Hell. Nothing can help this ache."

And then he felt her breath on his cheek and her fingers upon his face. "Except, maybe love?"

He looked up. "Are you offering?"

"Are you willing?"

His breath caught and his pulse leaped. She'd blindsided him with a truth he was ill prepared to face. Willing to love Gracie Moon? My God, he'd been ready and willing since the day he first set eyes on her. But did he dare risk it now, only to lose her later when she found out the truth?

She took his hand and placed it on her breast. "Feel my heart. It beats for you, Jake. Only you."

He shuddered on a breath and took her hand and placed it on his chest. "Can you feel my heart? I hope to hell so, because a minute ago, the damned thing stopped."

She leaned down and whispered against his lips. "I know a way to make it race. Make love to me, Jake. Do it now, before it's too late."

The urgency of her plea pulled him deeper into the need. "Aren't you afraid that I'll leave you?"

When she nodded there were tears in her eyes, but the tone of her voice was sure and firm. "Oh, yes, my love, on a daily basis. But I'm more afraid of never knowing what it's like to lie in your arms before you do."

She slid off Jake's lap as he stood, but he didn't let her go. His hands were firm upon her waist as he looked into her eyes.

"God help us that we don't destroy each other."

Gracie lifted her chin and met his gaze squarely on, refusing to be daunted by this man's dark past.

"If we do, Jake, we'll go up in flames."

The first thing he did was take down her hair.

Gracie lay naked on Lady Crockett's bed with no regrets other than this might never happen again. Jake dozed, his head pillowed on her breasts and one leg thrown over the lower half of her body, pinning her fast. She didn't care. There wasn't another place on this earth that she would rather be than lying in Jake Crockett's arms.

Her body ached, but it was a good ache. It was the pain in her heart that might kill her, instead. Her fingers lightly traced the path of scars across his back, and her belly clenched as she felt the one on his shoulder. In her heart, she knew Brady was responsible. What she couldn't understand was why. Was there a deep, dark secret between the two men that neither was ready to tell? Was there something going on that would destroy them all, including her?

She closed her eyes and said a prayer that somehow everything would work out all right. Gracie had never been the kind to be selfish, but she had a feeling that things were about to change. She didn't want to lose Jake to the zealots in New Zion, but she didn't know how to say what was in her heart without seeming like a traitor. So she held him in fear, praying for a miracle.

Jake stirred as he felt Gracie's fingers upon his back and knew without asking what was in her heart. He ached for her, wishing he could tell her that her life as she'd known it was about to come to an ugly end. But as badly as he wanted to trust her, his instincts for survival had been honed to a sharper degree, and not even the love of Gracie would make him break his code.

He felt her shudder on a breath and knew she must be close to tears. The thought made him sick, but this was nothing compared to what was going to happen.

"Gracie."

Startled by the sound of his voice, her fingers stilled, and her voice was a whisper in the silence of the room.

"What?"

"Are you all right?"

His tenderness was as unexpected now as it had been earlier when he took her virginity. She dug her fingers in the thickness of his hair and tugged, urging him to look up.

He did.

"Remember when you kissed me this morning and said it was something to remember you by?"

He nodded.

"Will you make love to me again? I want to make very, very sure that I never forget what it was like."

His eyes glittered dangerously as he rolled her beneath him. There was anger in his voice as he dug his fingers in her hair and parted her legs with his knee.

"Don't you dare forget me, Gracie Moon. Don't you dare."

But the anger was missing when he lowered his head. She heard him groan, and when their lips met, she felt his sigh. Thankful for what she could get, she wrapped her arms around his neck and gave herself up to his touch.

There in the gentle quiet of Lady Crockett's room, Jake made love to *his* lady on a threadbare spread. Her skin was satin to his touch. Her breath soft and urgent as he stroked her body in a slow, sensual path, following her pulse from her neck to her breasts to the middle of her belly and below. Circling, circling, ever circling, his fingers delved into places no man had gone before, and he felt humble that she'd let him be the first.

Gracie was lost in the passion that Jake had created. There was nothing in her world that mattered at that moment but getting to that breaking point with Jake deep inside of her and coming undone in his arms. His lips were on her body and his hands were between her legs and it wasn't enough. And when he slid lower, then lower still, and she felt his mouth on her belly, she gasped and then moaned.

"No, Jake. Don't make me do this alone."

Hard and aching, Jake understood all too well what she meant. He, too, wanted release from this need, but he wanted it to happen with her. With a groan, he shifted his weight and moved back up the length of her body.

When he did, Gracie parted her legs and guided him in, savoring the fullness of the man in her arms. He was hard and pulsing, and when he started to rock, she closed her eyes and gave herself up to the rhythm.

Time became meaningless. There was nothing in Gracie's world but the constant hammer of Jake's body against hers and the heat building low in her belly. Just when she thought it would go on forever, the heat boiled, shattering her senses and leaving her spinning and weightless.

Her climax caught Jake off guard. One minute he'd been savoring the pleasure, and the next thing he knew, he went out of control. But it wasn't the shattering burst of himself into her that he knew he'd remember. It was what she said afterward he would never forget.

Her arms were around his neck and her tears were on his face when she whispered his name.

"Jake, oh Jake."

"I know, darling, I know," Jake said.

"I love you, Jake. Whether you want to hear this or not, know that I love you."

He wrapped his arms around her, squeezing her as tightly as her words had squeezed his heart.

"My God, Gracie Moon, you sure know how to bring a man to his knees."

She shook her head. "I know nothing, Jake, except that I'm glad I waited for you."

Humbled by the sacrifice of a good woman's love, Jake's guilt increased two-fold. *What is this going to do to her?* But there were no easy answers to this mess.

She pressed a soft kiss against the lobe of his ear. "We need to be leaving. Father will have another fit if we come back late, and personally, I'm not in the mood to have this day ruined."

Jake braced himself above her, looking down at her face with a steely gaze. "Your father is a difficult man, Gracie. One of these days it's going to get him in trouble."

Gracie rolled out from under him and started pulling on her clothes. "He's already in trouble, isn't he?" When Jake didn't immediately answer, she added, "In fact, I'd lay odds that we're all courting danger on a daily basis."

Jake heard fear in her voice, and the slump of her shoulders was almost more than he could bear. He dressed in angry fits and starts while toying with the idea of kidnapping Gracie and sending her back to Washington, D.C., with Hudson. At least she'd be safe and out of the way when the fireworks started. She might never speak to him again, but at least she'd be alive.

And then she turned and held out her hand, and everything on his mind went blank. At that moment, Jake knew he would follow Gracie Moon to hell and back if that's where she wanted to go.

She glanced around the room, taking quiet note of the handmade doilies and tiny little knickknacks from an old woman's life.

"Is there something personal you're planning to take from here? You know, some sort of memento?"

Jake cupped the back of her head and tilted her chin up to his lips. "No. I already have it."

"Oh, what did you take?"

His whisper was soft against her cheeks. "Your love."

Brady was on Elijah's porch and waiting for Gracie. When he finally saw them driving up, he knew before they got out what had happened. He could see it on his sister's face. There was a look in her eyes that hadn't been there before. And when she got out of the truck, there was a sway to her walk that said *I know who I am*. She waved at Jake as he walked away, trying for a nonchalant attitude that just didn't wash with Brady. He knew what it felt like to want, and he hated her for what she'd done.

Brady's rage burned deep. He didn't want Gracie to share her life with another man.

"Took your own sweet time about getting home, didn't you, sister dear?"

Gracie moved toward the door without answering her brother's taunt.

His voice deepened. "I'm talking to you!"

"I have nothing to say to you," Gracie said, and started inside.

Brady caught her by the elbow. "Did you fuck that son of a bitch?"

"Brady, turn her loose before I break your arm."

Brady froze. He'd been so intent on punishing Gracie that he'd forgotten Crockett was still within sight. His anger shifted, and he turned, giving Jake the full brunt of his wrath.

"Have you been messing with my sister?"

Jake's expression stilled. "Gracie, go inside and close the door."

She gave Jake one frantic look and then bolted. The door clicked at the same moment Jake's fist caught Brady beneath the chin.

Brady went down like a felled ox, hitting the wall, then slumping to the porch. He tasted blood and spit it out as he rolled to his feet.

"I'll kill you for that."

Jake stepped forward until they were toe to toe. "You tried once and failed. You try again, and the consequences are on your head."

Before the fight could go any further, the door swung open and Elijah Moon came out. Hellfire burned in his eyes as he pointed at both men.

" 'Vengeance is mine, saith the Lord.' " And then he added, "Neither of you has the right to kill."

Jake shook his head. "Tell that to your son, old man, not me." And he walked away before either of them could respond.

Elijah stared into his eldest's son's face and even then turned a blind eye to the truth. He went inside with a heavy heart, and not even the Lord's own words eased his soul that night.

Brady waited on the path for Taggert Brown. His chin was throbbing, and his split lip was still bleeding, feeding the anger within him. When he finally saw the big man lumbering toward him, he went to meet him.

"You wanted to talk private?" Taggert asked.

"Crockett is a thorn in my father's side," Brady said. "He has challenged my father's teachings. He continues to refuse to associate himself with us in our endeavors. In my opinion, he is doing New Zion no good, and a whole lot of harm."

A feral smile broke through the brush of beard on Taggert's face.

"Could have told you that weeks ago. So why don't you tell him to go?"

Brady cleared his throat. He had practiced his speech and knew which buttons to push that would send Taggert into a frenzy. "Because I honor my father, and until he draws his last breath, Elijah Moon is the leader of New Zion, not me."

Taggert nodded. It was his interpretation of the Bible that had led him to Elijah Moon. It was also his interpretation of the Word that had gotten him sent to prison more than once. He was a firm believer in an "eye for an eye," even if it meant yanking the damned thing out and breaking a nose to go with it.

"Then it's up to us," Taggert said.

Brady nodded thoughtfully. "Yes, we must find a way to persuade him that it's in his best interests to seek his fortune in life elsewhere."

Taggert's little eyes turned dark. "I should have let him drown."

"Oh, no, Taggert. You showed what kind of man you are by throwing the rope that saved both their lives. In a way, it's you who should have been honored, not Crockett. You are the one who was strong enough to pull them both to shore."

Taggert's chest swelled with importance. "Whatever you decide, I will be with you all the way."

Brady clapped him on the shoulder and blessed

him with a smile. "I knew I could count on you, my friend. I leave tomorrow for a quick trip to New Orleans. When I come back, we'll deal with Crockett."

Taggert nodded, and they walked up the mountain toward their encampment, each in his own way plotting the demise of Jake Crockett—again.

The next day Brady was on his way to New Orleans, counting the hours to Miss Ophelia's. It was hell living where he was related to nearly every female. He was a man. He needed a release.

Besides that, he had a meeting scheduled with some people from Montana. Brady was of the opinion that if the militia-based groups all over the United States could band together, their power would be unstoppable.

It was midnight when he hit the city limits of New Orleans, and he was exhausted. Not even the thought of a roll in bed with one of Miss Ophelia's finest could make him drive any farther than the closest motel.

He checked in, weary in body, but not in spirit. All he needed was rest, and then it would be time to put his plans in gear. As he passed beneath the streetlights on his way to his room, a pretty young woman stepped out of the shadows and into his path.

"Hey there," she said softly. "Are you sleepin' alone?"

Brady stared. First at her long, dark hair, then at her face. In the dark, she reminded him of—

Impulsively, he grabbed her by the arm and began pulling her toward his room. "Not anymore, I'm not."

The woman giggled, and when he was unlocking the door, she reminded him, "Cash in advance."

"What's it going to cost me?" he asked.

"Forty dollars."

He nodded. It was a cheap way to get an unpardonable sin off his mind. He opened the door and then stepped aside for her to enter first.

"By the way," he asked, as she plopped down on the bed and kicked off her shoes. "What's your name?"

"Merla Jo."

He pushed her backward and climbed on top, stuffing the twenty-dollar bills down her bra. "That's a real pretty name."

She took the money out of her bra and rolled out from under him, putting it in the fanny pack around her waist as she began to undress.

Brady narrowed his eyes until all he could see was another woman's face and long dark hair spread out across a pillow. Unwilling to wait any longer, he sat up and reached for the whore, pulling her close, then pushing her down to her knees until she was kneeling between his legs.

Merla Jo giggled as she reached for his pants. "What is it, honey? Tell Merla Jo what you want."

Brady's face contorted into a grimace of pain. "Make it go away," he begged. "Make it all go away."

It didn't matter that she didn't understand him. She didn't have to understand what they said. Ultimately, she knew what it was that they wanted.

"Whatever you say, honey, whatever you say."

Angie Baretta stood at the edge of the yard, staring into the starlit night of a Wyoming sky. A coyote howled somewhere off in the distance, and she closed her eyes. Ever since they'd brought John home to bury him, she'd been unable to get past the thought that someday Jake would come home in the same condition.

Her fingers curled around the rough-hewn corner post as tears slid down her cheeks. Her soul was in mourning, and until she saw Jacob's face, she would not rest easy.

John parked the pickup at the steps and left the engine running. He cleared all five steps in one leap and hit the front door on the run.

"Mom! Can I borrow five bucks?"

Angie came out of the kitchen, drying her hands. "What did you do with the ten I gave you two days ago?"

He grinned. "Ate it. Drove it."

She rolled her eyes. "And have you paid that back yet?"

He made a face and then picked her up, dancing her around the room. "Now, Mom, how can I pay you back when I don't have a job?"

Angie swatted him on the arm. "Then why do you keep asking to borrow the money? Why don't you just come right out and tell me you need it?"

He paused, an odd expression on his face. "I guess because I didn't think of it."

"Well?"

He grinned. "Mom, I need five dollars."

She pointed to her purse.

Minutes later she was standing in the doorway watching the rooster tail of dust John's pickup was leaving behind and wondering where that wild, wayward son would end up in life.

Angie covered her face. Well, now she knew, and she would have given what was left of her life to change it. Wind lifted the hair from her neck, and as it did, Joe's hand slid in place, squeezing gently against the knotted muscles and rubbing at aches that couldn't be assuaged.

She leaned against him, taking comfort in his presence. Her voice broke on the words. "Oh, Joe."

Joe wrapped his arms around her, pulling her close against his strength. "I know, Angie, I know."

Long minutes passed as they stood in the dark. Suddenly Joe pointed. "Look, honey! It's a shooting star."

Angie teared, but she looked up with a smile. "It's probably John. He always did drive too fast."

Joe's heart shattered. It was all he could do to think that he'd buried a child while they still lived. "You know what, Angie? Parents should not outlive their children."

Angie turned and took her husband by the hand. "I think we should go inside. It's getting cold."

As they entered the house, she tried not to think

how cold and dark it was where they'd buried her boy.

D.C.

In his Washington, D.C., office, Ron Hudson slammed down the phone and rubbed his hands together in a gesture of satisfaction as he buzzed his secretary.

"Judy, cancel all of my appointments until next Monday. I'm going to be out of town."

Knowing that she would do as he asked, Ron began making mental preparations for what was about to occur. The wheels were already rolling in all the pertinent departments. The warrants were in place, and men were already being deployed. All he had to do was get to Little Rome with a buyer for Lady Crockett's house and then, as his dad used to say, "lower the boom."

For Hudson, it would be none too soon. Maybe after he brought them to justice, he would be able to get past the memory of John Baretta's coffin being lowered into the ground.

"Look at me, Jake. I can swing higher than you."

Jake's bare toes curled in the dust as he watched his brother go airborne.

"You better watch out," he warned. "You're going too high."

Johnny laughed. "You did it first," he yelled.

Guilt settled heavily on Jake's shoulders. He had been

the first one to touch toes with the leaves on the tree above them.

"But I was being careful," Jake reminded him. "You're not."

Johnny looked down as he flew by and made a face at his twin. "Careful is no fun," he teased, and even as he was grinning, he was starting to fall.

Jake saw him losing his seat and sail into space. Even before Johnny hit the ground, Jake was calling his mother's name.

Jake woke suddenly with sweat pouring down his face and his heart hammering against his chest. He got out of bed and headed for the sink to get a drink. Even as the water was sliding down his throat he was remembering the way John's arm had snapped, and how it had dangled uselessly at his side as he screamed in pain.

He set the glass aside and began sloshing his face and neck, washing away sweat and what was left of the dream, but when he lay back down and closed his eyes, sleep wouldn't come. Every instinct warned him that something was about to go wrong. After the blowup he'd had with Brady, he knew it was just a matter of time before something happened. The truth of the matter was, Jake had already stayed too long.

Chapter 9

*N*ew Orleans was Brady's kind of town. It was a place to catch up on every vice that his father had banned from New Zion, including poker. From where Brady was sitting, the back room of Rendezvous was the place to be.

The pot was a big one, and the hand he was holding was certain to be a winner. When the Cajun across the table folded, his elation surged. He had it won! With a flourish, he laid down his cards.

"Two pair, aces high." He started to reach for the pot when the man on his right caught his hand.

"Sorry, Moon, 'fraid I got you beat." He spread his cards, grinning wider with each one he revealed. "Royal flush. Beats 'em every time," he drawled, and pulled in the pot.

Brady froze. Every instinct told him the man had cheated. But Brady was the outsider in this game. In a place like this a man cut his losses in order to play another day.

"I guess this just isn't my night," he said, and stood.

A ripple of easy laughter followed his exit from the table, and he took a drink from the tray of a passing waitress. He leaned against the wall, savoring the whiskey as it hit the pit of his stomach. Almost immediately, he felt the kick and knew he needed to get something to eat.

"Hey, Moon. Long time no see."

Startled by the unexpected recognition, Brady turned. "Fats?"

Fats Quintella grinned. "One and the same." He slapped Brady on the back. "What the hell are you doing in this part of the world? I heard tell you had your own little thing going up in Kentucky."

Remaining noncommittal about what he was doing had held Brady in good stead all of his life. He saw no reason to change that trait now.

"Damn, Fats, you hear a lot of things. You ought to know by now not to put much stock in gossip."

When Fats chuckled, his jowls quivered and his belly shook. "Where I've been, that's about all you hear."

Brady understood the reference. "How long have you been out?"

Fats looked at his watch. "Seven days, twelve hours, and twenty-two minutes."

Brady laughed. "That bad, was it?"

Fats shrugged. "You know how it goes. Win some, lose some. Don't suppose you're needing any extra help?"

Brady glanced at Fats's broad body and soft hands and knew he would never fit into a place like New Zion.

"No, but I appreciate you asking," Brady said.

Fats nodded.

They stood for a bit, watching the women work the room and trading tidbits of information. Brady listened politely, his mind on other matters. It wasn't until Fats mentioned Kentucky again that his attention piqued.

"Say, Moon, aren't you close to a place called Little Rome?"

"Yeah, born and raised there," Brady said.

Fats nodded. "Thought so. You know, back in California, I shared a cell with a fella who got letters from there all the time."

Brady nodded. "That's good. I suppose letters from home help you do the time, right?"

"Wouldn't know. I don't know anyone who can write." And then he laughed, a big booming laugh that drew attention from several people standing nearby. "Naw, seriously, this guy, Jake Crockett, got a letter a week from some old lady. Always had a dollar bill in it. It wasn't much but it kept him in smokes."

Brady frowned. Crockett! It would seem he couldn't get away from the bastard. Stifling the urge to fling the drink in his hand against the nearest wall, he emptied it down his throat instead.

Fats continued, unaware of Brady's change of mood. "Yeah, he was one pissed-off guy when I kissed him good-bye," Fats said, laughing even louder.

Brady froze. "What did you just say?"

"I said, Crockett was one pissed-off guy when I—"

"You mean he's still there?"

"Unless he found a way to tunnel out in the last few days, he is. It will be at least six more years before he comes up for parole."

Panic shafted through Brady. There couldn't be two Jake Crockett's serving time in a California prison who had ties to Little Rome, Kentucky. And if one Crockett was still serving time in the pen, then who the hell was living in New Zion and sheltering himself beneath Elijah Moon's wing?

"Listen, Fats, it's been great seeing you," Brady mumbled. "But I have to be going."

"Yeah, same to you, Moon."

Brady bolted, running out the back room of the Rendezvous and onto the street, looking for street signs that would lead him back to his hotel. Yet no matter how fast he ran, he had a feeling it would be too late to stop what was already in motion.

With Brady gone from New Zion, there was a lull in the maneuvers that the men usually practiced. Instead of being gone most of the morning, they were visible around the cabins. Since school had resumed, Jake saw Gracie's focus changing from worrying about Elijah to fussing with the children. He marveled at her patience, and out of nowhere came the thought that she could already be carrying a child. His child. A great panic swelled within him. The urge to take her and run nearly overwhelmed him, but he knew this wasn't the time.

The school bell rang again, and the children began scurrying toward the hall, making one last game of the recess by seeing who could get inside first. As if sensing his scrutiny, Gracie paused on the steps and then turned. Across the distance, their gazes met and held.

She stood tall and proud on the steps of the great hall with the sun shining on her hair and a breeze trifling with the hem of her skirt. Just before she turned away she smiled, and Jake felt the impact. And then she was gone.

"Hey, Crockett, how about lending me a hand?"

The hail came from behind him, and Jake turned as Aaron Moon dumped an armload of split wood near his house and began stacking it for winter use.

"Getting ready for winter?"

Aaron nodded. "Sometimes the snow is so deep up here that we can't get out for days. It pays to have some wood nearby." And then Aaron smiled. "But you'll see that for yourself, won't you?"

Jake grinned and picked up an armload of wood. *Not by a long shot,* he thought. When winter came to Kentucky, he didn't intend to be around.

The persistent ring of Ron Hudson's phone wasn't nearly as startling as the fact that his secretary was not at her desk. He made a dash through the outer office and into his, catching it in the middle of a peal.

"Hudson, here."

"Sir, this is Wainright. I think we may have a developing problem."

Hudson frowned. The man on the phone had

been assigned to follow Brady Moon's every move, and the fact that Moon had made a second trip so quickly on top of the other one hadn't been lost on the bureau.

"I'm not going to like this, am I?" Hudson asked.

"Well, sir, I damned sure didn't."

"Then talk to me," Hudson ordered.

"Moon played poker last night at a place called the Rendezvous down on Bourbon Street. And after he lost all his money, he had an unexpected reunion with what appeared to be an old friend."

"Cut to the chase, Wainright. I'm late for an appointment."

"The old friend's name is Fats Quintella, who most recently was sharing a cell with an inmate by the name of Jake Crockett."

"Oh, shit."

"Yes, sir, my sentiments exactly," Wainright said. "Directly after a brief conversation, Moon made a rather quick exit and went to his hotel. He left early this morning."

Hudson's mind was reeling. "Baretta's cover may have been blown. Where are you now?"

"About ten minutes behind Moon and he's on the road home."

"Stay on him," Hudson ordered. "I think our plans have just changed. If everything is in place, we'll be making the raid sooner than planned. Keep me informed!"

"Yes, sir."

When the line went dead, Hudson dropped into

the nearest chair and reached for the antacids in the bottom of his desk.

"Son of a bitch," he mumbled. "This job is going to be the death of me yet."

It was nearing sunset as Jake started toward the river. The men were cleaning up for the evening meal, but sitting among them tonight seemed impossible. He could fix something later for himself, but right now all he wanted was to find a small measure of peace.

The woods were changing. There was a sense of quiet coming over the land. Jake moved through the trees like a shadow, watching where he was going as carefully as he watched where he had been. Ever cautious of the fact that John had been shot in the back, he changed directions several times, finally ending up at his destination.

The river looked red in the sunset. Its flow was slow, almost sluggish in places, but Jake knew there was a swifter current hidden beneath. It was the way with rivers—like people, it was what you saw on the surface that was often quite deceiving.

A great owl lifted off from a nearby tree, startled by Jake's arrival and unwilling to share its space. A fish flopped near the other edge of the shore, and just for a moment he wished he'd brought a pole.

The old beaver lodge to which Timothy Moon had clung so valiantly was gone, washed away in the flood just as Jake and the boy had almost been. It seemed strange to think that this sluggish flow of muddy water had almost taken two lives. Jake squatted down beside the water and picked up a stick, doodling in the damp dirt for lack of anything to do.

The first letter he scratched came without thinking, but when he stared down at the letter G, he knew what was going to come next. One letter after another, he spelled Gracie's name. For a while he stared without moving, and then finally his legs began to cramp. He shifted, starting to stand, when a twig suddenly snapped behind him. He spun in a crouch, and then relaxed and stood. It was Gracie.

"Are you lost?" he asked.

She slipped her arms around his neck. "Not anymore," she said, and then lifted her lips for him kiss.

It came as she knew that it would, followed by a hungry groan for more. Gracie gave without caution, because that was the way she loved this man.

Jake's hands traced the shape of her, from her shoulders to the sides of her hips, and he remembered what her skin felt like to the touch.

"This could be dangerous," he whispered.

She cradled his face with her hands. "The only time love is dangerous is when it's not returned."

His breath caught, and he held her close. "Oh, Gracie. If I'd known you were here waiting for me on this mountain, I would have been here sooner."

She hugged him back, drawing comfort and strength from being held in his arms.

Jake nuzzled the side of her neck. "I want to lay

you down on this riverbank and make love to you, Gracie Moon."

The thought was enticing, but the dangers were such that she just didn't dare.

"Oh, Jake, I'd like nothing more," she said softly. "But—"

He silenced her words with a kiss, breaking away after they were both breathless and hurting. "You don't owe me excuses or apologies. In fact, the apology should be mine for even suggesting it. I know better."

She let him hold her, taking comfort in his nearness. "I know better, too, but that doesn't make the wanting any less."

He kissed her one last time and then took her by the hand. "We'd better start back. By the time we get there it will be dark."

Gracie let him lead her, but as they started to walk away, she happened to look down and saw her name scratched in the dirt.

"Wait a minute," she said, and picked up the stick that he'd dropped.

While Jake watched, she added two more words beneath her name. In the grand scheme of things, they were only two little words. But for Jake, who was still grieving for his best friend and brother, the words went a long way toward helping the pain.

They walked away, leaving their epitaph behind.

Gracie loves Jake.

* * *

Hudson was cursing D.C. traffic and everything in between when he finally pulled into the airport parking lot. Except for his presence in Little Rome, the plan was falling into place. It was the delays here that were making him nuts. This case had been his baby from the start, and he'd lost a good man trying to bring Elijah Moon down. The fact that Jake Baretta was going to be caught unawares and might possibly suffer the same fate as his twin was frightening. All he could think as he ran for the plane was that if Jake Baretta died, it would be his fault.

Brady's hands were shaking as he took the curve in the road. His mind was reeling from the possible scenarios that could develop from the news he'd learned, and not a one of them was good. And yet the only thing that mattered about the entire mess was the fact that his father had brought a traitor into the fold—and that Gracie had taken him into her bed.

His face reddened at the thought. His pretty Gracie. Her slender legs. That tiny waist. All that long black hair. Naked in that bastard's arms. Unable to accept the mental image, he slammed on the brakes and pulled off the road before jamming the gears into park.

Without taking his eyes from the road, he began beating himself on the knees with his fists, trading one kind of pain for another. And when the feeling had passed, Brady leaned back in the seat.

"God help me, I'm going to make them pay," he

prayed. But as usual, Brady was praying to the right one for all the wrong reasons.

Jake was flat on his belly and sound asleep when the dream began. Somewhere within himself he knew that it needed to stop. But since he didn't know how he'd gone in, he had no way of knowing how to get out.

The phone burned the palm of Jake's hand as he punched in a series of code numbers. His gut was in knots as he waited, counting the rings. Outside the phone booth, a game cock strutted in the dust, while nearby a small fat woman hawked strings of red peppers that he knew would take the skin off your tongue.

"Come on, come on," he muttered, and as he waited, he felt his shoulder, still stunned by how sharp the pain had been and how fast the panic had spread inside him.

And then the ringing stopped, and a few seconds later a recorded message came on the line.

"At the beep, please enter your identification number."

Jake punched in the series. Four numbers, two numbers, three numbers, and a zero. This time the ring was brief.

"Division ninety-nine."

"This is Baretta."

"Where are you?"

"You know where I am," Jake said. "But I need you to find out where my brother is. He's been shot."

There was a pause. For a government man, it was a telling pause. This man was rarely caught off guard.

"If you don't know where he is, then how do you know he was shot?"

"Because I felt it, damn it. Now don't give me any bullshit. I know what I'm talking about. You call the ATF and find out where he's working, and then you tell them to go get John. He needs help."

"Look, Baretta—"

"I swear to God, if you don't do as I say, I'll make you sorry."

In spite of the fact that there were many hundreds of miles between them, the man shuddered.

"It's already done," he said, and then the connection was broken.

Jake stared at the receiver before finally hanging it up. His gut was in knots.

"Hang on, Johnny. They're coming."

Jake woke up from the dream just as he'd been boarding the first plane to get to John. But he didn't need to stay in the dream to know what came next. He'd been there when John died.

The urge to talk to his parents was so strong that he got out of bed and pulled on his jeans and boots and went to the door. He knew he couldn't call them, but he wanted to be outside. At least there they would be sharing the same sky.

When he walked onto the porch he stretched, inhaling the dampness of the cool night air. A scattering of stars shone overhead, but there were clouds moving in. It looked like rain.

Except for a raccoon he saw digging through trash by the hall, there was silence all around the camp. He looked at the mess the animal was making and knew that unless he chased it off, the women would have to clean it up tomorrow. Unwilling to go back to bed and the dream, he was about to step off the porch when he heard the sounds of a vehicle pulling up the steep grade outside the gates.

Instinctively, he stepped back into the shadows to watch. When he realized it was Brady's pickup, his nerves jerked. Brady wasn't due back for days. When the vehicle stopped in front of Taggert Brown's cabin, Jake started to worry. Taggert was Brady's right-hand man and all too willing in the ways that Brady's brothers were not.

As Brady got out of his truck and slammed the door, the raccoon scampered off into the night. At least one varmint had been dispatched, Jake thought. It was a damn shame he couldn't get rid of Brady as easily. So he stood in the shadows and watched, certain that whatever they were up to would be no good, except maybe to their own.

When Brady pulled into New Zion he had glanced at his watch and frowned. It was just after midnight, but this couldn't wait. Taggert Brown's cabin was nearest the gates, and when he stopped in front of it, it didn't take long for a light to appear. Brady got out, slamming the door loudly on purpose just to make himself heard. The last thing he wanted was for Taggert to think there were prowlers around. And when Taggert came to the door, Brady didn't have to look to know that he'd come out armed.

"It's me," Brady said, and only after the big man lowered his gun did he relax.

"What brought you back so fast?" Taggert asked.

"I thought you weren't coming back until day after tomorrow."

A soft, hesitant voice floated into the night. "Taggert, is something wrong?"

Both men turned toward the cabin. Moira was standing in the doorway, clutching her robe with both hands.

"It's nothing," Taggert said. "Brady's back. You get to bed where you belong."

The door closed softly behind her.

As badly as Brady wanted to share his news, now was not the time. "Anything happen while I was gone?" he asked.

"No."

"Then we'll talk tomorrow," he said.

Taggert frowned. "What's happening? Do we need to put out a guard?"

"No, Taggert. The enemy isn't outside, he's within. Meet me near the far pumpkin patch tomorrow after breakfast. We've got problems."

Jake slipped back into his cabin as Brady drove away, and then he did something he hadn't done since his first night here. He shoved a chair beneath the doorknob. In the grand scheme of things it wouldn't really foil an attack, but it could cause the delay he might need to make a break.

He turned to glance around the small one-room cabin and wondered how many times John had done the same thing. As he stood, he heard a scratching in the corner of the room, and then the sounds of tiny nails scurrying across the wood floor. He grinned. There was a mouse in the house.

Curious, he shoved aside a small table next to the wall, and reached for a flashlight. When he got down on his knees, he turned it on, searching the corners for the four-legged critter.

"Hey, fella, where did you go?"

The sounds had stopped, but he saw droppings where the mouse had been. "So, been here before, have you?"

Movement at the corner of his eye made him look, and he turned the flashlight just in time to see the mouse slip into a narrow crack and disappear beneath the floor. The crack couldn't have been more than a half-inch wide and Jake shook his head, marveling at the fact that the mouse had been able to squeeze that fat, little body into such a small space.

"So, there's your doorway," he muttered, running his fingers across the board and feeling the hole.

And as he traced the shape, he realized that it wasn't rough and splintered, as a hole might have been. In fact, if he didn't know better, he would have thought it had been whittled away smooth.

Lift it up.

Hair crawled on the back of Jake's neck as he rocked back on his heels. The thought had come out of nowhere, but now that it was in his head, he could no more have ignored it than he could his next breath.

Fitting his first two fingers into the small groove, he pulled back as hard as he could, and to his surprise, a neat, oblong chunk of the floor came away in his hands. He leaned over the hole, shining the light down inside. The mouse was nowhere in sight, but there was a small black notebook covered in dust. With shaking hands, he lifted it out and then sat down on the floor, shining the light by which to read.

Even before he opened it, he knew it must be John's, and as soon as he saw the handwriting, tears blurred his vision. He closed his eyes and held the book to his forehead, trying to come to terms with the fact that this notebook had survived when John had not.

"Hey, John, long time no see," he said softly, and then opened the book and began to read.

His eyes widened as he read page after page. He was holding all the information the ATF would need to bring down every resident of New Zion. He read it through, and then read it again. There were shipment dates on guns received. Notes made on the procurement of explosives. Memos about possible targets for retribution. Everything was here. Everyone was named.

He paused and then leafed through it again, and as he did, an inescapable fact began to emerge. Not once had John made mention of Elijah Moon's daughter. Not one time had he noted her involvement in any way. This wasn't like John. When it came to his job, he was as thorough as it got.

He closed the notebook and then slipped it in the top of his boot. Finding this had changed everything. Jake couldn't bring himself to wait any longer to leave. Revenge was going to have to take a backseat. John had given his life for this information. The least Jake could do was see that it hadn't been a lost cause.

His heart was heavy as he replaced the piece of floor. Tomorrow he was out of here, but how would he persuade Gracie to come with him? For leaving her behind was not an option.

Chapter 10

The next day Gracie stood beneath the overhang of the storage shed, holding her breath and clutching a pumpkin close to her breast. Brady and Taggert were on the other side of the shed, and only God could help her if they discovered her presence. Although she'd been in the process of accepting the fact that Brady was doing bad things, hearing it firsthand was horrifying.

And so she stood without moving, praying that they would not come this way when their conversation was finished.

"I'm telling you, Taggert, Crockett is a fake."

"Want me to get rid of him?" Taggert offered.

"We're going to do it together," Brady said.

"When?"

Gracie closed her eyes and bit her lip. *Dear Lord, they are going to try and kill Jake again!*

"Here's the plan," Brady said. "We need to get him alone first. If I have to, I'm going to beat the truth out of him before I watch him die. I want to know what he's doing here and why he was using Jake Crockett's name."

Using Jake Crockett's name? If Jake isn't who he says he is, then what have I done?

Little by little, Gracie died on the spot. Had she fallen in love with an imposter? And even if she had, that fact didn't change the other. Imposter or not, Brady was threatening to kill the man she loved, and she couldn't let that happen. She listened more closely, praying she'd be able to find a way to warn him.

"Tell me when," Taggert said.

"It's almost noon. We'll wait until after everyone eats."

"I'll be watching," Taggert said. "It would be my pleasure to send the bastard to hell."

Brady slapped Taggert on the shoulder. To Gracie's great relief, they walked the other way, unaware that their entire conversation had been overheard.

Her heart was hammering as she set the pumpkin down and took the back way to Jake's cabin. Earlier, she'd heard him telling Aaron he was going to wash up before the noon meal. Please God, let him still be inside.

Jake was drying his hands when he heard the tapping sound. When it came again he followed the sound to a back window and saw Gracie.

"What the hell are you doing?" he asked, as he opened the window and pulled her inside.

"Brady says you're an imposter. He says he's going to kill you."

Jake froze. Somehow—someway—he'd been made. And if it hadn't been for Gracie, he would have been taken unawares. Cursing the fact that the only phone was in the hall where they ate, he spun away, reaching for his shirt as he stalked toward the door.

"Jake! What are you going to do?"

He stopped, and there was a look in his eyes that made Gracie shrink back in fear.

"Something I should have done weeks ago."

She grabbed his arm in fear. "Don't go out there like this! These men will follow my father to his grave, and if he orders them to punish you, they will."

When Jake smiled, Gracie's stomach knotted. There was so much hate on his face she didn't know how to react.

"You listen to me, Gracie Moon. There's not a man up here who can hurt me, except maybe Taggert Brown. And I'm damned sure not afraid of him. You just pack your clothes and get yourself in one of those trucks. I've got something to say to your brother before I take my leave."

Before she could argue, he shoved her out of the door. Moments later, he heard the rapid sound of her footsteps as she began to run.

Outside, he could hear the sound of children's laughter as they were called to come wash for their meal. The muted clucking of chickens scratching in the yard was a lulling melody to the peacefulness of the day. But there was no peace in Jake's heart. Just a great big hole where his brother had been.

He glanced around the cabin, knowing it was going to be for the very last time. There was no time to pack, and whatever clothes he'd brought with him didn't matter. This morning he'd wrapped John's notebook in plastic and taped it to his belly. Gracie was the only other thing he refused to leave behind.

Moments later he was on his way out the door and searching for Brady Moon. When he saw him at the opposite end of the compound in a head-to-head conversation with Taggert, all he could think was that this was good. Metaphorically speaking, he was going to be able to kill two birds with one stone.

Brady was the first to see him coming, and there was something about the way Jake was walking that gave him pause. Crockett wasn't armed, but then neither was he, and it made him feel helpless—almost less of a man.

"Well, would you look what the dogs drug in," Taggert said.

"I see him," Brady said. "I wonder what the hell he wants?"

Taggert chuckled. "From the way he's comin', I'd guess maybe a fight."

Taggert was right.

Jake knew Taggert was there, but he never took his eyes off of Brady. When he was less than a yard from them both, he stopped, and his accusation shattered Brady's focus.

"I hear you have something to say to me."

Brady was momentarily speechless. How had he

known? But what the hell, it would save him the trouble of going to find Jake later. Confident that Taggert would back him up, he moved into Jake's space with a swagger.

"I don't know who you are, but you're not Jake Crockett."

"You don't know shit," Jake said.

"I know you fucked my sister and you shouldn't have done that." When Jake didn't deny it, Brady felt himself losing ground. Without thinking, he said more than he meant. "Gracie was pure. Gracie was everything a woman should be. I was always her favorite and you ruined it. You took her away from me, you piece of—"

The moment it came out of Brady's mouth, Jake froze. All he could think was, *My God, this is the reason John died.* Brady never knew John was working for the ATF. They didn't get in a fight over anything to do with what was going on up the mountain. Brady Moon was infatuated with his only sister, and Jake would bet his life no one, not even Gracie, was aware of the fact.

Jake's hands curled into fists. "You sick bastard! Is that why you shot me in the back? How many other men have you shot for looking at Gracie in a way that you can't?"

Spit ran from a corner of Brady's mouth. He forgot Taggert was behind him.

"You looked at her. You undressed her with your eyes. I warned you she was not to be touched. You wouldn't listen! I saw your smiles! I saw the way she laughed with you! I killed you. Why didn't you die?"

Jake's mind went nearly blank. All he kept thinking was now he had proof. He leaped toward Brady, choking off the rest of the filth coming out of his mouth and dragging him down to the ground.

Kicking and fighting, Brady struggled for breath as Jake's hands tightened around his throat, and he wondered why Taggert wasn't coming to his aid. But it wasn't the lack of air that frightened him most. It was what Jake whispered in his ear.

"You didn't kill me, you son of a bitch, it was my brother. I came back in his place to make sure you found the way to hell."

And then Jake shoved his thumbs into Brady's larynx. And if it hadn't been for Taggert Brown, within seconds, Brady Moon would have been dead.

Taggert had heard too much from Brady's own lips ever to forgive him. And as badly as he wanted to put his foot in Brady Moon's face, the urge to get Crockett was stronger. In the act of revenging himself upon Jake, he saved Brady's life. He reached down and grabbed Jake by the back of the shirt.

Jake flew backward, catching a glimpse of Taggert's face as he fell to the ground. He hit and rolled and came up kicking. The karate he'd learned years ago held him in good stead. The blow hit Taggert in the middle of his belly, and the big man staggered backward, then sat down on his butt with a thump. His face was red, and he was gasping for air as Jake landed on both feet, ready for the next blow.

"I'll kill you for that!" Taggert cried.

Jake was in no doubt that he would try. Shouts began to sound from far across the yard. He looked up, desperate for a sign of Gracie, but all he could see was a crowd of armed men heading his way and being led by the old man himself.

Damn it, Gracie, where are you?

Already Taggert was regaining his breath, and with it would come strength. Brady was moaning and gagging as Jake turned in place, still searching for Gracie. His panic grew. She was nowhere to be seen. Just as Taggert lurched for Jake's knees, he gave the big man another kick and then spun, darting into the trees and making a run for his life.

Limbs hit him in the face as he ran, stinging his eyes and making it difficult to see. He thought of John, wounded and bleeding and running through these very same trees. Running away from New Zion. Running for his life.

Behind him, the crashing of branches and the rustle of underbrush was proof enough that he was being chased. Although he didn't look back, somehow he knew it was Taggert Brown.

Jake increased the length of his stride, coming out of the trees into the open and running at full tilt. The river was right before him, flowing in a slow, moving current.

He hit the water headfirst, coming up moments later a little downstream, then swimming toward the opposite shore. Behind him, water continued to splash, and then he heard the loud angry roar of a madman, and he knew it was time to stop and fight. A shot sounded behind him, and a bullet zinged past his ear, plowing up a spray of water that splattered in his eyes. He spun around, his feet touching bottom and with water up to his chest. Taggert Brown was less than twenty feet away and still coming. Bracing himself, Jake doubled his fists and waited.

Mere seconds from Taggert's impact, Jake saw movement from the corner of his eye and froze as he saw what it was. A water moccasin. And it was swimming straight at him. Caught between a madman and a poisonous snake, Jake didn't think, he just reacted. Lunging sideways, he grabbed the cottonmouth behind the head and flung it up and out of the water like a whip. Writhing and coiling like a piece of dark rubber, it flew through the air with its mouth wide open.

When it hit Taggert Brown in the face, it struck with great speed, sinking its fangs into the big mountain man's cheek. Taggert was still screaming as Jake dove beneath the river's flow and swam away.

Gracie was in a panic. When she came out of the cabin, the fight between Jake and Brady was already in progress. Too late to save him from that, she headed for the nearest truck, then had to duck out of sight as the rest of the men suddenly appeared. Someone had seen the ensuing fight, and now everyone was racing toward their cabins. To Gracie's horror, moments later they all came out armed.

"God give me strength," she said, and jumped into the nearest truck, thankful that the keys were in the ignition.

The engine turned over on the first try, and her hands were shaking as she floored the accelerator, but she didn't let up. And even as she was barreling through the compound with the truck in high gear, she feared that she would be too late. Jake was already gone, and from what she could see, every man in New Zion was on his tail.

She drove without taking her foot off the gas, and as she came out of the main gate and started down the mountain, she kept glancing to her left toward the river, praying that Jake had at least made it that far. If he had, there was a very thin chance that she could intercept his flight and drive them both to safety. But everything depended on luck and timing, and Gracie had never counted on luck to get her by.

She flew down the narrow road with her heart in her mouth. Each time there was a break in the trees, she would look toward the river, searching for a sign of a dark head bobbing in the water, or hoping that she might see him safe and sound on the other side and disappearing into the trees. But neither happened, and still she wouldn't give up. It had taken her twenty-seven years to grow up and find a man she could love. Now that she'd found him, no way was she going to let him die.

Jake surfaced in deeper water, gasping for air. He could no longer touch bottom, but he wasn't satisfied with the distance he'd put between himself and the rest of the men.

"God help me." He started swimming with the flow and didn't look back.

Just up ahead was the narrow, single-laned bridge spanning the river, and he knew if he could get past that bridge, there was a chance he could disappear into the trees on the other side of the river. But when he saw a black truck parked in the middle of the bridge, his heart dropped. Just when he thought he'd escaped them, they were there and waiting.

When he heard someone shouting his name, he looked up, and an overwhelming sense of relief made him weak. It was Gracie, standing in the middle of the bridge and waving her arms toward the shore. He increased his kick and headed her way. Moments later his feet touched bottom, and he began running toward her through the water, unwilling to stop, afraid to look back.

"Give me your hand!" she screamed, and he did.

With more strength than he would have believed, she pulled him out of the river and onto dry ground, then started pushing him toward the truck.

"Get in the back," she ordered, and all but shoved him inside, slamming the tailgate before jumping behind the wheel.

Jake rolled over on his back, gasping for breath and staring up at the pure blue of a late-September sky as the truck began to roll. And as it gained speed, he breathed a sigh of relief.

Flat on his back in the truck, he never saw the phalanx of ATF vehicles that passed them on the main road. He didn't know and he wouldn't have cared. He couldn't let himself think how close he'd come to avenging John's death, and how frustrated he'd felt when he failed. He ran his hand across his stomach, breathing a sigh of relief as he felt the notebook. He'd done it. He'd gotten out with Gracie and the book. For now, that was all that could matter.

Gracie drove without slowing down or looking back. About an hour out of Lexington she was forced to stop for gas. When she pulled into the station she was shaking, and when Jake crawled out of the back of the truck she started to cry.

Ignoring the curious stares from the gas station's customers, he took her in his arms and held her close.

"Let it all out," he said softly.

She clutched at him, letting him hold her.

"It's all right, baby, it's all right," he crooned. "You did good. You did so damned good."

She staggered, and he caught her, refusing to let her fall.

"You saved my life, Gracie Moon." Then he blessed her with a kiss, whispering soft praise near her cheek.

Gracie covered her face with her hands. "Dear God, I thought you were dead."

Jake took her hands and kissed them palms up before holding them next to his heart.

"If you hadn't come, I probably would have been. You saved my life, sweetheart."

Gracie stared at the scratches on his face. When she trusted herself to move, she reached out, tentatively touching a welt that had long ago bled and dried. Her hands were shaking as she looked into his eyes.

"No, Jake, you don't understand. It wasn't just you I was saving, it was us."

Jake's heart filled with such love, and while he knew that this wasn't the time or place, he couldn't keep what he felt to himself any longer.

"No matter what happens in the next few days, you need to know that I love you. I think I have from the first moment I saw you."

Gracie sighed. "That seems like such a long time ago. You were laughing and talking to Brady a mile a minute." Then she frowned. "Now that I think about it, I don't believe I've seen you laugh like that since."

Here it comes, Jake thought. Now is the time to tell her the truth.

"That wasn't the first time *I* saw you, honey. It was the day I came to New Zion in July."

A frown creased her forehead. Someone honked a horn behind them, and she was suddenly aware of where they were.

"I don't understand." Then she remembered what Taggert and Brady had said about him being an imposter.

He took a deep breath, and even as he said it, a pain filled his heart. "The first man you knew as

Jake Crockett was my twin. His real name was John and he died in my arms."

Gracie's eyes rolled back in her head, and Jake caught her before she fell. Gently, he slid her into the seat. After filling the tank with gas he pulled out of the station and onto the highway. They had a long way to go to get to Wyoming. He glanced at his watch and then at her, wondering if she would hate him when she woke up.

The motel room was small and dark, and it suited Jake's mood just fine. Gracie had come to within minutes of their pulling out of the station, but she hadn't said two words to him since. Her eyes were wide and fixed toward a point somewhere down the road, and the few times he'd tried to get her to talk, she'd turned her head and cried.

Jake hurt and he was afraid to think why. The only thought in his mind was that she was mourning for the man she'd fallen in love with, not the one who'd taken her to bed.

But Jake couldn't have been more wrong. Yes, Gracie was mourning the death of Jake's brother, but not as the man she'd loved. The man she'd fallen in love with was the man who'd come back. She was trying to come to terms with the fact that a member of her family had killed a member of his.

In her mind, she kept looking at the years she'd imagined stretching out ahead of them and wondering how Jake would ever get past that. She didn't take into consideration that this wasn't news to Jake. He'd suspected Brady all along.

They'd taken the motel room with the intention to rest, but once inside, Gracie headed to the bathroom while Jake picked up the phone. When he dialed Hudson's number in D.C., he was upset to learn Ron was out of town.

"Just tell him I called," Jake said. "And have him call me back at this number. It's an emergency." He repeated it for the secretary, then hung up the phone as Gracie returned.

When she sat down on the edge of the bed without looking at him, his hopes fell. And when she covered her face with her hands, his voice started to shake.

"Gracie, for God's sake, talk to me."

"What's your name?"

"Jake Baretta."

Her smile was sad as she looked away. "At least there was a part of you that was real."

Jake dropped to his knees before her and grabbed her hands. "Don't do this, Gracie. Everything that happened between us is real. I might have been answering to a different name, but that's as far as the deception went."

And then the tone in her voice broke his heart.

"But Jake, why? Why did you have to lie?"

"You know what Brady was doing up there, don't you!"

Her gaze faltered, and then she nodded. "He's taken his games a little too far, hasn't he, Jake?"

Jake thought of Johnny. "He isn't playing games, Gracie. He's out for blood."

He felt her trembling as she continued to press for answers. "Are you a cop?"

"John was an agent for the Bureau of Alcohol, Tobacco, and Firearms. He was sent in to gather information on a subversive branch of a militia-based group."

She closed her eyes, swallowing harshly as she thought of her brothers and their wives. Of the children whom she'd taught. Of the peace and serenity of the mountains. The words *subversive* and *militia-based* seemed impossible for her to consider. Then she remembered the guns and Brady's hate and realized she'd known it all along and, like her father, had chosen to ignore it.

And as she sat listening to her world unraveling, she realized something good had come out of this after all.

"You've never been in prison, have you, Jake?"

He smiled, trying to tease some happiness back in her eyes. "No, although there were days in my life when my parents thought that's where I was headed."

Parents. She tried not to think of her father and what must be going on back in New Zion.

"Are you with the ATF also?"

He thought of dark alleys and foreign faces and shook his head.

"No, sweetheart. Like my brother, I also work for Uncle Sam, but in a different sort of role."

"Is my family going to be arrested?"

The pain in her voice broke his heart. "Probably."

She rolled over on her side and covered her face. Jake crawled into bed beside her and pulled her into his arms.

"I'm sorry, Gracie. I'm so sorry," he said softly.

She shuddered, remembering other days—better days—before the madness had taken them all.

"Will they come after me, as well?"

His arms tightened. "They'll have to come through me to do it."

It was almost dark on the mountain and Hudson was beside himself. The agents had been combing the cabins and the hills for hours and had yet to turn up a single living soul. The only person they'd found was a man floating facedown in the river. It had taken seven men to pull his dead weight out of the water, and when they'd seen his face, it hadn't taken a genius to figure out why he'd died. The fang marks of a snake were deep and purpling, as was the color of his skin. Hudson didn't have his files in front of him, but he was pretty sure the man was Taggert Brown.

He kept looking at the man and thinking of Jake and wondering if they'd be finding his body next. And then the message came that Baretta had called, and he sat down on the nearest rock and began to dial. Moments later, he heard Jake's voice and let out a heartfelt sigh. All he could think was at least he didn't have to face John Baretta's parents again to tell them their other son was dead, too.

"What the hell happened up here?" Hudson growled.

Jake glanced over at Gracie, thankful she was asleep. He shifted his weight, trying to ease her head down on a pillow so he could concentrate on Hudson's call.

"Other than the fact that Brady Moon is still alive and Taggert Brown is dead, I couldn't really say."

Hudson snorted. "Where the hell is everyone else? There's nothing up here but some damned scratching chickens."

Jake sat up straight. "What do you mean?"

Hudson stood up and began to pace "The vehicles are here. Their clothes are here. Hell, there was even food cooking on the stove when we came into the compound, but there wasn't a single soul in sight."

"That's crazy," Jake said. "Where could they go?" And then he thought. "Did you find the stash up the mountain like I told you? Maybe they hid up there."

"Like I said, we found everything but Elijah Moon and his followers."

Jake glanced behind him. "Gracie is with me."

Hudson stilled and then his face turned red.

"Damn it, Baretta, you're just like your brother. He didn't listen to me, either. You know she's going to have to—"

"She saved my life."

Hudson's tirade ended. "She did what?"

"She stole a truck from the compound and followed me downriver. If she hadn't pulled me out, they would have caught up with me."

Frustrated, Hudson thrust his hand through his hair. "That doesn't mean—"

"Damn you, Hudson, my life might not be worth much to you, but it means a hell of a lot to me. Now you get some people over here to this piss poor motel to pick us up. I want to go home."

"Okay, okay," Hudson said. "I'll figure out a way to make this right."

"You'd better," Jake warned him. "I've put my life on the line for my uncle too many times as it is. It's about damned time he pays me back."

At last, Hudson was beginning to understand. "I'll make some calls. Someone should be there within the hour." Then he glanced at his watch. "You should be in D.C. before midnight."

Jake frowned. "Not D.C.—Wyoming. Remember, I told you—I want to go home."

Chapter 11

*I*t was two in the morning when Joe Baretta heard it coming. He rolled over in bed and looked at the clock with bleary eyes. The windows were rattling and the roof was shaking, and all he could think was that the helicopter he was hearing was flying too low, and too fast. But when the noise increased, he got out of bed and went to the window. As he saw the landing lights coming down in the space between the house and the corrals, he reached for his jeans.

Angie came awake with her hair in her eyes and her gown hanging from one shoulder. Confused by the lights and the noise and the manner in which Joe was running, she reached for her robe.

"Joe, what's wrong?"

He grabbed her where she stood and gave her a hard, swift kiss. "Get your pants on, woman. I think your son just came home."

When Jake stepped out of the helicopter, a profound sense of sadness seized him. He was coming home for the first time, knowing that John would never be here again. The sensations staggered him, and when Gracie hesitantly threaded her fingers through his, he squeezed them until he feared he'd hurt her. Even then, she maintained her grip, somehow sensing he needed her support.

Before he could take a step, he saw lights coming on inside the house. When the porch light came on and his father stepped out of the house, he started walking, pulling Gracie with him.

When she hesitated, he nodded encouragingly, and she resumed following him until his mother came out. At that point he felt Gracie letting go and sensed she was telling him in the only way she knew how that he had to make the rest of the way alone.

Angie Baretta was coming down the steps. The wind from the helicopter blades was threatening to blow her off her feet, and still she kept on walking, straight into her son's arms.

Jake felt her shaking and knew that she was crying. Tears welled, and when his father wrapped his arms around them both, Jake let go of his pain. Within the safety of all that he knew, he was home.

They hugged without speaking, taking solace in the solid comfort of familiarity. And while they stood entwined in an embrace, the helicopter lifted off and quickly disappeared into the night sky, leaving Gracie as the lone spectator to the bittersweet homecoming. She watched with her heart in her mouth, certain that there would never be a place for her in their lives, convinced that once they learned who she was, it would all be over. So she waited, dying a little with each passing moment.

Jake took a deep breath, savoring the lingering scent of his father's aftershave and his mother's favorite bath powder. Even the cool, brisk air and the underlying odor of cattle and hay gave him a sense of peace.

Angie clutched at him one last time, and then stepped back and began fussing with his shirt. It gave her an excuse to continue touching him.

"I knew you'd come home," she said.

Jake heard her words, but he knew from the way she'd clung to him that she'd thought differently.

"You have someone to thank for that besides me," he said, and turned to Gracie. "Come here, sweetheart."

She took a tentative step forward, and only then did Joe and Angie realize someone else was with Jake. Their eyes widened, missing nothing of her bedraggled appearance and rumpled clothes. But they also saw the look on her face when Jake reached for her.

"Mom. Dad. This is Gracie Moon. She's the woman I love, and she's also the woman responsible for my being here. She saved my life."

Angie gasped, and then her eyes flooded with tears. "Welcome, my dear," she said, and extended her hand toward Gracie.

Gracie wouldn't budge. She looked at Jake with her heart in her eyes. There was nothing she wanted more than to belong to a family like this, but there was an insurmountable obstacle in their way. Her chin trembled, but her voice was firm.

"Tell them the rest, Jake. Tell them now before this goes any further."

Jake was taken aback. "No, Gracie, now's not the time."

"There will never be a good time to say this." And then she turned, taking the decision out of Jake's hands. "Mr. and Mrs. Baretta, it's true that I saved Jake's life. And I would do it again at the risk of my own because I love him more than I can say. But you need to know that my brother—" Her voice broke, and when Jake reached for her, she stepped away. "No, I can do this," she said, and lifted her chin, meeting their worried gazes. "You need to know that my brother is the one who killed your son."

Angie gasped, and Gracie started to cry. "I didn't know. I swear I didn't know. None of us did. I'm sorry. I'm so, so sorry."

The looks on their faces were more than Gracie could bear. She swayed where she stood, and it seemed to her as if the night was closing in. As Jake's face blurred in her vision, her legs gave way.

Jake caught her before she hit the ground, scooping her up into his arms and then holding her close. Tears were in his eyes and his voice was shaking, but his grip on Gracie was firm.

"Both of you know how I felt about John. For the rest of my life, a part of me will be missing. But all I ask is that you don't judge her, because as God is my witness, she had no knowledge or part in what happened to John, other than being related to a sick son of a bitch."

Joe finally spoke. "Bring her inside. If she brought you back to us, then that's good enough for me."

Angie's instincts for nurturing made her react without thinking. "Poor little girl," and she smoothed the tangles in Gracie's hair.

"Yes, Mom, how right you are."

It was nearing morning when Jake got out of bed. Careful not to disturb Gracie's uneasy slumber, he made his way across the hall toward his and Johnny's old room, then paused.

Wisely, his mother had put them both in the guest room, and it had been all he could do to calm Gracie enough for both of them to get some rest. But while she'd finally fallen asleep, it became impossible for Jake to follow suit. The longer he lay there, the worse the feeling became. There was a tension within him that wouldn't let go, and he knew until he laid one last ghost to rest, it would haunt him forever. With a heavy heart, he opened the door.

It swung inward on silent hinges. He stood at the threshold with his heart in his throat, letting his eyes adjust to the half-light of oncoming dawn, and then walked inside and closed the door.

"Hey, Johnny, I'm home."

There was no answer.

A band tightened around his chest as he moved to the dressers and then the twin beds. Two baseball bats were mounted on the wall, two well-worn leather mitts lay at the head of the beds in lieu of the teddy bears that had once been there. He was overwhelmed by school colors, old pictures, and when he opened the closets, even old clothes. Matching letter jackets hung side by side. For Jake, it was the last straw. He walked to the window and stared down into the yard below, remembering the life they'd shared and the years they'd left behind. Only life hadn't played fair with the Baretta twins. Jake was going to have to finish his alone.

He leaned his forehead against the window and let go of the pain. At first, there were tears. Blinding in intensity and burning as they filled his eyes and poured down his face. And then came the sobs. Gut-wrenching gulps for air that wouldn't let go. Last came the weakness. In his arms and in his legs as he sank to the floor. Everything that hurt came up and out, purging, cleansing, leaving an emptiness and a waiting that might never be filled.

Unknown to Jake, Gracie had heard him get out of bed. Not only that, she'd seen the look on his face when his mother had put them in this room the night before. It had such a look of impermanence about it that she realized it was the guest room, and with that knowledge came the reason why they were there.

Jake's mother had realized he would have to say good-bye to things in his own way and in his own time. So when he walked across the hall and then went inside the other room, shutting the door behind him, Gracie knew what must be happening.

She lay without moving, listening for a sound that would tell her what was going on. She heard nothing. Aching for what he must be feeling, she got out of bed and tiptoed to the door, listening closer.

At first there were the sounds of footsteps as he moved about the room, and she could only imagine what he would be thinking. And then there was a moment of total silence, as if he'd come to a stop somewhere within. But when she heard the first sound of a sob, her heart began to break. There in the quiet, in the darkness of an unfamiliar house, Gracie knew that she was hearing love die. The memories and the devotion that the brothers had shared would always be with Jake, but there would never be another day in his life when the love he had for his brother would be returned. She listened until she could bear it no longer and then she slipped inside.

Loneliness engulfed Jake as he sat on the floor between the beds. Everything he'd known, everything he'd counted on in life, was gone. He didn't know where to start to put the pieces of himself back together, because he'd marked who he was as much by his brother as by himself.

He felt a touch on his shoulder and heard the swish of fabric as Gracie knelt at his side. Her sigh was soft upon his cheek as she wrapped her arms around his neck and pulled his head to her breast. Without thought, Jake went where she led, for the first time in his life unable to be the strong one. "Oh, Gracie." It was all that he could say.

She held him tighter. "I will love you," she whispered.

And in Jake's heart, a small portion of the gap began to close.

Once Gracie got Jake to lie down in their bed, he'd fallen asleep within minutes. Knowing that he would rest better if he had the room to himself, she dressed quietly and slipped out of the room, leaving him to find his own peace.

Down the hall, Angie was buttoning her last button as she came out of her bedroom. Routine had always been the anchor to keeping her life from going awry, and since it was almost seven o'clock, it was time to make breakfast. When she saw Gracie standing alone outside the guest room door, Angie paused, absorbing what she'd been told against what she'd already seen. And while it was against every instinct she had to give shelter to an enemy, something within her knew that Gracie Moon was not the enemy, only another victim of what had befallen her son.

She thought of Jake, and of the love she'd heard in his voice when he said Gracie's name. If this was what God had handed her, then she was going to take it with both fists and never let go. And when she saw the young woman bury her face in her hands, Angie's heart went out and her footsteps followed.

"Good morning," she said softly, and then smiled encouragingly as Gracie jumped. "Sorry, I didn't mean to startle you."

Gracie didn't know what to say, but Angie did.

"I'm going to make breakfast. Want to come?"

Gracie didn't move as Jake's mother started toward the kitchen.

"Why don't you hate me?"

The poignant question stopped Angie Baretta in her tracks. She turned, and there was a look of acceptance on her face that was impossible to miss.

"Why should I, dear?" Angie asked. "Did you know what was going to happen to John?"

Gracie paled. "No! Oh no!"

"Did you pull the trigger?"

Tears filled Gracie's eyes. "Dear God, of course not!"

"Did you really save Jacob's life?"

This time Gracie looked away, remembering her wild ride down the mountain and pulling Jake out of the river only minutes ahead of the mob of angry men.

"Probably," she said. "They would have caught him eventually if I hadn't been there."

"Do you love him?" Angie asked.

A softness came upon Gracie's face. "With all my heart."

Angie took a deep breath. "Then why should I hate you?"

Gracie started to cry, and it was more than Angie could bear. She took the young woman in her arms and rocked her where they stood, much in the same manner that Gracie had held Jake earlier.

"Poor little girl," she said softly, and then pulled back enough to pat Gracie's cheek. "You had to learn it the hard way, didn't you?"

"Learn what?" Gracie asked.

"That a woman's role in life is to bear the most pain."

Angie wrapped her arms around Gracie's shoulders and pulled her close for a quick hug. "There now," she said briskly. "Let's go snatch a quick cup of coffee together before those men hit the floor. After that, in this household it's everyone for themselves."

It was the next day before the ATF found the shaft. Hudson was staggered by the ingenuity of it all. When Elijah Moon had built his smoke house, he'd butted it directly against the side of the mountain, concealing the open shaft to an abandoned mine. Their disappearance might have remained a complete mystery had it not been for a pack rat one of the agents had seen coming out of a small hole in the floor. One thing had led to another, and the discovery of an escape tunnel had been the explanation they were searching for. They'd followed the tunnel nearly a quarter of a mile through the mountain before coming out on the other side.

Myriad tire tracks and a couple of discarded items of clothing were proof enough that they'd gone this way. However, knowing how they'd gotten away, and knowing where they'd gone were two different things. They didn't even know what the vehicles they were driving looked like. All in all, Ron Hudson had to give it to the old man. He'd been wily enough to outsmart them all.

Cursing their luck in several different languages, the agents went back to D.C. Hudson had to be satisfied with the fact that at least the guns and explosives were out of their hands. And while Brady Moon's rag-tail army was on the run, he knew there was every indication that one day they'd surface again.

When Hudson landed in D.C., he knew that one phase of the endeavor was over, but the case was not. Jake Baretta had warned him that Gracie Moon was off limits. But Hudson had his orders, too, and if there was the slightest possibility that Gracie would know where they'd gone, she was going to have to tell or she'd find herself under arrest.

Jake had been up exactly two hours and fifteen minutes and was just getting used to the fact that he was actually home when the telephone rang. Something told him it wasn't going to be good news, and when his mother brought their portable phone outside to where he was sitting, he could tell by the look on her face he'd been right.

"What?" he asked.

"It's that Hudson man."

Jake frowned. "Where's Gracie?"

"I sent her to town with Joe. She needed something to do, and you know how useless he is in the supermarket."

He took the phone, wishing Gracie was within reach.

"This is Baretta," he said shortly.

"We found their escape hole," Hudson said. "It was an abandoned mine shaft. They're long gone,

every last one of them, and we don't have a snow-
ball's chance in hell of finding them without some
sort of lead."

"That's your department, not mine," Jake said.

Hudson frowned. "Maybe so, but when I tell
you what's going to happen, I suspect you're going
to want to be involved."

Jake sat up. He could tell by the tone of Hudson's voice that he wasn't going to like this.

"What the hell do you mean?"

"I'm coming out there."

Jake stood. "What for?"

"Like it or not, Baretta, Gracie Moon is the only
lead we have to finding her family. Now either I
talk to her there or you bring her in for questioning. You call the shots."

Jake started to curse, and Hudson held the
phone away from his ear until the man's anger had
eased.

"Are you through?" Hudson drawled.

"I haven't even started," Jake said. "If this has to
happen, you'll do it here. And, if she knows anything, she'll tell you and gladly. If she says she
doesn't, then she's telling the truth. But know this,
if I hear one little hint about taking her into cus-
tody, I swear to God you'll have to come through
me to do it."

Hudson winced. "Fair enough. I'm an understanding guy. Both the polygraph and I will know
if she's telling the truth."

Jake's voice lowered menacingly. "If you're half
as smart as I think you are, you'll leave that god-

damned machine at home. You know as well as I do that they're not admissible in court, and she's already scared half out of her mind."

Hudson sighed. He would have pressed the issue, but it wasn't really worth the effort. For some reason, he was beginning to believe Baretta.

"Okay, fine. It's a deal. Just make sure she's there when we arrive."

"When?"

Hudson glanced at his watch. "Say tomorrow around noon." Ron was about to hang up when Baretta spoke.

"Hudson."

"Yeah?"

"I want you to remember something."

"What's that?"

Jake's voice was cold, his words clipped. "I want them found a whole lot worse than you do."

"Yeah, I know."

"And I saw things in New Zion that you didn't."

"I know that, too."

"Then trust me when I say she's innocent."

Hudson sighed. "I hear you, Baretta, loud and clear."

Jake disconnected, then went in search of his mother. He found her making up the beds.

Angie could tell something was wrong when he came into the room, but she knew her son, and it wouldn't get told until he was ready to talk.

"Honey, get that other pillow, will you?"

Jake plopped the pillow in place and helped his mother finish making up the bed.

"They should be getting back from town any time now," Angie said.

Jake nodded.

"She's nice, Jake."

He looked up, and a slow smile spread across his face. "I know."

"She's caught in the middle of a terrible situation, isn't she?"

He dropped onto the bed with a thump. "They're coming to interrogate her tomorrow."

Angie's face paled. "Oh my."

"I don't know if she can take it," he said.

Angie smoothed the hair on the top of Jake's head, much as she had when he was a child. "I think she will surprise you, sweetheart. Your Gracie is tougher than you think."

Jake wanted to believe, but there was too much at stake to play loose with the rest of their lives.

"How do you know?" he asked.

"She loved you enough to leave everything she knew, and she loved you enough to risk her life to save yours. From a woman's point of view, that's the real stuff."

Jake sighed, and caught his mother's hand, holding it to his lips. "I love you, Mom."

"And I love you, Jacob."

Jake ran his finger along the snow white streak in his mother's hair. "Will you ever be able to look at her and not remember that her brother killed John?"

It still hurt even to hear the words, but there was more at stake here than grief. Angie's eyes darkened. "Jacob, darling, I think the more important question should be, can you?"

Jake's expression froze. For the longest time he couldn't find a way to say what was in his heart. Angie ached for her son, but she knew that whatever he was going through, he was going to have to do it alone . . . and for Jake, that was something he'd never had to do.

"Jake."

"What?"

"You haven't visited John's grave, have you?"

Jake paled. The thought of seeing his brother's name on a tombstone was more than he could face. He stuffed his hands in his pockets and turned away.

"Jacob, look at me when I'm talking to you," Angie said.

In spite of the emptiness in his heart, he grinned. "Yes, ma'am."

"As your mother, allow me the privilege of sometimes still being right."

"Okay, you've got it."

She nodded. "Then I think that it's time you did."

Jake took a deep breath, and all he could think was, oh shit.

"He's in the plot next to your grandmother and grandfather Baretta."

Plot? The word somehow offended Jake.

Angie handed him the scissors. "Here, go cut some of my chrysanthemums. But don't take pink. You know how John was about colors he considered sissy."

Jake grinned, but as he walked out the door Angie was remembering an incident in John's life that she'd forgotten until now.

John stood in the doorway with a pair of his briefs in each hand. "Mom, what in hell happened to my shorts?"

Angie looked up from the peaches she was peeling. John's face was almost as pink as his underpants.

"You put your red gym shorts in with the whites."

His voice was indignant. "My shorts are pink."

"That's because the red gym shorts ran on everything."

"Can't you fix them?" he asked.

Angie rolled her eyes. "No, John. You fixed them when you put the red shorts in with my whites. I now have pink towels, pink washcloths, and pink socks. I am not a lot happier about this than you are."

John couldn't believe what he was hearing. "So . . . are you telling me this won't wash out?"

By now, Angie had to grin. "Pretty much."

"Oh man!" John pivoted and stomped out of the room as abruptly as he'd come in.

Joe came in from outside just as John was making his exit.

"What's wrong with him?" he asked.

Angie's grin widened. "The same thing that was wrong with you when you got dressed this morning."

Joe flushed and then touched the seat of his jeans. "Man, if the guys down at the feed store knew I was wearing pink shorts, I'd never hear the end of it."

Angie started to laugh. "At least you don't have to strip down in front of a gym class like John has to do."

Joe grinned. "Knowing John, he'll think of something."

Moments later, Angie heard John coming back down the hall.

"See you later," he said, and grabbed a couple of cookies on his way out the back door.

Angie glanced at the clock. It was the boys' senior year in high school, and they had yet to get anywhere on time.

"You'd better hurry. You and Jake are going to be late for class."

"I'm on my way," he said, and blew her a kiss.

"Hey, John."

He paused at the door with a half-eaten cookie hanging out of his mouth like a lit cigarette.

"Yeah?" he mumbled around the bite.

"What did you do about your shorts?"

He grinned. "What shorts?" and pulled down the waistband of his jeans before bolting out the door.

He was bare beneath, and Angie was yelling for him to wait as the door closed behind him.

The day was sunny, the breeze soft but persistent, with a slight warning of chill in the air. Jake clutched the flowers in his hand, as if they were his link to the living, and headed toward the mound of dirt at the end of the row of tombstones. One step after the other he walked until he was forced to stop.

At first, he couldn't bring himself to look down. He couldn't face seeing that name, in that place, and so he looked over the tops of the markers to the highway beyond.

Trucks and cars sped by on their way to somewhere else. Like John. He was somewhere else. The scene blurred before him, and Jake inhaled past the pain and looked down.

John Jacob Baretta
Gone Too Soon

He went down on his knees and then on all fours, crushing the stems of the flowers as he let go of the last of his grief. Saying good-bye to the memories in their room had been one thing, but this was Jake's final good-bye. His words were choked, his emotions stripped bare for the world to see.

"Damn you, John. Damn you for leaving me behind."

If you don't forget me, I'll always be with you.

Jake lifted his head, tears streaming down his face as the notion settled. A hawk circled the sky above him in search of a meal, while on the ground at his feet a beetle scurried into a small hole.

He wiped his face with his hands. There was an apology in his voice as he stood over his brother's grave.

"I wasn't really mad at you," he said softly. "But you were always in such a big damned rush to do everything first. All I have to say is, you won."

The better man always wins.

Jake shook his head and walked away, and the flowers he'd laid on John's grave began to wilt in the sun.

* * *

When Joe and Gracie pulled up to the house, she could tell by the way Jake was waiting that something was amiss. Not even his casual offer to carry in the groceries was enough to throw her off the track.

"What's wrong?" she asked.

Jake paused on the top step, looking at her over the sacks in his arms.

"What makes you think something is wrong?"

She shook her head and then laid her cheek on his arm. "Because I know you, that's why."

Damn. "Let me put these sacks inside, and then we'll take a walk, okay?"

It wasn't what she wanted to hear, but she knew he would deliver the news in his own way and time. Joe winked at her as he passed by, carrying a bag of oranges and a carton of pop.

"He probably wants to show you the horses."

Gracie nodded, but she didn't believe it. She'd bet her life that the last thing on Jake's mind was horses.

Jake came out of the house and held out his hand. "Walk with me."

The wind had been brisk all day, and as they headed toward the corrals, it dug through Gracie's hair and pushed her shirt against her body, delineating her shape—the shape Jake knew so well. Impulsively, he tugged at her hand, making her look at him. When she did, he winked and she smiled.

"What are you thinking?" she asked.

He paused to stroke the side of her cheek with his thumb. "That you're beautiful."

"Thank you," she said, hugging the words to her heart.

"That I love you."

She grinned. "Thank you, again."

"And that I will never let you go."

The tone of his voice wiped the smile off her face, and she pulled back out of his arms. "Since I'm not threatening to leave you, then there must be another reason for that remark."

"Hudson called."

She paled but stood her ground. "And?"

"Did you know there was an escape tunnel in New Zion?"

He could tell by the look on her face that the question had taken her off guard.

"A what?"

"Behind the smoke house."

"You must be mistaken," Gracie said. "The smoke house was built right up against the mountain. There's not even a back door to the place."

"But there is. It leads to a tunnel that runs a quarter of a mile through the mountain and comes out on the other side. They got away, Gracie. Every single one of them—except Taggert Drown. They pulled his body out of the river soon after they got there."

A fear that had been with her since the previous day began to relax. "Then that means my father is safe."

"Probably."

"Thank God."

He couldn't deny her that measure of honest relief. Had the tables been turned, he would have wished the same thing. But the fact still remained that Elijah Moon and his followers were wanted by the law.

"Jake, you have to believe me. I didn't know, but don't expect me to pretend I'm unhappy that they weren't arrested."

He nodded. "That's fair enough."

Then a sadness swept over her, and she turned away and covered her face.

"This is a nightmare. I can't believe my father and brothers are fugitives from the law." She started to cry. "I'll never see them again, will I, Jake?"

He hurt—for her, as well as for himself. So much tragedy had come out of a place that had been built in the name of peace and love.

"Don't turn away from me, sweetheart." He pulled her to him, cradling her close. "Don't ever turn away from me. We'll get through this, but we've got to stick together, okay?"

She nodded, leaning against him and cherishing the knowledge that within his arms, she would be forever loved.

"That isn't all, is it, Jake?"

He didn't answer, but she felt the tension in his body, and she turned, refusing to move until he told her the truth.

"I asked you a question, Jake Baretta."

"Hudson will be here tomorrow. He wants to

ask you some questions. All you have to do is tell him the truth and—"

Worry yanked a knot in her belly. "But I don't have anything to tell. Oh, Jake, what if they don't believe me?"

His expression darkened. "Then that's their hard luck."

Chapter 12

"*Y*ou have the right to remain silent. You have the right to an attorney. Should you . . ."

The agent's voice droned into the stillness of the room, and Gracie's poise in the face of what was happening surprised them all, even Jake. As each man was introduced, she'd spoken graciously, acknowledging their presence as well as their right to be there. And when Hudson asked her to sit down, she had taken the burgundy wing-back chair in the corner of the room, smoothing the skirt of her dark blue dress as she settled.

When she met their gazes with an unblinking stare, Jake was startled by how regal she appeared. If it hadn't been for all the badges in the room, one might have believed that she was holding court.

Someone cleared his throat, and Jake realized the reading of the Miranda was over. Jake glanced at the agent. He seemed to be waiting for Jake to leave. Jake returned the stare without blinking.

When Jake didn't respond as expected, the agent looked to Hudson for guidance.

"Sir?"

"Let him stay," Hudson said.

The agent shrugged and turned back to his task. "Miss, please state your name for the tape."

And the questioning began.

One after the other, without letup, without consideration for the woman under scrutiny. And with each question, Gracie's shoulders grew straighter and her chin that little bit higher, but the tone of her voice never wavered. She was calm and rational, and Jake was about to explode. Two hours into the interrogation, he saw her falter. And when she closed her eyes and suddenly swayed, clutching the arms of the chair for support, he interrupted in anger.

"That's enough!" He reached across the table and punched off the power on the recorder. "You've asked her the same goddamned questions over and over for the last two hours, and she's given you the same answers. Now whether you like it or not, that's obviously all she knows. If you aren't satisfied with what she told you, then go talk to someone else."

As he scooped her up from where she was sitting, her head lolled against his shoulder, and he could feel her trembling. The natural pink in her complexion was almost gray, and her breath was rapid and shallow. When he started out the door, two of the men who'd come with Hudson stepped in front of him.

Jake's voice was soft, but the threat in it was unmistakable. "Get out of my way."

At a wave of Hudson's hand, they did.

"I'm sorry, sweetheart. I'm so, so sorry," Jake said, as he carried her toward their bedroom. Gracie couldn't even answer.

His mother had been sitting in the kitchen, anxiously waiting for the agents to leave, and when she saw Jake burst out of their living room with Gracie in his arms, she ran after him.

Jake was in the act of laying Gracie on the bed as Angie came into the room. Fear gripped her heart as she saw the young woman's pallor.

"What's wrong? Is she ill?"

Jake's hand was gentle as he smoothed away the hair clinging to her cheek.

"In spirit, yes." When he bent and kissed her cheek, fear shafted. Her skin was cold to the touch, and yet the house was comfortable, even warm. "She's in shock and exhausted."

Angie's expression softened. "You go deal with them and leave her to me."

And as she bent down to remove Gracie's shoes, Jake cupped her shoulder.

"Mom."

She paused and looked up. "What is it, honey?"

"I love you."

Peace settled in her heart. "I know that. Now turn on your tough side and get rid of those men. I don't like them in my house."

Jake grinned. "You know, maybe we're doing this backwards. You sure used to put the fear of God in John and me. I think I should turn you loose on them while I stay with Gracie."

At the sound of her name, Gracie rolled over in bed, only now aware that she was no longer sitting in the chair.

"Jake?"

He rushed to her side. "I'm here."

"What happened?"

"You just gave out, sweetheart, and it's okay. Mom's here. She's going to stay with you for a while. I need to do something."

She looked toward the door, her eyes dark and frightened. "Are they gone?"

Jake straightened. "They will be." After giving his mother a telling glance, he walked out.

Gracie started to sit up.

"Don't even think about getting up," Angie said. "Now here, let's get that dress off of you and get you under the covers. While you're resting, I'm going to make some of my special soup. It's good for what ails you."

Tears started to roll down Gracie's face. "Oh, Angie, my family is what ails me. My father . . . my brothers . . . they are all fugitives."

"I know."

"I don't think soup can mend a broken heart."

Angie sat down on the side of the bed and took Gracie in her arms. As she held her, Angie thought of the days and nights that had passed since they'd buried John, and her own heart tugged.

"I know, dear," Angie said. "But it's a good way to start."

While Gracie was being comforted, Jake was gaining comfort of his own in a different sort of way. He stalked into the living room with war on his mind.

Hudson was standing at the window with his hands in his pockets, rocking back and forth on his heels as he stared into the distance. The agent who'd been handling the interrogation was fiddling with the recorder, and some of the tapes they'd already filled. Another man was on the phone, and from what Jake could hear, talking to someone in D.C.

He gave the agent on the phone a cold, hard stare. "That better be on your nickel."

The man looked startled and abruptly broke the connection. Hudson turned around and knew the moment he saw Baretta that they were not going to be invited to lunch.

"Is she all right?" Hudson asked.

"She will be, no thanks to the lot of you," Jake said.

"It's not my fault she's Elijah Moon's daughter," Hudson said.

"Yes, well it's not hers, either," Jake snapped.

Hudson flushed. They'd pushed her, maybe harder than they should, but this was a serious case.

"Look, Baretta, there were things we needed to find out."

"And did you get the answers you needed?"

Hudson glared. "You know damn well we didn't. Hell, from the way she was telling it, we know more about the New Zionists than she did."

"I told you that."

"Yes, well, excuse me if I think your opinion could be slightly prejudiced."

Jake was in front of Ron Hudson before anyone saw him move, and there was a rage in his voice that froze them all where they stood.

"Shut up," Jake said. "For once, just shut up and listen and try to understand what I'm saying to you." He took a deep breath. "My name is Jacob John Baretta. I am an identical twin. Do you know what that means?"

Hudson paled. He figured he was about to find out.

"It means that once upon a time, at the point of conception, John and I were one living cell. There weren't two of us. There was only one. Somewhere within my mother's body, that little cell began to divide, and it separated everything it needed to separate to make two individual people. Two little boys who looked alike, but didn't always think or act alike."

Hudson was compelled by the fire in Jake's eyes and the fervor in his voice. He couldn't have moved if he tried.

"But," Jake continued, "there was one thing that John and I shared that never divided, and that was a split, or a soul, call it what you will. From the moment John died, a part of me died, too. There is a hole in my heart that will never be filled. There will forever be a part of me missing that Brady Moon took away. And if I thought for one moment that Gracie had anything to do with my brother's death, I wouldn't have touched her with a ten-foot pole, never mind fallen in love with her. Do—you—understand?"

Hudson exhaled. "Yes."

"Then get out."

Hudson nodded, and the agents began to pack. "Am I correct in assuming if anything comes up that could help me with the case that you'll get in touch?"

"You are correct."

Hudson held out his hand. "Baretta, I want to thank you for all you've done on behalf of the ATF."

Jake shook his head. "I didn't do it for you. I did it for John."

Hudson smiled. "I still want to shake your hand. You're a hell of a man."

Jake took it, squeezing the man's hand strongly and firmly. "So was John."

Finally they were gone, as quickly as they'd arrived. Jake stood in the living room, listening to the sounds of his mother as she worked about the kitchen. The aroma of chicken and tomato filled the air, and he smiled. Soup. His mother was making her cure-all soup.

A horse neighed and Jake looked outside. His father was in the far corrals working a horse. Suddenly, Jake wanted nothing more than to turn back time. To a day when the most complicated thing in his life was whether or not he'd get a date for Saturday night.

He walked down the hall to check on Gracie. She was curled up on her side with one hand beneath her cheek and the other clutching the covers beneath her breasts. His heart swelled with love, and as he watched her sleeping he realized that even good love hurt. Quietly, he closed the door and went to the kitchen.

"Mom, if you need me, I'll be down in the corrals with Dad."

Angie looked up from the pot she was stirring. "Is Gracie still asleep?"

He nodded.

"Are you all right?"

Even though it hurt to think of what wasn't right in his life, he managed a grin. "Well, if I'm not, I will be after you've dosed me up with that soup."

She arched a brow. "Get out of my kitchen and don't come back without your father."

"Yes, ma'am."

He grabbed one of his dad's old cowboy hats from a hook near the door and jammed it on his head as he stepped out on the porch.

The wind in his face was cleansing. The pure blue of a Wyoming sky was like a paintbrush on his soul, clearing away the darkness and the ugliness of the job that had become his life. As he walked, he became aware of the movement of his body, of the strength within his legs, of the beating of his heart. He heard the sound of his own breath as it slipped between his lips and felt the brush of his shirt against his belly as he stretched his arms over his head. When he was within shouting distance of the corrals, he whistled. His father, as well as the bay he was walking, turned toward him.

Joe had been cooling the horse down from a workout, and when he saw Jake coming, he walked the gelding to the watering trough.

"Hey boy, it's about time you showed up where the real work is."

Jake grinned. "Mom's making soup."

Joe rolled his eyes. "Glad it's you and not me that needs healing. She's hell on wheels with that stuff."

"Well, it's going to be coming out of Gracie's ears, not mine," Jake said.

Joe reached up to scratch the bay between the ears. "It was rough on her, wasn't it?"

Jake nodded.

Joe shook his head. "You know, sometimes the hardest part about life is just the living of it." When Jake remained silent, Joe continued. "Do you know what I mean?"

It took awhile for Jake to answer, but when he did, it left his father in no doubt as to what kind of a man he had raised.

"You mean the part about it being easier to quit, about giving up when you think you can't take another breath without bleeding, about being left behind when someone dies?"

Joe dropped the reins and took his son in his arms. "Yeah, boy, that's what I mean."

"Don't worry, Dad. I didn't say I liked it, but I'm damn sure not ready to quit on it."

"Considering the way your Gracie looks at you, I figured that's the way you would feel."

The wind circled the barn, tugging at the wide

dark brim of Jake's hat. He pushed it down on his forehead and pointed at the horse.

"Is he broke to ride?"

Joe's expression didn't change as he handed Jake the reins. "Find out for yourself."

Jake grinned. And when he vaulted onto the horse's bare back, just for a moment, he thought he heard Johnny laugh. But then he wrapped his long legs around the gelding's belly, and when he kicked him in the flanks, there was no time to dwell on ghosts. It was all he could do to hang on.

Joe swung the gate back as horse and rider came out of the corral, and he watched Jake ride away, until there was little to see but dust.

It was nearing dusk when Jake and his father came into the house. Gracie met Jake at the door, and before she could speak, he swooped her off her feet and into his arms. He put a blush on her cheeks that she was still wearing as Joe followed them into the living room.

Angie was buttoning the last two buttons on her best blue silk dress as she scurried into the kitchen.

"Joe Baretta, it's about time you got here. Now hurry up. We don't have much time."

Joe looked worried. Obviously there was something he'd forgotten.

"Where are we going?" he asked, as Angie grabbed him by the arm and started hurrying him toward their room.

"To dinner and to a movie." Then she called back over her shoulder, "And we're going to be late."

Jake grinned as Gracie's blush deepened. "Have we been set up?"

"I believe your mother thinks I need more than soup to make me better."

Down the hall, Angie waited impatiently while her husband showered. But the sound of her son's laughter was all she needed to hear to know she'd been right all along. There'd been too many tears in the house. It was time to remember the living and make peace with the dead.

The steaks Angie had left out for them to grill had been cooked and eaten. Gracie was wiping off the table while Jake put the last of the clean dishes in the cabinet. A radio was playing softly in the other room, and Gracie was absently humming along. In the middle of a verse, Jake took the dishcloth out of her hands and circled her with his arms.

As he pulled her close, he growled beneath his breath and bit the lower edge of her ear. "Don't tell Dad, but you taste a whole lot better than my steak."

Gracie laughed, and when she turned her head, his mouth slid over her lips, capturing the joy in the sound before it drifted away. She sighed. It was a miracle indeed how perfectly a man's body fit to a woman's when they were toe to toe. Jake's hands slid down her backside, cupping her hips and pulling her even closer. Her sigh turned to a moan, and she leaned back in his arms to look in his eyes. They were nothing but glitter in a face filled with passion. Her gaze slid to his mouth, remembering what it felt like on her skin. A trace of pink from her lipstick was on the edge of his lower lip, and she caught it with the edge of her thumb.

"You better be rubbing that in, not off," he warned her.

She laughed.

"Come here, woman." He swirled her out of the kitchen and into the hall where the music was louder.

"Where are we going?" she asked.

"Dancing. I'm taking you dancing."

When the music wrapped around them, she wrapped her arms around his neck. "Oh, Jake, its been so long, I'm not sure I can remember how to do this."

"Shoot, sweetheart, it's easy. All you have to do is follow my lead."

She cupped her hands behind his head. "I can do that," she said softly. And then she stood on tiptoe and kissed the edge of his cheek. "Whither thou goest . . ."

Jake forgot there was music, and just for a moment, there was nothing in the world but the single beat of their two separate hearts. The same rhythm, the same speed, the same constant pulse. Then he lowered his head, and just before their lips met, he whispered, ". . . I will go."

They danced all through the house and out the door, dipping and swaying in a waltzlike rhythm while the moon rose high in the night sky. Out on the porch, they danced, and with each step Jake drew her closer, held her tighter, loved her more.

The music faded, and they still moved to a song only they could hear. Gracie was lost in his eyes, in his touch, in the sweep of his breath against her cheek as he held her close. And when they finally stopped, they were far beyond the house, far beyond the corrals, and standing on a small grassy hill overlooking the land.

The night air was cool, and when Gracie shivered, Jake wrapped his arms around her, wishing it was as easy to shelter her from the ugliness in her life as it was to give her shelter from the chill.

"Are you too cold?" he asked.

"No, that wasn't a chill, it was just . . ."

He felt her sigh and knew that her unrest came from something other than him. "It's all right, darling. I understand."

She laid her face against his chest, relishing the strength of him, savoring the hard planes of his body against the soft contours of her own.

"Oh, Jake, I wish—"

He put a finger over her lips, stopping the words before they could be voiced. "You know the old saying, 'If Wishes Were Horses Then Beggars Would Ride.' Don't wish for things. Be thankful for what you already have."

"Only if that includes you," she whispered.

"You already have me, Gracie. What do you want to do with me?"

The question surprised her, but not the thought that came next. Without shame, without hesitation, she started unbuttoning his shirt.

"I want to lie with you beneath this Wyoming

moon. I want to feel the grass beneath my back and you inside me."

She saw his eyes glitter as he dropped his shirt to the ground. "I can arrange that."

He reached behind her back and pulled down her zipper. The dress, a borrowed one from Angie, fell at her feet, and she stood before him in bits and pieces of nylon and lace. Moonlight draped her figure in a cool ivory glow, and then she took his hand and pulled him down.

Forever after Gracie would remember that true ecstasy could happen anywhere, anytime. Even on a hillside—in the dark—beneath the vast space of a Wyoming sky.

Canada!

It was the last place Elijah Moon had expected to go. But they had, and in a run for their lives. When the men chasing Jake reached the river and found Taggert Brown dying from snake bite, Elijah had pronounced it a judgment from God. But when Brady had followed them down to tell the New Zionists that they'd had a traitor in their midst, Elijah became lost in the panic that ensued.

In Elijah's mind, even if the man they'd known as Jake Crockett was living under an assumed name, he didn't understand why it should matter. As long as a man lived under God's teachings, he could call himself anything he chose.

But that wasn't taking any of the militia activities into account, and that was because Elijah had turned a blind eye and deaf ear to it all. It wasn't until Brady revealed the hidden passageway in the smoke house that Elijah realized his dreams for an Eden were over. Only as Aaron was rushing him through the tunnel did he come to understand what Gracie had been trying to tell him all those months. With the children pale-faced and afraid of something they didn't understand and the women sobbing as they ran, Elijah was forced to face the fact that his eldest son had been carrying on his own objectives behind his back. Only then had he balked, and when he did, Brady took charge.

"No, Father, we have to go!"

Brady Moon was as adamant in his belief as Elijah was in his. And it was never more apparent than when he shoved his father aside and began moving people through the tunnel.

As they ran past, Elijah reached out to them in a beseeching manner.

"Wait! There's no need for fear! Just because a man lives among us under a name other than his own is between himself and God. It should not matter to us who he is, but how he behaved while he was with us."

One of the children fell and was almost trampled before his mother picked him up.

Kay clutched her sobbing child to her breasts. "Please, Matthew, maybe your father is right. I don't want to leave. We don't even have milk for the children."

But Matthew didn't listen. He just grabbed their child from her arms and pushed her on through, unable to look his father in the face.

Moira Brown came next, dragging her children by the hand, and while the others were crying, there was a hope in her eyes that had never been there before. Moira wasn't only running away from her old life. She was running toward a new one. If she was to believe what she'd been told, she was now a widow. Moira would not grieve because someone else would bury Taggert. It was an unexpected relief from the burden of her unhappy marriage.

"Please, my children," Elijah begged, "you don't know what you're doing."

Aaron came next, urging his wife, SueEllen, and their children to move on. He stopped to take his father's hand.

"Come, Father. It's no use. This was all set in motion a long time ago, and there's nothing we can do to take it back now."

Elijah was stunned. "What do you mean? What was set in motion? There's nothing we have to be ashamed about."

Aaron looked straight into Elijah's eyes, unwavering, unblinking. Finally, he spoke.

"You know in your heart that's not true. You've known for a very long time, haven't you, Father. And you've turned a blind eye to it all by letting Brady have his way, and we've let it happen by following Brady's will, just as we did when we were children. Only a spanking from you won't fix what we've done this time. Now run, Father. If Brady thinks they're coming, then they're coming. He hasn't been wrong yet."

"But who?" Elijah asked. "Who is coming? Who do we have to fear?"

"The law, Father. The law. We've been breaking it, and if we don't run now, we will be paying for the rest of our lives."

Elijah's shoulders slumped, and his chin dropped. "May God have mercy on our souls."

"That's all well and good, Father. But for now—and for God's sake—run!"

And so Elijah let himself be led north, just as he'd led them years earlier out of the cities in which they'd dwelled.

But now their running was over. They'd made it over the border with fake passports and little else to their names. Now they were huddled together in one room of the block of motel rooms that they'd rented only minutes earlier. There was time to talk, to plan, now that they were safe.

Chapter 13

*B*rady's fall from grace had been hard, but that was because he'd had a long way to fall. The pedestal Elijah had put him on had been high, and when he toppled, he'd taken all of them with him. No matter how hard he tried to explain to Elijah, the old man wouldn't heed his plea. In Elijah's mind, there was nothing left between them but the sharing of a name, and if he could have, he would have purged Brady of that, as well. He looked at his eldest son and realized that he'd never really known him.

Brady saw the look on Elijah's face and knew real fear. He'd already lost Gracie. He could not fathom losing the rest of his family.

"Father! You can't shun me like this! I'm your son. Your firstborn!"

But Elijah turned a deaf ear.

Brady turned to his brothers. "Aaron, please look at me! We're brothers. Burnett! Matthew! We were in this together. Why must I be the scapegoat?"

Following his father's lead, the brothers acknowledged neither Brady's presence nor his words.

And one by one the brothers turned their backs on him. Stunned by his family's total denial, Brady fell to his knees, clutching the back of his father's coattail.

"Father, I beg of you. Have mercy on me. Please give me another chance. I'll be the kind of son you want. All you have to do is show me the way."

"You are thirty-seven years old. If you don't know the way by now, you never will," Elijah said. "Now leave. You are no longer welcome in our world."

Crawling to his feet from his knees was the hardest thing Brady Moon had ever done. And by the time he was standing, there was a rage within him so fierce that it would take death to extinguish. He walked out of the Canadian motel with one goal in mind.

Refusing to accept the consequences for what he had done, he chose to lay the blame at another man's feet. A man who'd come into their midst under the guise of a friend. A man who'd called himself Jake Crockett. Who could have known there would be two men wearing the same face— two men who would come into New Zion posing as Lady Crockett's grandson? If the second Jake Crockett was to be believed, then the first one was dead. But where had the second man gone? Where was the man who'd lied—the man who'd taken Gracie away?

Brady's heart was heavy, but he drove away

without looking back. There was a thing within him that he knew must be done. Before he left this earth, he was going to find that man and make him pay.

Ron Hudson came out of his meeting with a handful of briefs and new information to add to an old case. The Bureau of Alcohol, Tobacco, and Firearms had it on good authority that Elijah Moon and his followers had made it over the border and were somewhere in Canada. The news rankled. Oh, there were avenues they could follow to get them back to stand trial, but all of those hinged on knowing where they were and being able to serve the papers that would get them back in the hands of the United States government. Right now, the prospects didn't look good.

Hudson's frustration mounted as he entered his office. Judy, his secretary of thirteen years, was gone. It galled him no end that she had the audacity to try motherhood at the age of thirty-six. He couldn't imagine what she'd been thinking. Didn't she know what a mess she would be leaving him in?

The substitute they'd sent up from the typing pool was a capable woman. She could answer phones and take messages and type letters. She even had a pleasant smile on her face. But she couldn't do two things at once. For the last week and a half, every time it got hectic, which it did on a daily basis, she seemed to lose control. And then she cried.

Ron nodded courteously as he strode by on his way to his office.

"Good afternoon, Tiffany."

She smiled at him and then jumped as the fax began to print. As she reached for the printout, the phone began to ring. Just then a delivery boy came in behind Ron, and he could already see her coming undone.

Damn, but he did hate a crying woman.

Hurrying to get out of her way, he entered his office and tossed the files on his desk, flopped down in his chair, and swiveled it toward the windows overlooking the parking lot. The leaves were beginning to turn, and it looked like rain.

He glanced back at the file with Elijah Moon's name. Canada. He thought of Gracie Moon. Did she know they were there? Somehow he didn't think so. Was he going to tell her? He had to give that some thought. If her family ever tried to contact her, would she let him know? From the very first day of this case, there had been more questions than answers. And for a man like Ron Hudson, that, and the impending thunderstorm, were all it took to ruin a good day.

But in the outer office, Tiffany Mead's day was getting better. The man she'd met the night before had just sent her flowers. Pink roses. Her favorites. She plunged her nose into the blossoms and inhaled slowly, savoring the scent and the memory of the man's gentle kiss. She'd never been partial to redheads—until now. There was something compelling about this man that she couldn't forget.

Finally, she set them aside with a sigh and returned to her work, and somehow Ron Hudson's hectic office became that much less of a hassle. There was someone new in Tiffany's life and she didn't intend to miss her chance. Maybe this time he was the one.

For Jake, the days since he'd come home were a balm to his soul. He felt a sense of peace within himself. And he knew that it was a healing time for his parents as it was for him. It had been years since he'd spent this long at home, and as he worked through the days at his father's side, he wondered why he hadn't done it before. There was a satisfaction in working the land and tending the cattle that he'd never found anywhere else.

He'd taken an extended leave of absence from his job with the understanding that the door was open for him anytime he wanted to come back. But both he and his boss had known the day that he called that it would be a long time, if ever, before that happened. Something had forever changed him. Part of him had died, and another part had been born. He'd never known it was possible to love a woman as much as he loved Gracie Moon.

But he worried. There were moments when he caught her crying. And there were moments when they made such desperate love that it scared even him. He might feel settled, but he knew she did not. There was no way he could actually blame her. His roots were deep in Wyoming. Gracie's people were as lost as seeds on the wind. All Jake and Gracie had going for them was the deep, abiding love that they shared. He prayed it would be enough.

Gracie woke in a cold sweat. Her stomach was lurching, and there was a four-step dash from the bed to the bathroom. She barely made it in time.

The sudden motion of her jumping from bed yanked Jake from a dreamless sleep. He sat up just as the bathroom door slammed behind her. The familiar sounds of retching could be heard, and moments later Jake was right beside her, holding her head and washing her face with a cold, wet cloth when it was over.

"Gracie, sweetheart, do you have a fever?" Jake asked.

She was sitting on the closed lid of the commode and leaning her head on the sink. Just the echo of his voice made her wince.

She barely managed a "no," before slapping the cold cloth on the back of her neck.

"Do you feel like getting back into bed?"

"No."

Moving seemed impossible. Breathing wasn't much better. But she managed to inhale without having to give it all back up.

"Want me to get Mom?"

Gracie moaned. "She can't help."

"You don't know Mom. Remember that soup she—"

It was the wrong thing to say. Several minutes later, when the second spasm of retching was over, Gracie trusted her stomach enough to lie back down.

Jake had never felt so helpless in all his life. His aim with a rifle was deadly. He knew how to track the most wily of perpetrators through several foreign countries. And he was pretty sure he knew all there was to know about being a man. But none of this expertise was worth a damn because he didn't know how to make Gracie better.

"Don't move, sweetheart. I'm going to go get Mom."

If she'd had the nerve, she would have laughed. Don't move? She was afraid to breathe.

"Tell her to bring me some saltine crackers," Gracie said.

Jake frowned. "Oh, honey, I don't think you should be eating anything just yet."

"It will help, trust me," she said, completely covering her face with the cloth, unmindful of the tiny drips of water running in her ears.

Jake headed down the hall and knocked on his parents' door. Only afterward did he think to look at the time. It was a little bit after six in the morning.

"Mom! Gracie's sick!"

It didn't take long to get a response. Angie was out of bed and pulling on her robe as Joe opened the door. They could tell by the look on Jake's face that he was worried.

"What's wrong with her, son?"

"She's been throwing up for more than thirty minutes. I finally got her back in bed."

Joe frowned. "Might be the flu. I heard it's going around."

"I don't know. She said to tell Mom to bring her some saltine crackers, but I don't think she should be eating at a—"

Angie stopped in her tracks, and Joe started to grin.

"She said what?" Angie asked.

"She said to bring her some saltine crackers."

Joe chuckled. "I'll get them, honey. You go see about her. I'll be right there as soon as I plug in the coffeepot."

This wasn't the reaction Jake had expected. "What's wrong with you two? She's sick, for God's sake."

Angie patted him on the arm, and then waved her husband on. "Hurry up, Joe. If she knows enough to ask for them, then she's far enough along to be sick as a dog."

Jake wasn't following at all. "Look, will somebody clue me in on—"

Angie turned in the hallway with her hands on her hips, pinning her son to the spot with a cool, green stare.

"Is there a possibility that Gracie could be pregnant?"

Jake forgot to breathe. "Oh my God." Possibility? Now that he thought about it, he realized it would be a miracle if she were not. Then a slow grin began spreading on Jake's face. "Some."

Angie rolled her eyes. "My stars. Some." She began to smile. "You always did understate the obvious."

But when she started toward their room, Jake caught her by the arm.

"Mom, give me a couple of minutes, okay?"

Angie nodded and patted his arm. "When you want the crackers, just yell. Your dad will come running."

"Thanks."

He slipped inside and closed the door. Gracie was right where he'd left her, flat on her back with the washcloth over her face.

"Gracie . . . sweetheart?"

She groaned.

"Can you talk?"

This time the groan sounded like a no.

"Then I'll talk and you listen, okay?"

He knelt beside the bed and pulled damp hair from beneath the cloth, smoothing it away from her face.

"Okay, here's how we'll do it. One finger means yes. Two fingers means no, okay?"

She held up one finger.

Jake splayed his hand across the flat surface of her stomach and took a deep breath.

"Sweetheart, are you pregnant?"

He felt her tense. For a moment she didn't move. Then ever so slowly she held up one finger. Jake caught it and lifted it to his lips, kissing the tip before turning it loose. "My God, Gracie, why didn't you tell me? Don't you know how much I love you?"

She lifted the washcloth from her face and

sighed. "You cheated. Those are not yes and no questions."

Jake leaned over and kissed her stomach. When he lifted his head, his eyes shone with unshed tears.

"I love you very much, Gracie Moon. Will you marry me?"

"And because I love you more, the answer is no."

Jake was stunned. He cupped her face with his hands and brushed a kiss across her forehead. "But why?"

"You shouldn't have to ask," she said, and looked away.

Once again, their pasts were rising up between them like a wall. A knot settled in his belly. "Don't do this to us, Gracie."

"Think about it, Jake. How do you tell a child that his uncle Brady killed his uncle John?"

Jake stood with a jerk and walked away from the bed to stare out the window. He was still for a very long time, and when he turned around, the expression on his face chilled her heart.

"Are you going to keep this baby?"

The question staggered her. Abortion was abhorrent to her, and she couldn't believe that he'd asked.

"Dear God, yes." She laid a hand across her stomach, as if protecting the tiny spark of life from such an ugly thought.

"Well, not without me, you're not. We made this baby in love. It will be raised with love. The rest will have to sort itself out."

"But—"

"No buts," he said shortly. "Now, do you still want those damned crackers, or what?"

She started to laugh and then she started to cry.

Jake went to her, lifting her in his arms. "Make up your mind, Gracie Moon. Either you're happy or you're sad, but you can't be both at the same time in this house. It's a rule."

Gracie clung to him. "That's the silliest rule I ever heard," she said.

"It was one Mom made when John and I were small. We were so opposite in personality that it wasn't unusual for one of us to be happy while the other was having a bad day. She made a rule. We could both be sad. Or we could both be glad. But we couldn't be one of each."

Gracie smiled. "And why not?"

"Because she said she didn't have time to laugh and cry at the same time."

"Your mother is priceless."

Jake grinned. "I know. She still scares the hell out of Dad."

"He's a lucky man."

"And so am I." Then he nuzzled her neck. "Are you ready to break the good news?"

"Will it be all right?" she asked, suddenly ner vous all over again.

Jake rolled his eyes. Puting her on her feet, he took her by the hand. "Just wait and see."

When they entered the kitchen, Joe and Angie were head to head and leaning over a piece of paper while Angie chewed on the end of a pen.

"Hey, what are you guys doing?" Jake asked.

"Making a list of names to suggest for the baby."

Jake looked at Gracie and grinned. "I rest my case."

And when Joe handed her the crackers, Gracie found the joy within herself to smile.

Tiffany Mead was in love. She stood naked before the mirror, eyeing herself from one side and then the other, pulling her hair up on the top of her head, testing it to see which way it looked best. As she turned it loose, it slid down her back and she shivered. She loved the sensual feel of it against her skin.

She glanced at the clock and began to dress. Tonight he would come and she couldn't wait. They'd been dating for weeks now, and she'd almost talked him into going to her parents' house for Thanksgiving. He was the best thing that had ever happened to her, and she was convinced that he was going to propose. He'd told her he had something special to ask her. What else could he have possibly meant?

Tiffany reached for her dress and slipped it over her head, then lifted her hair from the neck. She was thankful she hadn't followed the urge to bleach it. He liked it long and black. He said it was his favorite color. Carefully, she applied mascara to her eyelashes, then stepped back to view her work. She liked this color. It made her brown eyes look even darker. He said he liked brown-eyed women.

Tiffany was even thinking of going back to college and finishing her degree. She'd always wanted to be a teacher, and she was only twenty-two hours from gaining her teaching certificate. He said he admired teaching more than any other occupation in the world.

When the doorbell rang Tiffany turned away from the mirror. There was a smile on her face as she opened the door.

"Bradley, darling, come in. Dinner is almost ready."

Bradley Packard strutted in bearing a small bouquet of flowers. He thrust them in her hands. Sniffing the air, he said, "Something smells wonderful. I can't wait."

She buried her face in the flowers and inhaled, then batted her eyes over the blooms and giggled.

"Me either."

He shoved the flowers aside and pulled her into his arms for a kiss. His hands slid down her backside, cupping her hips and pulling her closer against him.

He moaned as she ground herself against him. "Oh, sweetheart. Dinner can wait."

Tiffany smiled as he swept her off her feet and carried her into the bedroom. The scent of talcum powder and perfume was still in the air, and there was a wet towel lying in the corner that she'd forgotten to hang up. But none of that mattered. They were caught up in the moment.

He laid her down on the bed and stood back, admiring the way her long black hair spread out across the pillows and gazing deeply into her dark brown eyes. He removed his jacket and kicked off his shoes, then followed her down on the bed.

One kiss led to another, then another, and then he was yanking down her panties and unzipping his pants. He was hard and aching, and she was moaning in his ear and clutching at his shoulders, begging him to complete the act.

And he did, jamming himself between her thighs over and over until he thought that he would go mad. Her hair was tangled in his hands, her legs wrapped around his waist. His face was buried in her breasts as the climax came upon him, and at the height of his joy, he turned loose of the secret that had been his ruin and his shame.

Clutching her to him with every breath, he let slip a name, a name that didn't belong with this act. He clutched Tiffany closer and groaned aloud.

"Oh, Gracie. My God, my Gracie."

Teetering on a climax of her own, Tiffany heard what he said and stiffened with a shriek.

"You sorry son of a—"

The moment she screamed, he lost the image of Gracie's face and his erection, all at once. Furious, he raised up and hit Tiffany with his fist. Her eyes rolled back in her head, and she went limp. Disgusted with himself, he rolled off her and walked into the bathroom to clean himself up. With purpose in every movement, he completed the job and then dried his hands before going to retrieve his jacket.

With a casual glance toward the bed to make sure she was still unconscious, he thrust his hand into the pocket and pulled out a loaded syringe, holding it up to the light to see that the contents were still intact.

He smiled. There was enough stuff in there to make her talk for days. But the way Brady had it figured, it wouldn't take days for him to find out what he needed to know. All he needed was the date and time of the ATF's next computer check. Then his break-in to their system could be coordinated with their next maintenance check. As soon as the computer was back on-line, the hacker he'd hired could get all the rest. It was risky, but Brady thrived on risk. He needed to get in and out of the files before the hacker's location was revealed.

Using Tiffany had been a stroke of genius on his part. Her resemblance to Gracie had been the bonus he hadn't expected. He glanced back at her limp, half-naked body sprawled on the bed and grimaced. As badly as he'd wanted her before, he felt nothing but distaste for her now. She'd served her purpose in one way. It was time for him to complete the job.

He went to the bathroom and filled a drinking glass with water, then tossed it in Tiffany's face. She moaned and soon after started to sob. Ignoring her pitiful cries for understanding, he jabbed the needle into her flesh, emptying the syringe in her arm.

"What are you doing to me?" Tiffany cried, trying without success to crawl out of bed.

Something was wrong! Her legs wouldn't work and her eyes wouldn't focus, and she fell face forward, with her head hanging off the side of the bed.

Brady grabbed her by the hair and yanked her backward. She hit the pillows with a thump.

"Tiffany, can you hear me?" he asked.

Her eyelids were fluttering and her lips were slack, but he knew she could hear.

"Now I want you to listen to me. There's something I need to know."

Ron Hudson entered the office, expecting to see Tiffany Mead's round face smiling up at him. The blonde sitting behind the desk was a surprise, but not nearly as much as the reason she gave him for her sudden appearance.

"Good morning, Mr. Hudson. My name is Alicia Ryan. I'm your new secretary. I've put your mail on your desk. You've already had a couple of calls. One to cancel a luncheon engagement, the other to remind you that your mother's birthday is next week. If you want to reschedule your appointment, let me know, and if your mother likes crystal, I noticed that Brouchard's Jewelry and Gifts is having a marvelous sale. I'd be glad to pick something up for her on my lunch hour."

Hudson was stunned. "Uh . . . yes . . . I guess that would be fine."

She smiled. "Very well."

He started toward his door.

"There's fresh coffee on your desk."

He actually grinned "Why, thank you, Miss . . ."

"Ryan. Alicia Ryan."

"Yes, Miss Ryan."

His hand was on the doorknob when he thought to ask, "Say, what happened to Miss Mead? Is she sick?"

Alicia Ryan's smile disappeared. "Oh no, sir. I assumed that you heard."

Hudson frowned. If she knew something he didn't, this didn't seem right. "Heard what?" he asked.

"Why, about Tiffany! She was found dead in her apartment this morning." And then she dropped her eyes, as if hating to say it but knowing it had to be said. "They're guessing it was a drug overdose, although I'm told the autopsy has yet to be performed."

Hudson couldn't find the impetus to move. He kept thinking of Tiffany as she'd been yesterday— laughing and full of excitement. She'd even dropped a couple of hints about a possible marriage proposal.

He shook his head. "I'm sorry, really sorry," he said, and when he reached his desk, he realized that he was. Poor Tiffany. He wondered if she'd been crying when she died.

Brady was riding a high that wouldn't come down. He was certain that he had what he needed to get back in good standing with his father. Gracie had been the delight of Elijah Moon's life, and her disappearance from their midst had caused his father great pain. Even though they'd known she helped the traitor escape, in their world, blood was thicker than water. Gracie was the baby, the only daughter. In spite of her wayward ways, Brady knew that Elijah would welcome her back with open arms.

With what he'd learned, he was certain that all he had to do was go to his father, tell him where Gracie was, and everything would be forgiven. And Brady needed to be forgiven.

For him, the drive back to Canada was long and dangerous. But with his fake identification, shaving off the beard that he'd grown, and a dye job on his thick red hair, his appearance was drastically changed. As Bradley Packard, he crossed the border with no problems, his hopes high. It was late November and threatening snow.

But when he got to the town where the New Zionists had been, to his horror he found that they'd gone. Panic seized him as he staggered back to his car and crawled in behind the wheel. His hands were shaking, and he felt sick to his stomach. For all intents and purposes, Brady Moon had just been orphaned. Everyone he knew and loved in the world was lost to him. He didn't know where any of them were—except Gracie. And knowing where she was didn't do him any good. Not this way. Not if he couldn't find Elijah to give him the news.

He leaned his head on the steering wheel and willed himself not to cry. Not now. There was no need to waste the tears if there was no one around to witness them. Besides, all wasn't lost. He knew his father's ways. There were only a certain number of places he was bound to go. It might take awhile, but Brady knew he could find him.

With a lighter heart, he started the car and drove away, remembering better times and happier days. By the time he'd gone a few miles down the road, he had a smile on his face. There would come the time when he would find Gracie again, and when he did, there was a man who was going to pay for taking her away. For now, he would concentrate on locating his family. Wherever they were was where he belonged.

Chapter 14

*G*racie's morning sickness had finally passed. Only on the rare occasion did she suffer any queasiness, and when she did, she found herself flat on her back. With three Barettas watching her every move, there was little danger of overexertion. In fact, it was beginning to get on her nerves.

She was standing on a small step stool and reaching for a bowl on the top shelf of the cabinet when Jake came in the kitchen.

"Gracie, sweetheart, be careful," Jake said, and dashed across the floor. He lifted her down from the stool and handed her the bowl, then kissed her cheek. "Is there anything else you need while I'm in here?"

She set the bowl down and turned around. Her hands were on her hips, and there was a fire in her eyes he hadn't seen in months.

"Yes, by the way, there is. I need for you to back off."

"But—"

"You are driving me nuts. I have never been so

looked after in my life. I'm not sick. I'm not dying. I'm just pregnant, remember?"

He grinned and took her in his arms. "Ooh, yeah, I remember how it happened really well."

Slightly taken aback by his audacity, a sideways smile tipped the corner of her mouth before she poked him in the chest.

"Stop that. You're supposed to be in trouble."

His grin widened. "But honey, I'm not the one in trouble. You are. I heard some no-good jackass up and got you pregnant."

She pursed her lips, then arched a brow. "He might be a jackass, but I can't say he was no-good. In fact, I have to admit he really had his moments."

This time, Jake was the one caught off guard. And then he hugged her.

"Okay, I get the message," he said softly, nuzzling on a spot beneath her ear. "But I have one to give to you, too."

"If you would get your tongue out of my ear, I could hear you better," Gracie said.

Jake laughed aloud. "Damn, woman. You're downright sassy. And that's good," he said. "Because there's something we need to be doing, and I think you're just about up to the task."

"What's that?" Gracie asked.

All the teasing was suddenly gone from his voice. Gracie was unprepared when Jake dropped to his knees and laid his cheek on her belly, hugging her to him.

"Marry me, Gracie. I've already given you my child. Please let me give you my name."

The plea was so poignant and so unexpected, Gracie found herself near tears. She brushed her hand across his head, loving the springy feel of his hair against her palm.

"In spite of the unsettled manner of my life, you're sure?"

"I've never been more sure of anything in my life," he said.

"Okay."

He was so keyed in to convincing her that her acceptance didn't register at first.

"Please, Gracie. You aren't thinking things through. If there's enough love, there's always a way to work things out."

Jake had such a frown on his face that Gracie started to smile.

"I said, I will."

"We aren't responsible for the actions of—"

She dropped down to his level and held his face between her hands until he was forced to meet her gaze.

"Jake! Listen to me."

His eyes focused. On her face. On her mouth. On the sound of her voice.

"I said, I will marry you."

He went limp, then pulled her into his lap and held her, cheek to cheek.

"Thank you, thank you. I swear, you will never be sorry."

The back door slammed, and they looked up to see Jake's father standing in the doorway and grinning from ear to ear.

"What's going on?" Joe asked.

"We're planning a wedding," Jake said.

"I knew that," he said, and sauntered past them to get a drink. He emptied the glass and filled it again, this time turning toward them before he took another swallow. "You know, someone had better be letting Angie in on the news, or there will be hell to pay. You know how she likes to plan things out."

"Help me up," Gracie said, holding out her hand to Joe.

Joe lifted her off Jake's lap and Jake rose, too. "Mom can plan all she likes, but she's going to have to go through Gracie to do it," Jake said. "It's her wedding."

"No, Jake, it's ours," Gracie said. "I will welcome all of your mother's help."

"My help with what?" Angie asked as she came in the back door with an armload of clean jeans that she'd just taken from the clothesline.

Joe winked. "A wedding. Jake and Gracie are planning their wedding."

Angie's expression lit. "It's about time. Just let me dump these clothes on my bed, and I'll be right back. The first thing we need to do is make a list."

She was still talking as she walked out of the room.

"Told you," Joe said, and downed the rest of his drink of water. "I've got to get back to the cattle. The truck will be here any time."

Jake nodded. "I was on my way out there when Gracie changed my mind."

"Oh, so it's my fault that you're late," Gracie said. "Well, that's all I need to hear. Get, the both of you. I have things to do."

Joe disappeared quickly, but it took Jake longer to let go. He couldn't quit looking at her. At the way she stood. The way she tilted her head. The way her body moved beneath her T-shirt and jeans. The way her hair caught the sunlight and seemed to take fire, burning dark, burning black. And she stood there so strong and so proud, carrying his child, and he knew she felt so alone.

"I love you so much, Gracie Moon."

She smiled and she walked into his arms.

"And I love you, Jacob. More than you will ever know."

He held her close, conscious that he was holding his world in his arms. "You've had so much taken away from you, girl. Let my family be yours. Let me give you that much."

Gracie looked up at him, and there was a sadness behind her smile. "Yes, I've lost a lot, but I've also found more. When you came into my life, I found happiness and I found joy. I found a man I loved enough to risk everything to keep. I will take anything and everything you give me, including your family. Thank God they are willing to have me."

A horn honked outside. Jake looked up. "There's the trucker. I'd better go help Dad load the cattle. We'll talk some more later, okay?"

"Okay."

"Don't let Mom push you into something you don't want to do."

She grinned. "Go load cattle. I can take care of myself."

But even after the door had closed behind him, Gracie couldn't let go of the feeling she had. It was one she'd carried with her all the way from New Zion. It had slept with her, stayed with her, every step of the way. It was an overwhelming feeling that everything was going to come undone.

She knew her family in a way Jake did not. Elijah was a man who lived his whole life by his interpretation of the Bible, and he was a harsh judge of those who did not see the world in the same manner. But even though she knew he would consider her a fallen woman, it was her brother Brady she feared the most.

She looked back at the cabinet. The bowl that had started this sequence of events was right where she'd put it.

"Get over this," she told herself, as she began gathering ingredients for the cake.

But it was easier said than done. Brady Moon held grudges more than anyone she'd ever known in her life. And she could only imagine what was going through his head now that his empire was in ruins.

She glanced out the window over the sink and saw Jake on a horse and his father near the trailer. They were laughing, even as the dust was boiling and the cattle were being loaded. That was the kind of relationship father and son should have. She thought of the child that she carried. Thank God it would be raised in a healthy, loving environment instead of one that revolved around judgment and strict rules.

She turned back to the business at hand. As she stirred and measured the cake she was going to bake, she could almost forget that her brother had killed . . . almost, but not quite. Gracie knew in her heart that having killed once, the killer would find the act easier the second time around.

She kept thinking of John Baretta, the man she'd first known as Jake Crockett. He'd been a part of Jake in a way only identical twins could understand. And because of Brady, John Baretta was dead. All she could do was hope that Brady was far, far away, because if he and Jake ever met again, one of them would wind up dead.

People were pouring out of the church sanctuary. Everywhere Jake stepped he ran into one old friend or another. Their comments were mixed up with condolences that John was not there to be his best man. And no one was more conscious of the fact than Jake. He couldn't believe that this was happening without his brother. Only once in their lives had the subject of marriage ever come up, and when it had, John's words had stunned Jake, just as their memory did now.

Jake was sitting on the edge of the corral and watching the sunset. As always, John was right beside him.

"Hey, Jake, Cherry said that June Dunson has a crush on you."

Jake shrugged. He knew it. But he didn't like June

Dunson. She was only a freshman, and she giggled too much and she didn't know how to stand still.

"So, that doesn't mean I have to like it."

John grinned. "No, but it means you could take advantage of the situation . . . if you wanted to."

Jake glanced at John and, for one of the few times in their lives, took a mental step back and looked at him. The smile on John's face slowly died as he stared into his brother's eyes.

There was something in his expression that John recognized. A look that could almost be called disapproval. Above all else in his world, John valued his brother's goodwill.

"What?" John finally asked.

Jake's gaze never wavered. "You would take advantage, wouldn't you, John?"

John laughed a little and then looked away. The question made him uneasy.

Jake didn't push the issue, and the sunset regained their attention. A fly buzzed past, and they each reached up, swatting in unison, and then exclaiming in disgust the same curse. And when they did, looked at each other and grinned. Being twins was something they were used to, but once in a while, even they saw the humor in their identical behaviors and thoughts.

"Boys! Supper is ready!"

Their mother's cry sent them into a different frame of mind, and they slid off the corral fence and started toward the house, always ready to eat.

Halfway there, John stopped, and Jake turned to see what was wrong. There was a pensive expression on John's face.

"What's wrong?" Jake asked.

"Jake, you know what you said earlier, about me taking advantage of the situation?"

Jake grinned, but John didn't.

"I would have, you know."

The smile slid off Jake's face, and he saw the fear in John's eyes.

"That doesn't mean—"

John interrupted him. "You're going to be the better man."

Jake frowned. "Damn, Johnny, what made you start thinking all serious like this?"

John shrugged. "I don't know. I just suddenly saw us down the road a few years. You're the kind of man who will probably fall in love only once, and when you get married it will last for a lifetime."

Jake grinned. "When I do, you will be my best man."

Jake's mother grabbed him by the arm and pulled him out of the vestibule.

"What are you doing out here? We've been looking all over. The preacher was beginning to think you'd stood Gracie up at the altar."

Jake shook off the mood and grinned. "Not on your life," he said.

"Come on, then," Angie said. As they hurried down the hallway, she glanced up at Jake. "Did your father tell you?"

"Tell me what?" Jake asked.

Angie patted her hair, and there was a twinkle in her eye that made Jake smile.

"That our wedding present to you is a trip to Florida for us."

Jake laughed aloud. "You're going to have to run that by me one more time."

"Well, we figured Gracie wasn't up to a lot of traveling, and you needed some time alone. And I am getting too old to appreciate Wyoming winters, so . . ."

"So you're leaving me all alone on that ranch with all those cattle and horses and all that snow."

"And a brand-new wife and a baby on the way. You better enjoy your time alone, because it's going to be brief."

Jake stopped and swept his mother off her feet, kissing her grandly and swirling her around where they stood.

Angie was grinning and grabbing at her hair. "Jacob Baretta, you put me down this instant. I'm going to be a complete mess."

Jake laughed. "Mom, you're beautiful and you know it. Now go take care of Gracie. I know what I'm supposed to do."

"Sometimes I wonder," she said, scurrying off down the hall to where the bride was dressing.

Gracie stood before the mirror, looking at the reflection of the woman in the glass. She saw her mother's eyes and her father's brow. Her brother Matthew's smile and her grandmother's thick, black hair. She was a part of everyone who'd come before her, and yet on this most special of days, she was alone. *If only I knew.*

The thought had been with her for days. The uncertainty of where they were or if they were even alive was killing her. She was going on with her life as if they'd never been part of hers, and it was more than she could bear. When she turned away there was a droop to her shoulders that a bride shouldn't wear.

Angie burst into the room, bringing energy and joy. She had a portable phone in her hand.

"Telephone for you, dear." When she handed it to Gracie, she whispered, "Tell whoever it is to make it short. The preacher is waiting."

Gracie took the phone as Angie left, shutting the door behind her.

"Hello?"

"Gracie, it's me, Ron Hudson."

Gracie stiffened.

"I wanted to call and wish you and Jake all the very best."

She started to relax. "Frankly, I'm surprised you called me instead of him."

Frankly, Hudson was a little surprised with himself. But he knew the moment he heard her voice that he was doing the right thing.

"I have a little gift for you," he said quietly. "It's an intangible thing, but as information goes, I thought it might make your day a little bit happier."

She waited for him to continue.

Hudson cleared his throat. "What I'm about to tell you could get me in trouble, so I'm assuming that you'll keep it to yourself."

"I'm listening," she said.

"As far as we know, they're safe and somewhere in Canada."

A weight came off Gracie's shoulders as swiftly and suddenly as a bird taking flight. The smile that lit her face was beautiful to behold, and she started to cry quiet tears of relief.

"Oh."

Hudson heard her breath catch and knew that he'd done the right thing.

"Are you all right?" he asked.

Gracie closed her eyes and pressed her fingers to her lips to keep from crying for joy.

"Oh, Mr. Hudson."

When her voice broke, Ron smiled to himself.

"Well, I just thought you'd want to know."

"If you were here, I would hug your neck," Gracie said softly.

His grin widened. "I will remind you of that when we next meet." He added. "And that would be strictly on a friendly basis, you understand."

"Thank you, sir. This means a great deal to me."

Hudson nodded to himself. "It's been my pleasure. Have a happy day. Have a happy life."

"And that will be *my* pleasure," Gracie said softly. "Good-bye."

The line went dead just as Jake's mother opened the door.

"They're ready," Angle said.

Gracie set down the phone and lifted her chin. "And so am I."

The house was quiet. Gracie lay in the crook of Jake's arm, listening to the even rhythm of his breathing. This man who was her husband was strong. So strong. And yet she knew the love between them could bring him to his knees. She prayed that it wouldn't destroy them, as well.

Ron Hudson's call had been unexpected, but oh, so welcome. It had lifted the guilt she carried with her all these weeks. And even though she knew Jake had seen her sadness, it had been something she was unable to share.

If Hudson was right, if her family was in Canada, she was certain they would be all right. She was also certain that her father would never allow the same mistakes to occur again. But she wished she could be as sure about Brady as she was about them. Brady always had been—always would be—the wild card.

She turned toward Jake, and even as he slept, he instinctively reached out for her and pulled her close. A deep, heartfelt sigh slipped out between her lips as she lay beside him. She might not have a family, but she had a home and a man who loved her and a baby that needed her to be strong. For Gracie, it was definitely enough.

A day behind. A town too late. For the past six weeks that had been all Brady knew. It was winter in Canada, and today the weather was miserable. Christmas had come and gone, and he couldn't believe they'd had it without him. Ever since he was sixteen years old it had been his honor to carve the turkey. He wondered who'd stood in his place and hated them for doing it.

It was strange, this yearning he had to reinvent

himself within the Moon family. He knew it wouldn't take much to reconnect with his old contacts. If he wanted to, within a year, maybe less, he could build a new company, arm and organize with a whole new strategy, but he didn't seem to care. That might come later, when he was in a better frame of mind. Right now he needed to sit at the right hand of his father and feel his smile upon his face and his hand upon his brow and know that he was the chosen one. And he wanted Gracie back in his life. That's what Brady needed, and he would go to any lengths to get it.

Aaron draped a large towel around his father's neck and combed through the long white length of hair.

"Just a trim," Elijah warned him.

Aaron smiled. His father had been saying the same thing for as long as he could remember.

"I know, Father."

Elijah relaxed as Aaron began to snip, and he considered it as good a time as any to broach the subject that had been on all of their minds.

"Father?"

"What?"

"Do you blame Gracie for leaving the way she did?"

Elijah's shoulders stiffened, and for a moment Aaron didn't think he would answer.

"It's not my place to blame," Elijah said. "God judges, not man."

Aaron sighed. He should have known his father would answer in biblical fashion.

"I know, but if she were to want to come back, would you let her—or would you shun her the way you did Brady?"

"She will not be back," Elijah said.

"But how do you know? What if she's out there now, looking for us?"

"She will not be looking."

Aaron was getting frustrated. "But how do you know, Father? I know she's not a helpless woman. I know she's educated. But she's family. She's my little sister, and truthfully, Father, we all miss her something dreadful."

Elijah's countenance fell, and it was then that Aaron knew how terribly his father was suffering.

"I miss her, too, son. More than I can say. But she is a woman, and when a woman chooses her man, he will become beloved above all others, save God. It's the way it should be."

Aaron tried one more time. "I suppose. But I wish—"

Elijah interrupted. "No more than I, son. No more than I."

The first hint Brady had that he was on the right track was when he saw one of their old trucks sitting in a used-car lot in a small village he was passing through. He slammed on his brakes and made a U-turn in the middle of the road.

His legs were shaking when he got out of his car, and when the salesman came out of the office, it was all he could do not to grab him and beat the information out of him, rather than ask.

"Hello!" the salesman called. "How may I help you?"

Brady pasted on a smile and stuffed his hands in his pockets, hoping he looked more relaxed than he felt.

"I'm looking for a second vehicle. You know, the kind to do some rough hauling and clean-up work around my place."

The salesman smiled. "I have just what you need." He strolled toward the old truck. "I haven't had it long, and if you're interested, I'd advise you not to wait. I don't come by vehicles like this often. It's a workhorse of a truck, and the best part is the low mileage."

"Really?" Brady said, and ran his hand over the fender, feeling the dent and remembering all too well how it had come to be there. Burnett had almost dropped a case of ammunition. Only the fender had stopped it from spilling everywhere.

"Yes, really," the salesman said.

"I'd like to talk to the former owner," Brady said. "You know, to ask if it burns much oil, what kind of mileage it gets, that sort of thing."

The salesman frowned. "I'm sorry, sir, but they aren't from around here. In fact, I got the impression they were just passing through and needed money."

Brady was getting antsy. He could almost feel the touch of his father's hand upon his shoulder. And he knew that with the information he had about Gracie, they would forgive and forget.

"Gee, that's too bad," Brady said, glancing at the

truck. And then he grinned. "I guess they thought they couldn't get much farther in that one. I wonder where they were going."

The salesman shrugged. "I don't know. I heard them saying something about a campground outside Ruta."

Brady pretended great interest in the truck's tires. "Hmm, Ruta? I never heard of the place. Where is it located?"

"It's an old gold-mining town about a hundred and fifty miles north and then a little to the east."

Brady nodded, then pointed to the truck. "Mind if I look under the hood?"

The salesman didn't mind. In fact, he would have been surprised if Brady hadn't asked.

A short while later, Brady left with the man's card in his pocket and a smile on his face. It wouldn't be long now.

Chapter 15

*G*racie was standing at the sink with her hands in the dishwater when she suddenly gasped and grabbed her stomach. Water ran from her hands and onto the floor as she turned to Jake.

"Jake! Oh, Jake!"

The dish he was drying shattered on the floor as he reached for her in a sudden panic.

"What's wrong? Do you hurt? Are you—"

She grabbed his hand and slipped it beneath her shirt, pressing the palm of his skin against her belly.

"I felt the baby move!"

Confusion slid away, leaving behind a look of pure wonder on Jake's face as he felt that gentle push and roll against the inside of Gracie's stomach.

"Does that hurt?"

She was smiling. "No. But it feels strange. I knew the baby was there, but this is the first time he's said hello."

"He?"

She nodded. "For some reason, I always think of the baby as he."

Jake frowned. "It stopped."

She laughed. "It will happen again."

He shook his head in disbelief and looked in Gracie's eyes. "It's a miracle, isn't it, sweetheart?"

She nodded.

"We made that miracle, didn't we?"

She wrapped her arms around his neck. "We're going to make a lot of things in our life, but I can guarantee that so far, this is definitely our best effort."

He grinned. "How do you feel about going to bed with me?"

"Jake, it's only nine-thirty in the morning. We just got out of it."

"So, are you saying this is a problem?"

She pulled his head down and whispered against his lips, "What I'm saying is, there are other places to make love besides that bed."

He laughed aloud.

Brady's heart was pounding as he pulled into the small campground outside of Ruta. When he spotted his father's pickup beneath the security light, anxiety gave way to an overwhelming relief. He had to stop at the side of the road and calm himself before he drove any farther.

It was warm inside his car, but the weather was cold and spitting snow. Trees towered over the campground, sheltering the small travel trailers the Moons had been pulling, and yet Brady could only imagine how miserable they must be. He felt guilty over the hardship they'd been enduring since fleeing New Zion. But he would make it better. When they heard what he had to say—when they listened to his plans—all would be forgiven.

When he felt it was safe to procure it, he even had some money stashed in a Louisiana bank. He would bring them out of the wilderness, just as Moses had done in the Bible.

Filled with a sense of importance, Brady put the car back in gear and drove up to the trailer and parked. He pulled the hood of his coat up around his ears and jumped out of the car, then leaped up the steps. He started to knock, picturing his entrance as a grand surprise, but decided to dispense with the preliminaries.

Aaron's wife, Annie, screamed in fright as he burst inside. She started running toward the back of the trailer, scattering children before her. Aaron stepped from behind a curtain and thrust them behind him as Elijah looked up from his Bible. Stunned by Brady's arrival, Elijah closed the book with a resounding thump and stood.

"Father!" Brady shouted. "I've come with great news! I know where Gracie is! I've come to tell you my plans to bring her home."

The cold wind tunneled through the small trailer. Papers flew off a table, and a candle went out, leaving a single electric light as the only source of illumination in the small dingy room. The frost in the old man's voice was more frigid than the ground outside as he pointed toward the door.

"You have no place here anymore! You are an outcast, a disbeliever! You shamed us all for your own selfish needs."

Brady's stomach lurched. This wasn't the prodigal son's welcome he'd expected.

"But, Father, I found Gracie. We need to get her and bring her back."

Behind the curtain Annie could be heard trying to calm her children. Aaron frowned and pushed past his brother to close the door, shutting the wind out, and Brady inside.

Brady turned to him, holding out his hand. "Aaron, we need to proceed quickly. Under cover of darkness is best, and since there's snow in Wyoming, it's possible that will help cover our tracks."

Aaron couldn't help but ask. "She's in Wyoming? Is she all right?"

Brady laughed, almost clapping his hands with delight. "Yes, on a ranch outside of a town called Cutter. The owner's name is Baretta." And then his expression changed, as a wild, vicious look came in his eyes. "I don't know about her welfare. What I do know is she needs to be saved from that man who took her away."

Elijah felt sick. Brady was his child, his firstborn, and his soul was as barren as a desert.

"Gracie is no longer our concern," Elijah said. "She made her choice. She desires to be a part of a world that we reject as carnal. And while I do not agree with her, I recognize her right to make that choice."

Brady couldn't believe what he was hearing. "But she's living in sin."

"How do you know?" Elijah asked. "Did you see her? Did you talk to her?"

"No, but—"

"There are no excuses, Brady. And once again, I tell you to go. Do not come after us again. We are trying to start a new life, and by coming here, you could have led the authorities straight to us."

Brady paled. "No, I swear, Father. No one knows anything about me. Why, I was even in Washington, D.C., a short while ago. I moved among them. They are so caught up in messing with other people's business, they didn't even know I was there."

"Oh, dear Lord," Aaron muttered, and dropped into a chair, hiding his face in his hands. "They will find us for sure."

"No, I swear!" Brady cried. "They won't. I didn't leave any witnesses to—"

The moment it came out of his mouth, he knew he was lost. Elijah's eyes widened, and what was left of Brady's soul withered inside of him.

"Oh my God. No, Father. I didn't mean that like it sounded."

Elijah pointed an accusing finger in Brady's face. "Don't lie to me! It's quite the opposite, isn't it, Brady? You never did know when to keep quiet. Who did you kill this time?"

Brady was shaking from the inside out. He felt like he was in a tunnel that kept getting smaller and smaller, and pretty soon there would be no room to stand, let alone breathe.

"What do you mean?"

It was all Aaron could do to say the words. "Taggert Brown didn't die instantly. He was screaming and cursing your name, as well as the name of the man who called himself Crockett."

Brady started backing toward the door. Everything was coming undone. He couldn't look at his father. He wouldn't look at his brother. If it had been possible, he would have chosen to die on the spot. But he kept drawing breath, and the ache kept getting bigger.

"I never touched her," he said, and then winced as he heard himself whine. "I would never ever touch my Gracie. I loved her, Father. I loved her."

Elijah stepped past his son and threw open the door himself. The fierce blast of cold that came back in the trailer was a cleansing to the ugliness that Brady had brought in tonight.

"You are an abomination to the Lord," Elijah said. "Get out! Get out! Never darken my doorway again!" And then he ducked his chin, shamed that this man was his son. "And may God have mercy on your soul, because I do not."

Brady staggered backward out the door and stumbled as he stepped onto the dirt. He couldn't think. He couldn't move. There was nothing inside him. Nothing to live for. No reason to care. Elijah stood on the threshold, his hair and beard blowing wildly in the wind, and at that moment, Brady believed himself to be in the presence of God Almighty.

"You're wrong!" Brady screamed, waving his

fists toward the sky. "You're wrong! Gracie doesn't belong with him! She belongs with us . . . with me! I don't care whether you believe me or not, I'm going after her and the traitor who took her away from me, and so help me God, I will make him pay! I will make them both sorry for what they've done!"

He spun and ran, disappearing into the night like a shadow moving out of the light.

Elijah dropped to his knees and started to pray. The shouts had alerted the other family members, and one by one the brothers came out of their trailers on the run. All they could see were the disappearing taillights of a car and their father on his knees in prayer.

Although Jake had no reason to, he'd felt uneasy for days. The new year had come and gone, and the baby Gracie carried was growing by leaps and bounds. Compared to some winters in the past, this one had been mild. And they had at least another month before his parents were due back from Florida. Everything should have been perfect. But he'd lived on the edge too long to ignore his instincts, and so he prepared himself for a disaster, even while going through the motions of an ordinary life.

Gracie was unaware of Jake's concern and spent her days wrapped in a cocoon of his love and protection. She wanted for nothing. It was a time of tenderness and sharing, and it was coming to an end she would never have imagined.

*　　*　　*

Brady was crazy. Even he knew it now. He didn't eat. Didn't sleep. He couldn't focus on anything except seeing Gracie's face and watching the man who'd taken her away from him die. The inside of his car was like a pigsty. Days'-old food wrappers were scattered on the front and back floorboards of his car. Empty beer cans and pop cans littered the seats and the dash. There was a map on the seat beside him with his route traced in red, and he'd drawn a circle around the area of Joe Baretta's ranch. His dark red hair was long and shaggy, and he hadn't shaved or bathed in days. He reeked, both of evil thoughts and foul smells.

There was a rifle in his trunk, a revolver in the glove compartment, and a semiautomatic in the pocket of his coat. Surrounded by guns, he felt himself above the powers of an ordinary man.

He was driven. With every mile that passed, his thoughts grew wilder, more disconnected. At one moment, he saw himself as the avenger of all the wrongs that had been done to his family. At another, he saw himself as the aggrieved, the one who had been wronged. And always, he saw himself meting out the justice that was due.

Somewhere between sunset and midnight he ran off the road. When he finally came to a stop and realized he was still alive, he drove back onto the highway and began watching the road signs, pulling into the first rest stop he came to.

A couple of truckers had beaten him to the best parking spaces, so he pulled onto the grass behind their rigs. Once the engine had been loud in his ears, now he heard nothing but the absolute silence. A car sped past on the highway beyond, and he shuddered at the sound. The high-pitched whine of the tires on pavement sounded too much like the scream in his mind. He looked up, catching a glimpse of himself in the rearview mirror. Startled, he looked over his shoulder, certain that there was someone in the seat behind him, and then he realized that it was himself he had seen. He moaned and covered his face.

Sometime later, a Wyoming highway patrolman drove through the rest stop as a matter of routine, checking to make sure everything was all right. Just as he was about to pull up to Brady's car to investigate, one of the truckers stepped out of his rig. The trucker waved, and the patrolman moved on to talk to him instead, thereby saving Brady from being caught. Again, Brady Moon seemed destined to succeed in his dark and dangerous mission.

When the sun rose over the horizon, his car was gone, and there was nothing to mark his passing except the trash that had blown out of his car when he got out to piss.

Jake sat on the edge of the couch, watching Gracie knit. Her fingers flew as she wound the needles in and out of the baby-soft yarn. Her face was beautiful in repose, and there was such a glow to her person he could have believed she was an earthbound angel. Her hair was loose, pulled back at the sides and clipped at the crown of her head. When she moved, it slipped across her shoulders like soft, black silk.

As she worked the pattern in the baby afghan she was knitting, she would stop periodically and hold it up for inspection, and each time she did, she would smile. Jake was suspended by her serenity, and at the same time, so on edge that it was all he could do to sit still. Last week he'd cleaned every gun in the house. Last night he'd loaded them. Tonight, he had an urge to sleep with one beside the bed, and he still didn't know why.

Twice during the day he swore he heard John's voice, and each time he had turned around with an expectant smile on his face and then had to face the fact that what he'd heard must have been in his mind. Maybe it was some old memory, or maybe an old echo from the days when John's voice had been alive between these walls. At any rate, the hair on the back of his neck kept rising, and he kept looking over his shoulder. And all the while, Gracie moved about the house, unaware of the imminent danger he sensed coming.

Yesterday, he'd been so certain that something was about to happen that he fed the animals twice as much feed as usual so that he wouldn't have to leave Gracie alone in the house today. And now the night was growing colder, and if the weatherman was to be believed, they might have snow before morning. Jake didn't mind. He'd grown up wading through snow to feed livestock, but the thought of being snowbound with a pregnant wife and no means to escape made him nervous as hell. And yet he kept asking himself, escape from what?

The wind rattled a windowpane, and Gracie looked up from her knitting, startled by the sudden sound.

"It's just the wind, sweetheart."

She nodded, then smiled and held up the afghan. "Look, Jake. Isn't it pretty? I just love yellow. It makes me think of sunshine and flowers and homemade butter."

Jake's smile was slow, his voice soft. "Yes, sweetheart, it's beautiful, and so are you."

She dropped the afghan in her lap and just looked at him.

"What?" he asked.

"You," Gracie said.

"What did I do?"

She shoved the afghan aside and crawled into his lap. "You made me love you."

A sudden sense of urgency swept over him, and he pulled her close and tightened his hold. "I'm an easy person to love," he whispered. "Want me to show you?"

"Yes, please."

He carried her back to their bedroom and laid her down among the covers that had been turned back. The room was warm and in shadow. When Jake slipped into bed beside her, she was waiting for him with open arms.

"We've got to be careful," he said, rubbing his hand across the swell of her belly. "I'm holding precious cargo here and I don't want anything to happen to either of you."

Gracie stretched, loving the feel of his hand on her skin. "Oh, Jake, that feels so good."

"How about this?" he whispered, as his hand dipped between her legs.

She arched to his touch, grabbing his shoulders for balance as the bed started to spin. She felt his mouth at her neck, then her breasts, and as he kissed her taut belly, he increased the pressure of his hand.

The climax was quick; startling in intensity, it left her breathless and shaking. Before Jake could move away, she found the strength to return the favor.

It was nearly midnight when Jake woke up, and when he did, he automatically reached for his gun. He didn't know why, but something inside him said the time had come.

Without rousing Gracie, he slipped out of bed and into his clothes, pulling on his boots as quietly as possible. And yet as careful as he'd been, she still sensed he was gone and rolled over.

"Jake?"

At the door, he paused and looked back. "Go back to sleep, sweetheart. I'm just going to check on some things."

Gracie glanced at the clock. "But it's midnight. Surely the livestock don't—" She saw the gun in his hands and reached for her robe. "What's wrong?"

Damn, he should have known he couldn't fool her. "I'm sure it's nothing," he said.

"Did you hear something?"

"No, go back to sleep. I'll be right back."

She was out of bed and looking for her house shoes. "Then why are you taking the gun?"

Something clattered outside and he pivoted in a crouch, the gun aimed toward the curtained window.

"Get down," he whispered, and she huddled on the floor in sudden terror. "Now stay there until I get back."

His anxiety had become contagious. "No! Jake, please don't go out there alone."

"Gracie."

She was shaking. "What?"

"Do what I say."

There was a tone in his voice she couldn't ever remember hearing, and she knew that this was the side of him that Ron Hudson had known. She bit her lip and crawled into a corner of the room. When she looked back, he was gone.

Jake slipped out the kitchen door, using darkness as a shelter to make his way around the house, constantly searching the perimeter of the yard for signs of an intruder. Although he saw nothing, the feeling was even stronger, and he knew his instincts had been right. Something—or someone—was out there.

And it started to snow.

When Brady saw the armed man circling the house from the back to the front, he jerked back in shock.

The bastard! How did he know?

Yet it was obvious to Brady that Crockett, or Baretta as he now knew him to be, was on the defensive. Even though Baretta was standing in the shadows, Brady could see the gun in his hand. Brady clenched his teeth to keep them from chattering and stood without moving, becoming one with the night as the snow swirled around him and into his eyes. He was cold, so cold. And he was so damned tired. When this was over, he was going to sleep for a week.

Jake slowly turned, and Brady could almost feel his gaze as he suddenly paused, staring into the darkness and straight at him. *He can't see me,* Brady thought, but he was also certain that somehow the man knew he was here. When Jake hefted his gun to a firmer grip and started walking toward him, Brady shivered. The anticipation of blowing a hole in the middle of Jake Baretta's gut was better than a four-day high.

Come on, you bastard. You took something from me. I came to get it back.

It had been so long since he'd seen his Gracie. She would be glad he'd come to get her, he just knew it. Poor Gracie. He could only imagine how she must be missing the family—as he was. Together. They'd go back together. Then it would be all right.

He aimed his rifle, squinting just a bit to adjust to the lack of light and the swirling snow.

I want you to remember this, Baretta. I'm going to make sure it takes you a long time to die.

The shot came without warning, and the gun

flew of out Jake's hand before he could think to react. He spun, intending to dive for cover, when someone screamed out his name.

"Baretta! Don't move!"

Spotlighted by the security light and with nowhere to hide, Jake froze. He stared into the place where the sound had come from.

A large, hulking figure came out the darkness and into the light like something up from the pits of hell, and in spite of the drastic change in his appearance, Jake knew who it was.

Brady Moon! And dear God, Gracie was alone inside the house!

No sooner had he thought Gracie's name than he heard the door slamming behind him, and he spun, terror for her uppermost in his mind as she came running out the front door.

She came down the steps, screaming her brother's name. "No, Brady, no!"

The knot in Brady's stomach began to relax. Gracie! His Gracie! And then his joy turned to horror as he watched her run. Her belly! His lips went slack, and he turned the gun toward Jake again.

"You bastard! You shouldn't have touched her like that! She was pure and you soiled her. Now she's ruined."

Gracie slid to a stop, putting herself between Jake and Brady's gun.

"Damn it, Gracie, get back!" Jake yelled, and tried unsuccessfully to shove her behind him, but she fought him, certain that if she moved, Brady would kill Jake.

"He's my brother!" she cried. "I can make him listen to reason."

"No, you can't. He's beyond reason. Look at him!"

Gracie turned, and for the first time, she really looked at the man her brother had become.

"Brady, for God's sake, have you gone mad? Look at yourself."

Brady never moved but continued to stand with the gun aimed chest high at them both. And the longer he stood, the louder the sounds inside his head became. Finally, he could stand it no longer and shook his head, like a dog shedding water.

"You bitch! You left our family for this? You're living in sin. Have you no shame? Have you no sense of decency for the way Father raised you?"

"Gracie, for the love of God," Jake begged. "Get out of the way."

She wouldn't listen and continued to stand between Jake and the gun.

"Don't talk to me about shame," she said, pointing at Brady, unaware it was much in the same accusing manner that her father had done. "You're the one who dragged our family into your little military games. You're the one who bought illegal weapons and played war and God only knows what else. It's your fault everything was ruined, not mine."

Snow was falling now, heavier, obliterating from sight all but the nearest objects. Brady shifted the gun and stepped closer, unwilling to let Baretta get the upper hand.

"Shut up, Gracie. Just shut up," he yelled. "You don't know what you're talking about."

Snowflakes fell on her face, melting with the tears already on her cheeks. Though dressed only in her gown and a long, heavy robe, she was unaware of the cold, only the dark bore of the gun barrel aimed at them.

"Why, Brady? Why did you do it?" she begged.

Jake's gut clenched. Gracie didn't know why John had been killed, and he'd never intended to tell her.

"Let it go, Gracie," Jake muttered.

"No! I have a right to know."

Brady took a deep breath that sounded like a sob, and his teeth shone like fangs through that dark red beard. "He shouldn't have touched you. I told him to leave you alone. You didn't belong to him."

A gust of wind blew shards of icy snow in their eyes, and as it did, Brady blinked.

"Run," Jake said urgently, but Gracie wouldn't budge, and he groaned beneath his breath when she leaned against him, determined not to let Brady get a clear shot. Jake's mind was caught in a whirl of possibilities, but he knew unless a miracle occurred, none of them would work. Brady was just crazy enough to shoot them both.

Gracie continued. "Brady, Jake and I are married. He's my husband. He's the father of my child. Please, just go and leave us alone. We won't tell anyone you were here, I swear."

Brady swayed. Married? "No." His voice broke,

and then he said it even louder. "No, damn you, no! You can't be married!"

"But we are," Gracie said.

Brady's finger tightened on the trigger, and Jake knew it was only a matter of time. He had to do something. He couldn't just stand there and let Gracie and their baby die.

"Come on, Brady. This is your sister. You don't want to hurt her now, do you? What would your father say?"

Brady's eyes widened, and Jake knew that somehow that had been the wrong thing to say.

"Father? My father? It doesn't matter what he says. I've been shunned." He waved the gun in their faces. "And it's all because of you. I killed you once, you son of a bitch. I can do it again."

Gracie covered her mouth to stop a scream. She couldn't panic. Not now. Not when their very lives depended on keeping Brady focused on talking instead of pulling the trigger.

"Brady. You need help. Please put down the gun and let me help—"

He laughed, and the sound was lost in the wind. "Help? I don't need your help. I needed your love, Gracie, and you gave it away to the wrong man . . . twice."

"You always had my love until you started acting like a fool," Gracie said.

Brady couldn't take his eyes off of Gracie's belly. He kept thinking of Baretta rutting her like an animal, of the seed spilling into Gracie, his Gracie.

"You chose the wrong man, Gracie. You were mine. You were always mine."

Gracie stiffened, unable to believe what Brady had just said. "But you will always be my brother. It shouldn't have mattered who I married, it wouldn't have changed our—"

Jake held his breath. Brady was going to say it, and he didn't know how Gracie was going to react.

Suddenly Brady swung the gun in the air and shot off a round before swinging it back their way.

"Shut up!" he screamed, and he was almost crying. "Just shut up! You don't understand. I loved you best. You were mine. Mine."

Gracie's legs went weak, and if she hadn't been leaning against Jake, she would have collapsed. Everything had just fallen into place. The reason for John Baretta's death. The reason Brady had come after Jake. It had nothing to do with his militia-based games, and everything to do with her. She covered her face, unable to look at him and bear the shame of what he'd just insinuated.

Without thinking, she dropped to her knees, her body shaking, the tears freezing on her cheeks. "Oh my God. Oh my God." Nausea bubbled at the back of her throat and all she could do was rock back and forth in the snow.

Jake dropped beside her, cradling her in his arms, shielding her as best he could from the bitter winter blast. He looked up at Brady through the snowfall and knew that they were going to die.

Brady aimed the gun. "Gracie! Come here! Come stand by me."

Her head jerked up, and her eyes were suddenly blazing with a fury and disgust he'd never seen.

"No! Never!" she cried.

"Gracie, I won't hurt you. Just come here by me. I'm your brother. You know what it says in the Bible about blood being thicker than water. You belong with me, not him."

"I'd die with him before I'd let you touch me," she screamed.

Rage shifted Brady's mind from reason to retribution. He didn't think. He just took aim.

Jake was rolling with Gracie in his arms when the shot went off. When he jerked, Gracie screamed. And then there was nothing but the warmth of Jake's breath on her face and the feel of his arms around her, shielding her. As they lay without moving, the snow began to blanket their bodies while Gracie waited to die.

Jake tensed. He kept waiting for the pain, but it didn't come. He could feel Gracie's panic in the way she clung to him, but to her credit, she hadn't moved or spoken since she screamed. He took a chance and rolled over, coming within inches of Brady Moon.

What was left of his face was covered in blood.

Chapter 16

*I*t didn't make sense. Jake was still trying to figure out what had happened when they came out of the falling snow and into the light. Three bearded men, each dressed in heavy down parkas, and the one in front was armed.

Jake couldn't believe what he was seeing. Elijah Moon was carrying a gun. Their hair and beards were icy and covered in snow, and the old man walked as if the burden of just being there was more than he could bear.

Dear Lord. Elijah shot his own son!

Jake stood and gave Gracie her first clear sight of her brother's face. She gasped and then looked away. When she started to moan, he bent down and lifted her out of the snow and into his arms. She went limp.

"Sssh, sweetheart. It's over. It's all over," he whispered. Her head lolled against his arm.

"Is she all right?" Elijah asked.

Gracie was in a near faint, probably from shock and the cold. He nodded.

Elijah slumped. Looking down at the rifle in his hands, he let it drop. As it fell to the ground beside Brady's body, the old man wiped his hands across his face, as if to wipe away the horror of what he'd just done.

Aaron Moon stood on one side of his father, Burnett on the other. They looked at their sister, and then they met Jake's gaze. Speech was not necessary. They'd seen Gracie standing between Jake and Brady's gun. They'd seen Jake throw himself in front of her just as Brady would have pulled the trigger. Aaron touched Elijah's arm. "Father?"

Elijah looked down at the snow collecting on his firstborn's body. In a few more minutes, it would be hard to tell where Brady lay. Then he looked up. Although he seemed bent by the strain of the past few months on the run, his voice and his spirit seemed strong.

"I gave him life, and God forgive me I took it away." His voice broke, and he took a deep breath before continuing. "It's over. I swear on the Book that you will never be bothered by me or mine again." He looked at Gracie and his expression softened. "She is a good and loving woman. I would ask that you care for her always."

"Come inside," Jake urged. "She'll come around as soon as I can get her warm."

Elijah shook his head. "No. She made her choice just as we've made ours." He glanced back at Brady, then up at his two other sons. "We'll take what we came for and no more."

Aaron lifted Brady's feet, Burnett took him by the arms. "Father. We need to go."

He nodded, then glanced back at Gracie one more time, as if fixing her face in his memory.

"Tell her . . ." He hesitated. "No, it's not necessary to tell her anything," he said quietly "In her heart, she already knows."

They disappeared into the darkness as silently as they'd come, leaving nothing behind of their passing except the rifle that had marked the end of Brady Moon.

Jake kicked it toward the porch where he would be able to find it tomorrow and hurried inside with Gracie. When he had time, he would put it away in the barn. When spring came, he would find a place to bury it. What had happened here tonight was the end of one way of life for Elijah Moon's family. For Gracie's sake, the least he could do was give the old man a chance to begin another, and hopefully one that would be better.

As soon as he got her inside, he carried her into the bedroom and laid her down on the bed, stripping off her clothes.

A few minutes later, he eased her down into a tub of warm water, watching nervously until the color returned to her skin. When her eyelids fluttered, he knew she would be all right.

"Gracie, sweetheart, can you hear me?" he asked.

Slowly, she opened her eyes, and as she did, he saw the memories coming back in her mind. Her lips trembled, and huge tears spilled out of her eyes to roll down her cheeks.

"Jake?"

"Ssh, it's over. It's all over," he said softly.

She covered her face with her hands, her whispers faint and broken as she spoke. "I didn't know. I swear to God I didn't know he felt like that about me."

Jake felt sick for her and for everything they'd lost. He'd lost his brother and she'd lost her family, and all because of one man's twisted mind.

"I know, baby, I know," he said softly "It's not your fault. It's not anyone's fault." And what he said next was the hardest thing he'd ever had to admit. "Hell, maybe it's not even Brady's fault. I can't pretend to understand a mind like that, but I know how easy it is to love you. Maybe Brady just got his love for you all twisted up in his heart."

She shuddered. "He never once . . . If he hadn't said it just now I would never have—" Her voice broke, and she looked up at Jake in new horror. "Dear Lord, he killed John because—"

Jake tilted her chin. "Look at me, Gracie."

Her eyes shimmered with tears, but she met his gaze without faltering.

"None of this is your fault, and John would have been the last one to lay blame." A thought crossed Jake's mind and he almost smiled. "John's probably laughing right now because he died for a woman's love. Knowing him, he'd say it was a hell of a way to go."

Gracie covered her face, but Jake took her hands away.

"Never turn away from me. Never be ashamed of who we are. Know that I love you."

She caught his hand and lifted it to her cheek "I know how much you love me, Jacob." She thought of the way Jake had thrown himself between Brady and the gun. "Enough to die for me."

He traced the edge of her lip with his thumb. "A thousand times over." Then he smiled. "I think you're warm enough. Let's get you dry and back into bed. We don't need the baby making an early arrival."

He held her in his arms all night long.

In the morning, the snow had stopped and the land was white and glittering in the winter sunlight.

Gracie stood at the kitchen window, looking toward the barn and watching as Jake fed the livestock nearby. Later, she knew he would have to take the tractor and go feed the cattle in the far pastures. Taking care of a ranch and livestock was a full-time job.

The baby rolled in her belly, and she rubbed at the spot where it had last kicked in an absent and soothing motion. A caretaker, that's what Jake was. He'd spent most of his life in the service of others. Caring for his country. Protecting the security of others, and now her and their child.

There was a pensive smile on her face as she turned away from the window. She didn't remember a lot of what had happened the previous night after seeing Brady's face. But she knew who had saved them, and she knew at what cost. She walked into the library and sat down at the desk, rifling through some papers until she found the number she was looking for. She picked up the phone, dialed, then counted the rings.

"Mr. Hudson's office, may I help you?"

Gracie took a deep breath and closed her eyes. "I need to speak to Mr. Hudson, please."

"I'm sorry, miss, but he's about to leave for a meeting. If you'd care to leave your—"

Her voice was quiet and low. "Please tell him it's Gracie."

The secretary paused. Something in the woman's voice told her to give it a try. "Just a moment, please."

Seconds later, Ron Hudson picked up the phone.

"Gracie! Don't tell me! It's a boy, right?"

Her throat tightened. Today was not a day for joy. "That's not why I'm calling."

He was pacing in front of the window, but when he heard the tremor in her voice, the smile died on his face.

"You know something, don't you?"

Gracie's fingers clutched the receiver until her knuckles turned white. Know something? Dear God, she knew too much.

"It's over."

He heard what she said, but he knew it meant so much more. He paused, looking out the window at the traffic moving through snow-packed streets.

"It snowed here last night," he said.

Gracie swallowed. "It snowed here, too."

The silence between them lengthened. Finally, it was Hudson who broke it. "You're not going to tell me anymore, are you?"

"There's nothing to tell other than to guarantee you that Brady Moon is no longer running from anything other than God."

"What the hell happened out there?"

Gracie shuddered. "Judgment day."

"Are you and Jake all right?"

She thought of Elijah and what he'd done. "Yes."

"You know the file will remain active."

She thought of a family forever on the run and swallowed past the lump in her throat. "Yes."

Hudson sighed. "Gracie."

"What?"

"Thank you for calling."

This time, she was the one who sighed. "I owed you one, didn't I?"

He grinned. "You're a hell of a woman, Gracie Moon."

"Baretta," she reminded him. "Gracie Moon is gone."

Hudson shook his head. "No, ma'am, I beg to differ, and don't ever be ashamed of it, either. The Gracie Moon I knew saved a good man's life, as well as her own. That took more than guts, lady."

The back door slammed, and Gracie looked up. "I have to go now," she said. "Jake's in from feeding the livestock."

"You're not going to tell him you called, are you?"

She thought about it for a moment. "No."

"You didn't ever tell him I called you the day of your wedding, either, did you?"

"No."

That surprised him a little. "Why?" he asked.

"I don't know. One day I probably will."

"Take care, lady."

"I will."

"The next time I hear from you two, it better be good news."

She smiled. "It will be."

She hung up just as Jake came into the room. His face was red from the cold, and she knew when he grabbed her up that his hands would be cold, too. She didn't care. She loved this man enough to warm a thousand cold hearts.

"There you are," Jake said, wrapping her in a great bear hug just as Gracie had known he would. "I couldn't find you."

She put her arms around him, holding him as close as the baby would allow. "I'm right here, love," she said softly. "You couldn't lose me if you tried."

Jake nuzzled her ear, grinning when she squealed about his cold nose. And then he remembered she'd been on the phone when he came in.

"Who were you talking to?" he asked.

She looked up at him and then shrugged. "Just a friend."

Jake paused. There was something in her voice that worried him. He thought of last night and all she'd endured.

"Are you all right?"

Gracie laid her cheek against Jake's chest, right where she heard his heart beating loudest. It was solid and strong, just like him. Then she looked up and saw the strength in his face and the love in his eyes.

"My darling, Jake, as long as I have you, I will always be all right."

Epilogue

$\mathcal{E}$xcept for the low murmur of nurses' voices in a nearby room, the hospital floor was quiet. And it should have been. It was almost midnight, and Joe and Angie had gone home hours ago after making no apologies for the fact that their grandchild was cuter than all the others.

Jake stood over Gracie's bed, watching her sleep. The love he felt for her was overwhelming, and every time he tried to say what was in his heart, the words choked him. Nearby in a hospital crib, their day-old son lay sleeping, replete after just having been fed.

As Gracie shifted on the bed, a slight moan slid from her lips. Jake frowned. The birth had been hard on her. Almost too hard. Another half an hour and they would have had her in surgery. He moved to her side and felt her forehead. It was cool. At his touch, she stilled. He leaned down and brushed a kiss against the side of her cheek.

"I love you, Gracie."

She smiled, and he knew that wherever she was,

she'd heard him. The baby squirmed and then squeaked, and Jake moved to the crib. Such a tiny bit of life to hold so much hope for their future.

"Just look at you," Jake whispered, as the baby came awake. "You're supposed to be asleep."

He scooped little John up in his hands and then cradled him next to his chest. The comfort of being held next to a warm body, as well as Jake's deep voice, seemed to soothe the baby's mood. Instantly, the fussing stopped.

"Already calling the shots, are you, buddy?" Jake said, as he carried him to the window and pulled the cord to open the shades, giving him a clear view of the night.

He looked past the tops of the buildings to the sky above. It was dark and clear and still bitterly cold, although it hadn't snowed for days. The three-quarter face of a big blue moon hung clearly against the velvety blackness of star-speckled space.

The baby squeaked, and Jake traced the side of his tiny face with the tip of his finger, marveling at the absolute perfection and softness of a newborn's skin.

"Hey, Johnny, want to see the world?"

He turned the baby in a playful manner, aware that clear sight and the ability to focus was something that would come to his son later. But the fantasy of being the first to show him was strong in Jake's heart, and he couldn't resist.

Jake watched Johnny's face, grinning to himself at the way the tiny mouth seemed to be in constant

motion seeking sustenance. But when he turned
the child toward the window, the baby stilled, and
Jake watched as his little eyes opened wide. It was
a silly notion, but the baby seemed to be looking
up at the sky.

"What are you looking at, fella?"

He followed the path of the baby's gaze and
didn't believe what he saw. Again, he looked down
at the child and at the intent expression on his face.
The baby was staring at the moon.

I think he takes after me.

The skin crawled on Jake's neck, and he closed
his eyes. He didn't have to turn around to know it
was John that he'd heard. When Jake spoke again,
his voice was thick with unshed tears, and his remark was more statement than question.

"So, little John, you're going to be a moon
chaser, too." His voice was tender as he put the
baby up on his shoulder and began rubbing his
back in a slow, soothing motion. "Well, that's okay.
I know something about chasing the moon. When
you're a little bit bigger, I'll sure show you how."

Gracie had been watching them, almost from the
moment Jake had taken the baby from the crib.
They were her boys. One slightly bigger than the
other, but each in his own way in desperate need of
her love. And she had more than enough for them
both.

She smiled to herself, listening as Jake talked to
the baby in such an adult manner. She supposed it
was their first man-to-man talk. But when Jake
stilled and looked up at the sky, she sensed his

change of mood. He stiffened and cocked his head, almost as if he was listening to someone talk, although she knew nobody was there.

And as she watched, somehow she knew he was remembering John, and the thought that he was suddenly sad made her want to cry.

"Jake."

He turned. "I'm sorry, sweetheart, did we wake you?"

She held out her hand. "Not really. I won't sleep soundly until I'm in our own bed."

Jake looked down at the baby in his arms. "And maybe not then either, I'm thinking."

She patted the side of her bed. "What were you two talking about?"

Jake laid the baby in her arms and then scooted onto the bed beside her. Even though Gracie had the baby in a firm grip, he couldn't stop himself from reaching out and holding on to them both.

"Just guy stuff," he said, and then grinned when she rolled her eyes.

The baby was fussing now, and Gracie loosened her gown to let him suckle. As Jake sat back and watched, he knew he would never see a more beautiful sight.

"Gracie."

She looked up. "What, darling?"

"Dad gave me some land. If we wanted to, we could build a house up above that high spring that you like."

Gracie's eyes widened. "Oh, Jake, are you ready to settle down like that?"

He slid his hand along the blanket covering her legs. "Sweetheart, I've been waiting for you all my life. I'm not about to take chances with what I have now. You're both too precious to me."

"I thought you might go back to—"

"Never."

"You'd quit because of us, or because you're ready?"

"To me, the reason is one and the same."

She thought of the lifestyle he'd lived before her. "What will you do . . . besides ranch, I mean? Will that be enough excitement for you?"

He looked down at the baby who'd fallen asleep with his mouth still attached to her breast. And in that moment, his heart was at peace.

"More than enough. Besides, with that little fellow in our lives, I don't think there will be time to get bored."

"As long as you're sure."

Jake's touch was gentle as he brushed the hair from Gracie's cheek. "Sweetheart, you don't understand. Besides everything else that he'll be learning, I have to show him how to chase the moon."

The World of Sharon Sala

When a man meets a woman in the books of Sharon Sala, there is no question that it is meant to be—that it is *fate*. For in the wonderful world of this bestselling author, who also writes as Dinah McCall, love is often left in the hands of destiny—threatening danger, the bonds of family, a terrible accident, or even just the whims of Mother Nature. Now, experience the romance for yourself, with these excerpts from a few of Sharon Sala's classic stories. Whether first love remembered or a new passion like no other, her stories will inspire your faith in destiny, and remind you that love is always around the next corner . . .

Chance McCall

In one of Sharon Sala's most emotional love stories, amnesia takes Chance McCall *away from innocent Jennifer Ann Tyler, who has been secretly in love with him for as long as she can remember. When Chance returns to her father's ranch, remembering nothing, Jenny knows it's up to her to help speed Chance's recovery—and perhaps heal her broken heart at the same time.*

Chance watched Jenny flit from one group of men to the other, playing hostess one minute, and reverting to "one of the boys" the next. She kept slipping glances in his direction when she thought he wasn't looking, but, true to her claim, she'd more or less left him alone. He didn't know whether he was relieved or disappointed. His fingers curled around the cold bottle of beer in his hand and knew that holding that beer was not what he wanted to do. Holding Jenny seemed much more necessary . . . and important.

"What's for dessert?" Henry asked, as Jenny scraped the last of the potato salad onto his plate.

"Movies," she answered, and grinned at the men's cheers of delight. "Roll 'em, Henry," she called as she walked away from Chance. "And the first one to start a fight has to clean up the party mess."

Chance grinned as the men muttered under their breaths. Jenny knew them well. They'd rather feed pigs than do "woman's work." And a cowboy does not willingly set foot around a pig.

Images danced through the night on the beam of light from the projector and jumped onto the screen, bringing a portion of the past to life. It didn't take long for the laughter to follow, as Henry's weathered face and hitched gait filled the screen.

He was leading a horse toward Jenny, who sat perched on the top rail of the corral. The smile on her face kicked Chance in the gut. And when she vaulted off the fence and threw her arms first around Henry, and then around the horse's neck, he swallowed harshly. It was a Jenny he'd never seen. This one wasn't scolding, or wearing a continual frown of worry. She was unconscious of her beauty, unconcerned with her clothing, and looked to be in her teens.

Firecrackers went off beneath a bystander's feet, telling Chance that it must have been a Fourth of July celebration that was being filmed. A man walked into the picture, and Jenny's face lit up like a roman candle. Absolute and total devotion was obvious. When the man turned around and made a face at the camera, Chance caught his breath. *It's me!* He had no memory at all of the occasion. Jenny was handing him a bridle that he slipped over the horse's head. She was smiling and laughing and clapping her hands as the crowd around her began singing.

It took Chance a minute to decipher the song, since this movie had no sound. Happy Birthday! They were singing Happy Birthday to Jenny! His breathing quickened and he stiffened as he watched Jenny throw her arms around his neck and plant a swift kiss on his cheek before allowing him to help her mount the horse. Because he was looking for it . . . because subconsciously he'd always known it was there . . . he didn't miss the intense look of love that Jenny gave him before she turned to the horse's head and rode off amid cheers and birthday greetings from the crowd.

It was too much! Chance knew that the rest of the night would simply be a rerun of similar scenes and similar people. He didn't have to remember it to know that Jenny Tyler loved him. He'd felt it through the darkness in the hospital, when he had no memory at all . . . when there was nothing in his life but misery and pain.

What he didn't know, and what he couldn't face, was the depth of his own feelings for the boss's daughter, and memory of what, if anything, had ever happened between them. He turned and walked away, hidden by night shadows.

Jenny saw him go and resisted an urge to cry. It would do no good. And it would be too obvious if she bolted after him. *Damn this all to hell*, she thought. *Why can't you remember me, Chance McCall? Injury or not, I'd have to be dead not to remember you.*

Second Chances

Weather stranded both Billie and Matt in the same airport, but it was fate that made them meet in Second Chances. After disastrous holidays, Billie Jean finds herself trapped in Memphis on New Year's Eve. She is alone, until she meets a tall cowboy lingering in the shadows and passion takes over. What seems like a fluke is really the hand of destiny, changing Billie's and Matt's lives forever.

Matt sensed, rather than heard, her approach, as if someone had invaded his space without asking. Instinctively he shifted his absent gaze from the swirling snow outside to the reflection of the woman he saw coming toward him from the rear.

At first, she was nothing more than a tall, dark shadow. It was hard to tell exactly how much woman was concealed beneath the long, bulky sweater she wore, but she had a slow, lanky stride that made his belly draw in an unexpected ache. Just as he was concentrating on slim hips encased in tight denim and telling himself he'd rather be alone, she spoke.

"Would you like something to drink?"

Every thought he had came to a stop as her voice wrapped around his senses. Men called it a bedroom voice—a low, husky drawl that made his toes curl and his breath catch.

But when their hands touched, Matt wasn't the only one in a state of sudden confusion. Billie lost her train of thought, while the smile on her lips froze like the snow against the windows. There was a look in his eyes that she'd never before seen on a man's face. A mystery, an intensity in the dark blue gaze that she hadn't bargained for. Several staggering breaths later, she remembered what she'd been about to say.

"I thought you might like to . . ."

She never got to finish what she was saying. He took the can and set it down on the ledge without taking his eyes off her face. Mesmerized, she stood without moving as his hands lifted toward her cheeks. When his fingers sifted through the strands of escaping curls that were falling around her eyes, she caught herself leaning toward his touch and jerked back in shock. Then he grinned, and she felt herself relaxing once more.

He lifted a stray curl from the corner of her eye. "That face is too pretty to hide."

A surge of pure joy made Billie weak at the knees. Embarrassed, she looked away, and when she looked back, found herself locked into a wild, stormy gaze and dealing with another sort of surge. Ashamed of what she was thinking, she pretended interest in the storm and knew that she was blushing.

"Where are you going?"

I wish to hell it was with you. Wisely, Matt kept his wishes to himself.

"Dallas."

She nodded and looked down at the floor.

"I was in Memphis for Christmas vacation. I'm on my way back to California." When she got the nerve to look up, those dark blue eyes were still staring intently.

They shared a long, silent moment, then the noise of the crowd behind them broke the tension. It was obvious by the loud chanting voices that the countdown to midnight had begun.

"Ten . . . nine . . . eight."

Billie looked up. His eyes were so blue. So compelling. So lonely. She took a deep breath.

"Seven . . . six . . . five."

She bit her lower lip, then took a step forward. Just in case. Hoping—wishing—needing him to want what she was wanting.

"Four . . . three . . . two."

Matt groaned beneath his breath. He saw the invitation in her eyes as well as her body language. So help him God, there wasn't enough strength left in him to deny either of them the obvious.

The merrymakers were in full swing as they shouted, "Happy New Year!"

Matt cupped her face in his hands, then waited. If she didn't want this, now was her chance to move. To his utter joy, she not only stayed but scooted a hair-breadth closer to his chest until he could almost feel the gentle jut of her breasts against the front of his shirt. Almost . . . but not quite.

"Happy New Year, Memphis." He lowered his head.

Finders Keepers

Molly Eden thinks fate is not on her side. Ever since her chance at a baby was robbed from her, grief has only been a few steps behind. Then, on a warm summer day, someone comes toddling into her life to change it forever. Joseph Rossi's baby son, Joey, is that darling someone, and when Joey Jr. asks Molly to be his mother, he proves that children can be wise beyond their years and see love where there was only loneliness before in Finders Keepers.

"Isth you my momma?"

Molly didn't know what startled her more, the unexpected question or the touch of a child's hand on her bare thigh.

"What in the world?"

She spun. The food on her barbecue and her solitary picnic were forgotten as she stared down in shock at the small boy who waited patiently for an answer to his question. She was startled by the unexpected pain of his innocent question—it had been years since she'd let herself think of being anyone's momma. But the child's expression was just short of panicked, and his hand was warm—so warm—upon her thigh; she couldn't ignore his plight just because of her old ghosts.

"Hey there, fella, where did you come from?" Molly bent down, and when he offered no resistance, she lifted him into her arms.

But he had no answers for Molly, only an increase in the tug of his tongue against the thumb he had stuffed in his mouth. She smiled at his intense expression, and patted his chubby bare legs. Except for a pair of small red shorts, an expression was the *only* thing he was wearing.

"Where did you come from, sweetheart?"

His chin quivered and then he tugged a little faster upon his thumb.

It was obvious to Molly that the child was not going to be any help in locating missing parents. She turned, searching her spacious backyard for something or someone to explain the child's appearance, but nothing was obviously different from the way it had been for the last twenty-two years when her parents first moved in—except the child.

"Are you lost, honey? Can't you find your mommy?"

His only response was a limpid look from chocolate-chip eyes that nearly melted her on the spot.

She frowned, patting his sticky back in a comforting but absent way and started toward the house to call the police when shouts from the yard next door made her pause.

"Joey! Joey, where are you? Answer me, son!"

Even through the eight-foot height of the thick yew hedge separating the homes, Molly could hear the man's panic. She looked down at the child in her arms and sighed with relief. If she wasn't mistaken, the missing parents were about to arrive, and from a surprise location. The house on the adjoining lot had been vacant for over a year, and she'd been unaware that anyone had moved next door.

"Hey! You over there . . . are you missing a small boy?"

"Yes . . . God, yes, please tell me you found him."

Molly smiled with relief as she realized her unexpected guest was about to be retrieved. "He's here!" she shouted again. "You can come around the hedge and then through the front door of my house. It's unlocked."

The thrashing sounds in the bushes next door ceased. Molly imagined she could hear his labored breathing as the man tried to regain a sense of stability in a world that had gone awry. But she knew it was not her imagination when she heard a long, slow, string of less-than-silent curses fill the air. Relief had obviously replaced the father's panic.

Molly raised her eyebrows at the man's colorful language, but got no response from the child in her arms. He didn't look too perturbed. But he did remove his thumb from his mouth long enough to remark, "My daddy," before stuffing it back in place.

"Well, really!" Molly said, more in shock for herself than for the child, who had obviously heard it all before.

She turned toward the patio door, expecting the

arrival of just an ordinary man, and then found herself gaping at the male who bolted out of her door and onto her patio.

It had been a long time since she'd been struck dumb by a physical attraction, but it was there just the same, as blatant and shocking as it could possibly be. All she could think to do was take a deep breath to regain her equilibrium and then wave a welcome. That in itself took no effort, and it was much safer than the thoughts that came tumbling through her mind.

She saw the man pause on the threshold, as if taking a much-needed breath, and then swipe a shaky hand across his face. He was tall, muscular, and, oddly enough, quite wet. His hair lay back and seal-slick against his head like a short, dark cap, while droplets of water beaded across his shoulders.

He stared at her backside and then tried not to. But it was an impossible task. Her long, tan legs made short work of the distance to the grill. He tried to remember his manners as he followed behind.

Deep in the Heart

In Deep in the Heart, *it is danger that brings Samantha Carlyle back to her rural Texas hometown, and back
into the world of John Thomas Knight, the stunning
local sheriff. She left him behind once for the bright
lights and big city, but the success she found there—or
the threats that came with it—is exactly what brings
her into his arms again . . .*

There were no tears left to cry. Unmitigated terror
had become commonplace for Samantha Carlyle.
She was waiting for the inevitable. Day by day the
stalker came closer, and there was nothing she
could do to stop him.

She could barely remember her life three months
ago when she'd been a highly valued member of a
Hollywood casting agency, calmly and compe-
tently going about the business of fitting the fa-
mous and the not-so-famous into starring and
supporting roles.

"And look at you now," Samantha whispered to
her own reflection as she stood in the window
overlooking the courtyard below. "You have no
job. You're running from the devil and your own
shadow. You're just hiding . . . and waiting to die."

Until now, she'd never considered what it meant

to be "living on borrowed time." She looked again at her reflection and wondered what there was about her that could drive a man to insane threats of vengeance.

Her face was no different from many others—heart-shaped, but a bit too thin, and framed by a mane of thick, black hair. Her nose was still small and turned up at the world, but there was no longer a jut to her chin. It only trembled. Her lips were full but colorless, and the life that had once shone from her eyes seemed dim . . . almost gone. She shuddered and dropped the drapes, rearranging them to shut the sun out and herself in from prying eyes.

When the harassment had gone from hate mail to phone calls with spine-chilling messages left in an unrecognizable voice, she'd nearly lost her mind and, soon after, she did lose her so-called friends.

As if that wasn't enough, she'd moved her residence twice, certain each time she would outwit the culprit. And then came the day that she realized she was being stalked. But by then going back to the police was out of the question. They had convinced themselves that she was concocting the incidents herself. In fact, they had almost convinced her.

Her anger at their accusations had quickly turned to disbelief when they had proved to her, without doubt, that the hate letters she'd been receiving had been typed on her own office typewriter, and that the calls left on her answering machine were traced to an empty apartment that had been rented in the name of Samantha Jean Carlyle. It was enough said. When LAPD reminded her that perpetrating fraud was a crime, she'd taken her letters and her tapes and gone home, having decided to hire a personal bodyguard. Then she'd reconsidered her financial situation and given up on that idea.

That was the day her boss put her on indefinite leave of absence, after reminding her, of course, that when she got her act together she would be welcomed back.

The victim had become the accused. At first she'd been furious over everyone's lack of sympathy for her situation or concern for her life. Then she'd become too busy trying to stay alive.

It was the constant frustration and the growing fear that no one was going to save her, let alone believe her, that made her remember Johnny Knight.

Touchstone

In Touchstone, *a Dinah McCall classic, fate doesn't bring two lovers together, but instead tries to tear them apart. Rachel Austin has buried her father, and now her mother, and finally they are coming for her family's land. She cannot bear staying in Mirage, where all she'd ever known is lost, but she soon discovers that without her first—and only—love, Houston Bookout, she will never stare down the demons of her past. Look for* Touchstone *in reissue from HarperTorch December 2003.*

"Rachel!"

He heard fear in his own voice and took a deep breath, making himself calm. But when she didn't answer, the fear kicked itself up another notch.

"Rachel! Where are you?"

He started toward the house, then something— call it instinct—made him turn. She came toward him out of the darkness, a slender shadow moving through the perimeter of light from his headlamps, then centering itself in the beam. She was still wearing the clothes she had on this morning, when he'd seen her last: worn-out Levi's and an old denim shirt. She came toward him without speaking. Fear slid from him, leaving him weak and shaken.

"Damn it, Cherokee, you scared me to death. Why didn't you answer me? Better yet, what the hell are you still doing here in the dark?"

Then he saw her face and knew she was incapable of answering.

"Jesus." He opened his arms.

She walked into them without saying a word and buried her face in the middle of his chest.

He rocked her where they stood, wrapping his fingers in the thickness of her hair and feeling her body tremble against his.

"It's going to be all right," he said softly. "I promise you, girl, it's going to be all right."

She shook her head. "No, Houston. It will never be all right again. It's gone. Everything is gone. First my father. Then my mother. Now they're taking my home."

He ached for her. "I know, love, I know. But I'm still here. I'll never leave you."

But it was as if he'd never spoken.

"The land . . . they always take the land," she muttered, and dropped to her knees. Silhouetted by the headlights of Houston's truck, she thrust her hands in the dirt and started to shake.

Houston knelt beside her. "Rachel . . ."

She didn't blink, staring instead at the way the dust began to trickle through her fingers.

"How can I give this up? It's where I was born. It's where my parents are buried."

He didn't have words to ease her pain.

She rocked back on her heels and stood abruptly. Fury colored her movements and her words.

"Everything is over! Over! And all because of money."

Houston reached for her, but she spun away. A knot formed in Houston's gut. He grabbed for her again, and this time when she tried to shake herself free, he tightened his hold.

"Stop it!" he said sharply, and gripped her by both shoulders. "Look at me, Rachel."

She wouldn't.

He shook harder. "Damn it! I said look at me!"

Finally, reluctantly, she met his gaze. She saw concern and anger; to her despair, she saw fear and knew it was because of her. She went limp.

"Houston."

He groaned and pulled her to him. "Damn it, Cherokee, don't turn away from me, too."

She shuddered. Cherokee. She couldn't deny her heritage any more than she could deny her love for Houston.

"I'm sorry," she whispered.

"It doesn't matter," he said. "Nothing matters but you."

He took her by the hand.

"Wait . . . my car," Rachel muttered.

"Leave it," he said. "You're coming home with me."

"But the sale. I need to be here by seven."

Houston frowned. "I'll have you here by sunup if it'll make you happy. But you're still coming home with me."

They made the drive back to his ranch in total silence.

Rachel felt numb from the inside out until she walked in the front door of Houston's home. The odors of cleaning solutions and pine-scented furniture polish were startling. She inhaled sharply, and as she did, tears blurred her vision. He'd been cleaning for her. Her anger dimmed as shame swept over her. She turned.

"Oh, Houston."

"Come here, girl. Don't fight your last friend."

She shuddered as his arms went around her. Last friend? If he only knew. He was her best and last friend, and in a couple of days he was going to hate her guts. A sob worked its way up her throat, but she wouldn't give in. No time to cry. Not when she wanted to remember.

She tilted her head to look up at him. "Make love to me, Houston. Make me forget."

Chase the Moon

Chase the Moon *will always be remembered as one of Sharon Sala's—here writing as Dinah McCall—most passionate, thrilling stories of love. When Jake Baretta goes looking for his twin brother's killer, he finds instead beautiful Gracie Moon—a woman he could easily fall for, if only she didn't believe he was his dead brother. Sheltered and innocent, Gracie doesn't know about the evil that lurks under the surface of her idealistic Kentucky hometown—but she is in danger of finding out, far too soon. Look for* Chase the Moon *in reissue from HarperTorch December 2003.*

Less than an hour later, Jake was startled by a knock on the door, but even more so by the woman behind it.

All Gracie said was, "Oh, Jake," and then walked into his arms.

He froze and tried not to panic. *Damn, Johnny, why didn't you warn me this would happen?*

Her arms were around his waist, her cheek against his chest, and he felt her shoulders trembling. Her long dark braid felt heavy against his hands as he tentatively returned her embrace. The thrust of her breasts, the feel of her slender body against his, were startling. He hadn't prepared himself for this, or for the supposition that John could have had a personal relationship with anyone here—no less with a woman as damned beautiful as this one. Worst of all, she thought he was John.

It took a moment for Jake's shock to pass. He didn't know who she was, but he suspected that this was Elijah Moon's only daughter. From the files he'd read, Gracie Moon was the only unattached female in New Zion. He hoped to God this was Gracie, because if John had been seeing a married woman, then that would pretty much explain why he had been shot.

He said a prayer and took a chance.

"Gracie?"

Gracie sighed. She loved to hear her name on his lips, and then she remembered herself and took a quick step back. There were tears in her eyes as she laid her hands on his shoulders.

"Father said you'd been shot." Her chin trembled, and she bit her lip to keep from crying. "He said you didn't trust us anymore." Tears hovered on the edge of her lashes. "Does that mean you don't trust me, either?"

Jake stifled a groan. My God, how could he answer her? For all he knew, she could be the one who'd pulled the trigger. Just because she was beautiful as sin, and just because there were tears in her eyes, did not make her an innocent woman. But he had to play the game. It was why he'd come.

"I guess what it means is, getting shot in the back put me off balance. Trust isn't something that's happening yet. But I'm glad to see you, too. Does that count?"

Gracie ducked her head, fighting tears, and when she looked up, there was a sad smile on her face.

"Of course it counts," she said softly.

She kept looking at him. At his eyes. At the shape of his mouth. At the cut of his chin. Finally, she shrugged.

"You look the same . . . but in a way you're very different. Harder, even colder." A gentle smile accompanied her apology. "But I suppose surviving being shot in the back would do that to anyone, right?"

"It made me hate," Jake answered.

Gracie touched his arm. "Just don't hate me."

Give Your Heart to
New York Times Bestselling Author

SHARON
SALA

(also known as Dinah McCall)

Lucky
0-06-108198-1/$6.99 US/$9.99 Can

Queen
0-06-108197-3/$6.99 US/$9.99 Can

Diamond
0-06-108196-5/$6.99 US/$9.99 Can

Deep in the Heart
0-06-108326-7/$6.99 US/$9.99 Can

Second Chances
0-06-108327-5/$6.99 US/$9.99 Can

Finders Keepers
0-06-108390-9/$6.99 US/$9.99 Can

Chance McCall
0-06-108155-8/$6.99 US/$9.99 Can

Touchstone
0-06-108702-5/$6.99 US/$9.99 Can

Chase the Moon
0-06-108445-X/$6.99 US/$9.99 Can

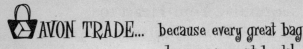